ALWAYS
THINK of ME

www.mascotbooks.com

Always Think of Me

Cover Design by Dave Stonehouse
Cover photo: 121958829 © Rolffimages Dreamstime.com

For more information, please contact:
Mascot Books, an imprint of Amplify Publishing Group
620 Herndon Parkway, Suite 220
Herndon, VA 20170
info@mascotbooks.com

Library of Congress Control Number: 2023921116
CPSIA Code: PRV1123A
ISBN-13: 978-1-63755-725-9

Printed in the United States

For Kevin, Drew, and Nate. But most especially to you, Ty. You rocked my world when you arrived and then when you left.

ALWAYS
THINK of ME

A NOVEL

Lori Keesey

MASCOT
BOOKS
an imprint of Amplify Publishing Group

PROLOGUE

Today, May 30

Georgie, my brindled goofball of a canine, hated the river. Despite my cajoling, he'd dig in his paws and pull against his leash. Treats or no treats, he wouldn't go into the water. I probably should've followed his example. Because the river deceived me. It's there where my story begins or ends, depending on your point of view, and sets the stage for my unexpected, otherworldly reunion with Ginny—a special woman I fell for a year ago.

But I'm getting ahead of myself.

Let me introduce myself. My name is TC, short and sweet, an abbreviation for Tyrus Cal. Why my parents foisted this ugly name on me, their then-scrawny firstborn, is beyond me. Something about famous baseballers, my dad's heroes…but come on. No one names a kid Tyrus Cal these days.

Whatever. I can't worry about my name now. Other concerns

press on my mind. I don't know where I am or why I'm going. All I know is that I'm headed for Ginny's, torn about seeing her again. But I'm told she needs me. This is a shot at a do-over. Today is the day to set things right.

CHAPTER ONE

Today, May 30

My only intention seconds, minutes, or maybe even hours ago was to cool off and comfort myself in the river's soothing waters, not to head off to see Ginny. Foul didn't come close to describing my mood.

All day, working in the heat and humidity, I'd obsessed about my anemic bank account and how I'd make enough money to pay the month's mortgage. I'd considered asking my folks for a temporary loan but dashed that. Mom's questions, her worried tut-tutting, would've made me feel worse. That, of course, then led to an hours-long fixation about my career choice, and whether I was really cut out for the real-estate game. Why couldn't I figure out what I wanted to be when I grew up?

No answers.

So, I'd fumed. Scowled. Spoke little, even to my dad who'd agreed to renovate the bathroom of a house that my client wanted to list in short order. Dad was doing everyone a favor, including myself who'd get paid for being his gofer, and I was barely being civil. Even at quitting time, the bathroom finished, my bad temper hadn't abated, and nothing would shake it—not even a nice, cold beer.

I know because I'd tried.

I needed an attitude adjustment, and the river—an overgrown creek is a more accurate description—had always worked its magic in the past. But instead of bobbing around, practicing my backstroke, and forgetting life's irritations, I'm getting ready to go to who-knows-where.

So, I'll stick to what I do know. The facts that led to this unforeseen, otherworldly mission to see Ginny again.

As soon as I arrive, park my car, and open the door, business cards, marketing fliers, and a week's worth of fast-food wrappers strewn across the floorboards fly out, annoying me to no end. I toss the mess back into my ride and slam the door, giving my sweaty brow a good swipe before heading for the riverbank.

I see only two other people: a kid chucking rocks into the river and an older guy, probably his grandfather, leaning against his truck, too busy with his phone like everyone else these days.

I approach the water.

Kick off my flip-flops.

And I jump.

Within seconds, it becomes clear that I've made another hasty, ill-advised decision, one of many in a long list of mistakes. A long, cold shower would've done the trick just fine.

I know that now.

The undercurrent surges fast. Too fast. And in a flash, I hurdle over the dam.

I can't hear the birds chirping from the trees, only the muffling sound of water roaring over the dam. My mind feels disconnected from my body. No pain. Just a feeling of nothingness, weightlessness, but my mind won't stop. *Why didn't I pay better attention to what was happening before taking the leap?* Obviously, no one, aside from myself, thought it a good idea to go swimming today.

This is where things get weird.

As I floundered on the down-river side—below the dam, maybe thirty feet from where I jumped—I see a person. Not the grandfather or the boy . . . another man. He has coarse dark hair and a trimmed beard and is wading through the water toward me. His khaki shorts hang from his narrow hips and a pair of sunglasses dangle from the collar of his cotton shirt. He looks like every other hipster I know, except he stands out for two notable qualities: his otherworldly calm and deep, espresso-colored eyes.

He extends a hand toward me. "Let me help you out of the water, TC."

He seems familiar. But I can't place him. *How does he know my name?* His friendliness erases my suspicions, so I take his hand, impressed by his firm grip and sinewy forearms. I glance around and catch sight of the dam, the trees, and a large sign warning swimmers of hazards.

But the rock-throwing kid and his grandfather appear to be gone. What has happened to them? My mind can't compute.

"Uriah, help me," the man with the nice eyes says as he drags me out of the water. Mud and river rocks make standing difficult, giving me the balance of a newborn colt. My legs quake, and my knees buckle. They refuse to support my water-logged frame.

"Sure thing, boss."

I swivel my head to see who's speaking. Another man . . . standing on the pebbled shore. He leans down and grabs my other arm, and together, they set me on both feet.

I pull my shirt down over my paunch and look closer at the guy named Uriah. He seems vaguely familiar, dressed similarly in a pair of threadbare shorts and fraying T-shirt, *also* pulled tight around his gut. His stocky build reminds me of my own.

So focused on this Uriah dude, I don't notice that the man with the gentle gaze has left. What happened to him? I shake my head, hoping the movement might rearrange my brains and help riddle the revolving-door scene where people appear and disappear, without so much as a sound.

"Good to see ya," Uriah says, treating me to a big, happy grin.

He then starts to speak to me about things I'd done and said, in some cases, years ago. "Remember that time you ran your car up on that concrete road divider? You know, it could've been a lot worse." He throws his head back and laughs. Claps me on the back. Like we've been best buds for years.

"How do you know about that?" I ask. I feel my eyes getting squinty. "You weren't there."

Uriah raises an eyebrow and continues jabbering, stopping briefly to run his freckled hands through his tousled ginger-colored hair. I can talk circles around most people, but this dude won't shut up about me or his now-missing companion whom he calls the "Big Man."

He obviously knows me, but how? Social media? A bar? The cosmos, somewhere? I'm wracking my brain trying to place him when he brings up Georgie.

"That dog of yours is something else. Got some pit in him?"

Whoa. Whoa. Whoa. I don't know if I should be weirded out or delighted. Uriah certainly wasn't there when an old man stopped Georgie and me on our ritual walk through the neighborhood the other day.

The image of that memory flashes back to mind. While we were walking, the old man had bent down at Georgie. "Sho is a purty dawg." With a trembling hand, the senior rubbed Georgie's head. Georgie's tail twirled. His backside wiggled maniacally. The old guy seemed smitten. "Yes, indeedy. Purty dawg." He scratched Georgie's ears and glanced up at me through rheumy eyes, and asked, "Got some pit in 'im? I could take this here boy home with me."

The memory fades, but I have no time to ask the source of Uriah's knowledge. Because at this moment, a feeling of light-headedness and detachment rushes over me. My body feels like it's hovering high above the ground, and then picks up speed, drawn toward a blindingly bright light. *What is happening?* Uriah fades, reappears, and fades again. He is talking but his voice sounds far away. Images and snippets of moments in my life then flash through my mind. I see these bits and pieces as an observer, not a participant, which gives me a different perspective. Someone must've drugged me because this isn't normal.

That's when the man with the tender bearing comes back into view. I wobble as a wave of nausea rolls over me.

"Uriah, enough. Give him a minute to adjust," the man says. "You'll have plenty of time to talk later." He grabs my arm to steady me and angles his head to get a better look at my face. A warm, tingly sensation of abiding love fills me. Although I want to look away, I can't. I'm mesmerized.

"You know Ginny's situation," the man says to Uriah, never taking his eyes off mine. He squeezes my shoulder and smiles. "You know what TC needs to do. You know dreams save lives. Take him."

And that's all I know right now, just that I'm going to Ginny's. Don't ask me to explain how or why. Don't ask me about dreams either. I'm still trying to work that out.

But here's the deal. I don't want to go with Uriah. I'd rather stay in this man's presence and drink up his warmth.

But he doesn't let me. He tells me I still have a job to do. Says it could be my finest hour.

After all, Ginny needs me.

CHAPTER TWO

Today, May 30

Did we dematerialize and reconstitute like something you'd see on Star Trek? Uriah is at my side outside of my friend Ginny's bedroom. We stand at the threshold of her opened doorway. How we got here is a blank. The neurons don't fire inside my brain. I rub my temples.

Am I hallucinating? Did I smash my head against a rock? Why can't I remember the trip here?

I ask Uriah, but he ignores my questions.

"Pay attention." Uriah places his hand on my shoulder. "You're a smart guy. You'll figure this out."

Understanding comes. Not all at once, but in fragments like I'm putting together a jigsaw puzzle and can finally recognize the big picture.

Since I first met Ginny at the outdoor music festival last spring, she's occupied a fair bit of my headspace. I can't count the times I've wanted to see her, talk to her, and make her laugh. Now, I'm maybe twenty feet from her and feel like a creepy voyeur, peering uninvited into her life. *This is the last place I want to be.*

Uriah seems able to read my thoughts and what I'll say next. He shakes his head and puts his finger to his lips. He will not indulge my protests. In silence, we stand side-by-side just beyond the threshold and stare at Ginny, sitting on the edge of a king-sized bed, rocking, and whispering to a baby in a light pink onesie. A pink headband is affixed to the baby's head, and her blonde hair sticks up in all directions. Does the baby belong to Ginny? The little one grasps her dimpled hands and then clumsily shoves them into her mouth, gurgling.

Ginny must not be able to see or sense our presence. She doesn't look up the way people do when they suspect someone staring at them. Another head scratcher. *Were we that quiet when we landed here, or are we invisible?* I pinch myself. I feel the sting. *So, why can't she see us? I don't like this.* Being in the spotlight is my stock and trade.

I narrow my eyes and look harder. Something is wrong. In more ways than one.

Though she sits in a beautifully outfitted room, with custom plantation-style shades and tasteful furniture available only in designer showrooms, she, herself, looks like she lives in the streets with strung-out people who warm their hands over barrel fires amid the trash and used needles that litter the sidewalk.

Her honey-blonde hair is unwashed and stringy. It hangs in

her face, and her clothes look dirty and several sizes too big. The Ginny I knew stayed spotless even after a deluge and, like a cat stretched on its side licking and grooming its paws, she would spend several minutes scrubbing mud off her white cowgirl boots. It was one of the personality traits that attracted me. Made me want to do better. Take better care of myself. And here she is now . . . rode hard and hung up wet. That's not the Ginny I know. The girl I knew would light up even the darkest corners, her eyes shining as she talked about her future and the possibilities.

Who or what has smothered her inner light?

I scan the spacious bedroom. The initial perception of perfection gives way to a different reality. An empty baby bottle sits on top of the nightstand next to an empty bottle of wine. A crystal wine glass, tinged with the residue of fermented grape, teeters on the table's edge, and another empty bottle lays atop a large red stain on an otherwise unblemished gray rug. When we said our goodbyes a year ago, Ginny didn't drink alcohol. A life choice I personally didn't share.

What happened to her?

My concentration is interrupted. Footsteps pound up a flight of stairs and across a hardwood floor. Ginny hears them too. She stops whispering in the baby's ear and pulls the child protectively to her chest. Her head swivels as if she's looking for an escape hatch. Finding none, her body shrinks like a deflated balloon.

I turn my head to look down the hallway.

Jacob. He's headed our way.

He looks exactly as I remember him. He accentuates his

movie-star looks with perfectly pressed, stylish clothes and coiffed, auburn-colored hair. Even his five o'clock shadow looks manicured. All artifice.

Although Jacob seems in a hurry, he stops at a hallway mirror. He adjusts his collar and smooths his hair, then tilts his head side-to-side to check all angles. Satisfied, he sweeps past me and Uriah, as if we don't exist, and positions himself directly in front of Ginny still sitting on the bed with his hands on his hips.

I look at Uriah. He draws in a deep breath, his mouth forming a hard, straight line.

"Gotta go. Have a plane to catch." Jacob's voice sounds friendly enough. He bounces on the toes of his polished Italian loafers. "Back tomorrow night or early Friday morning."

If Jacob notices the bottles, the wineglass, or the baby, he doesn't show it. His smile reveals perfectly aligned, overly bleached teeth. In his confident voice, he tells Ginny that he's hours away from scoring the biggest business deal of his life. Jacob glances at his expensive-looking watch, something I wouldn't wear even if I *could* afford it. My Android works just fine. I check my pockets, another rote behavior, and realize the phone's gone.

Ginny rests her chin on top of the baby's head and studies an invisible spot on the wall behind him. I can now see her unfocused eyes. Her pallor. Caring people normally notice things like this and ask what's wrong. Not Jacob. He reaches down, grabs her chin, and forces her to look at him.

"Don't bother calling or texting." His eyes narrow and he shakes his head.

She tries to pull away, but his grip on her chin is too strong. The fingers on his other hand flex. *Is he going to hit her?*

"I don't want to hear from you." He stops, moves back, and takes in the room. "Look at this place. Who's worked hard to give you this lifestyle? These clothes? This beautiful home? You don't appreciate anything I've done. Who lifted you out of your squalor, Ginny?" He waits a few seconds and sneers. "Do the names Jimmy and Audrey ring a bell?" He laughs.

All color drains from her face.

She jumps up and thrusts the baby into his arms. "I'm going to throw up." She stumbles to an open interior bedroom door, a hand clamped over her mouth. He frowns and places the baby on the bed. He wipes his palms on his khaki pants and turns to leave. But then he stops when he hears the toilet flush.

"I'm not done with you yet," he yells. "When I get back, we're going to sit down for a little talk. I want *you* to tell me about Jimmy and Audrey."

Ginny emerges from the bathroom, dabbing her mouth with a towel.

"You're pathetic. You know that? I can smell you from six feet away."

He turns and resumes his strut across the room, kicking aside a pile of clothes as he sails past Uriah and me, again oblivious to our presence. The sounds of his footsteps recede as he progresses through the hall and down the stairs, punctuated by a slammed door.

The muscles in my jaw tighten. I've never started a fistfight in my life but can hardly resist the urge to run after Jacob and sucker punch him. I want to send him sprawling across the floor. I want to hurt him.

Why didn't Ginny defend herself? Moments before walking out of my life, she had stood up to that creep.

Uriah places his hand on my forearm. "Jacob's not your concern. Concentrate on Ginny."

CHAPTER THREE

Today, May 30

Jacob's exit refocuses Ginny's attention on the baby, who is still lying on the bed where Jacob dropped her. Ginny picks up her child. "Time for bed, baby girl. Mommy's done."

Though she slurs her words, her warm and welcoming Southern drawl charms me just as it did when we first met at the festival. Right after she hoisted me from the mud.

She rubs her chin and shuffles across the room toward a small crib in the corner. She trips over a pair of shoes but manages to stay upright. She lays the baby down, removes the headband, and kisses her forehead. Her smile doesn't reach her eyes. "Go to sleep now. Mommy needs a long rest too."

Long rest? What does that mean?

As Ginny starts toward the king-sized bed, she changes directions and heads for the dresser instead. At the mirror, she licks her finger, and rubs the smudges of black mascara beneath her eyes. "Pointless." She glances down at her stained misshaped black T-shirt, lifts it to her nose, and sniffs. "Maybe, I'll take a shower later. Maybe I won't. Who cares anyway?"

I look at Uriah and raise my eyebrows. Ginny's a mess. Was it only Jacob who contributed to her misery? He's certainly capable. But what else has happened since we said goodbye?

I feel helpless. Ashamed. Back when I first met Ginny, I knew what lay ahead if she stayed with Jacob. But I said nothing. I was too caught up in my own doubts. Think of all the heartache I could've prevented had I just opened my mouth. Now what can I say? She hasn't seen me in a year, and I show up like *this*?

Uriah tilts his head, looking at me. I get the sense that he doesn't agree with my unspoken assessment and isn't in the mood to hear my arguments and excuses.

My attention is drawn to Ginny's herky-jerky lurch toward the bed, but she stops when she notices the empty bottle and crystal wine glass. She takes a few more clumsy steps toward the bed and falls to her knees in front of the nightstand. "Where are they?" she mutters, pushing aside papers and books, sweeping the wine bottle to the floor. The wine glass cracks when it falls on the table next to the baby bottle.

Ginny's frenetic search reminds me of a moment we'd shared hours after we met. It was a magical time for me. She was rummaging through her super-sized satchel looking for an item lost among the crackers, notebooks, pens, sunglasses, and other girly detritus. I'd snatched the bag playfully, dumped the contents on the ground, and explained the virtues of traveling light. Our hands brushed and I knew this girl could be the one for me.

So lost in my memory, her voice startles me, jolting me to reality.

"Get real. Jacob's never gonna stop," she slurs. "What does he know about Jimmy? Audrey? I can't do this. Maybe I'll beat him to the punch...with these."

A plastic sandwich bag dangles from her fingers. It's filled with multi-colored pills bouncing around in a lewd dance because of her twitching fingers.

My mind can't process what my eyes see. Is she planning an overdose? I glance at Uriah. His eyes shimmer with tears.

She drags herself onto the bed and dumps a few pills in her hand. She examines each and then places them back, one by one. "Not yet but soon." Her voice is a whisper. "Gotta take care of the baby. Call Melinda." She starts scouring the nightstand drawer.

If I hadn't seen the drugs, heard her retching, then the scene would have been laughable. She could never find her stuff. She shuffles the drawer's contents until she finds her phone and scrolls through her numbers, taps a name, and lifts the phone to her ear.

"Hey, Melinda, Ginny here." She pauses. "No, I'm not drinking. Why would you say that?" She eyes the baby bottle and broken glass on the table and the bottles on the floor. She stares at the wine-stained rug and closes her eyes. "I'm tired. Laurel had a rough night. Cranky. Out of sorts. She hasn't slept much today either." She listens and clears her throat. "No, he didn't help. Because of her fussing, he told me to put her in our room and he slept in the other. Said he needed his sleep."

She pulls the phone away from her ear. The woman's voice is muffled, her words undecipherable.

"Don't worry. I'm okay," Ginny says, lifting her voice. "Don't come over. Things are under control. I fed Laurel and put her down. I'm going to bed. I need sleep . . . lots of it." She rolls her eyes. "I know it's only seven o'clock, but I'm beat. Only called to see if you would pop in tomorrow morning."

Ginny glances at the baggie in her left hand. "No, he won't be here. He left a few minutes ago for a business trip and won't be home for a few days." She secures the phone between her shoulder and ear, punches a pillow, then shoves it to the floor. Some of the pills scatter all over the bed.

"Good grief. Sorry, wasn't talking to you. I just dropped something." She puts each pill back inside the bag. "Look, I'll be upstairs, so don't bother knocking. Let yourself in. You know where the key is."

Ginny places the phone on the nightstand and falls back onto the mattress. The sheet and blanket are bunched in a knot at the foot of the bed. She tries to untangle them with one hand but gives up and curls herself into a tight ball instead.

And then she starts bawling. The howling intensifies. The baby doesn't react. *Is she used to this?*

I try to ask a question, but Uriah shushes me. He's waiting.

Within a minute or two, Ginny's cries turn into whimpers. She soon falls asleep with the bag secured in her clutched hand.

"Time to go, TC." Uriah faces me. He wipes his eyes. Probably trying to hide his tears the same way my dad did when he didn't want us kids to catch him crying during a sad movie. "Our girl is in trouble. She's lost all hope. You gotta help her, and you don't have much time."

My head spins. Sweat forms in my armpits, and my heart pumps.

I hate seeing Ginny like this. Now that I've witnessed Jacob's manhandling, I suspect he's the source of her downfall. I hate everything about this situation and blame myself for it.

I should have warned her when I had the chance.

"What if she doesn't remember me?" I rub my nose, a tic some people assume is a cocaine habit of mine. But only because they know nothing of my deep-seated insecurities. My feelings of inadequacy that I mask behind a super-sized persona.

Uriah laughs and grasps my shoulders, looking straight into my eyes. "You have a lot to learn my friend. This could be a mountaintop moment for you and her, but *you* need to get out of the way. Stop underestimating yourself. Do what you've always done best. Talk to her. She'll listen to you." A small smile forms on his lips. "Look at Ginny's wrist."

I glance toward her. She wears the memory bracelet I had given her before Jacob yanked her out of my life.

"Ginny Carmichael wants you to come," Uriah says, bringing my attention back to him.

"Carmichael? That's her last name? Never knew it."

"Go." Uriah guides me closer to the bedroom entryway. "Stop her."

I bite my lip and nod.

And then I step past the threshold . . . and into the unknown.

CHAPTER FOUR

Today, May 30

Within moments of crossing over the threshold, a strange physical force takes over. It's as though I've stepped onto an invisible roller coaster that is unlike anything ridden before in my life. My body feels like hot mozzarella, stretched and elastic until it seems to break apart into a stream of subatomic particles, now circling a dark, eerily quiet drain.

Have I stepped into another dimension? My entire sense of time and place have vanished. One minute, I'm standing next to Uriah outside Ginny's bedroom door and then I'm shrouded in darkness.

Just as I want to freak, yell at Uriah and the Big Man, a light comes into view. A room.

Ginny.

Before I stepped over the threshold, she was curled up in a fetal position on her bed. Now, she sits upright in her bed, propped up on pillows. She gazes at the corner where the crib sits, absently rubbing two reddish bruises on her chin. *What is going on here? How much time has passed?* Because now she looks different. Her complexion looks pale and sickly, and her eyes are puffed, but she appears sober and alert—a huge improvement.

Nothing makes sense.

The baby still sleeps in her crib. The wine bottles and heaps of clothing lie on the floor, and the pills rest on top of the sheet. But the room feels ethereal now, as though fairies draped it in strands of shimmering gossamer. Has the soft glow from the table lamp created this effect or is it caused by something else? It didn't look like this before.

Not knowing if she can see me, I give it a go and rap the door jamb with my knuckles before taking a few hesitant steps forward. If she can see me in the flesh . . . *what will I say then? How am I supposed to help her?* My nose itches. Uriah and the Big Man had provided no details, only that she'd likely listen to me. That I would know what to say when the time came. It certainly seems the tables have turned where Ginny is concerned. Wasn't she ministering to me a year ago?

She looks at me and her eyes widen. "TC, is that you? Oh my gosh. Your hair is longer. You've shaved your beard. Wow. You look great." She looks flushed as she slides over to the side of the bed. "How did you find me? Did Jacob let you in the house?"

I run my hands through my unkempt hair, not barbered since I last saw her. The dirty-blond strands are slicked back off my forehead, tucked behind my ears. I don't return the compliment because I don't want to lie. She looks awful.

"Yeah, I caught him just as he was headed out the door. He thought I was the pool guy."

Her dimples play at the corners of her mouth and light returns to her eyes. "So glad he did. Don't stand out there skulking. Come in. Sit." She pats a spot on the bed. "This is a dream. Must be. I woke up this morning thinking I needed to talk with you. And here you are. How did you find me?"

Thank God, she spares me from telling another lie. Pool guy? Where'd that come from?

She bounces from one topic to the next and asks about my real-estate business and friends—the people she'd met at the festival. When did she last talk with a good friend? Out of the corner of my eye, I see her slide the pills beneath the pillow.

If they were legit, why hide them? *Should I confront her now?* The thought is vetoed. Getting in her face could backfire, shut her down completely, make her suspicious. She knows me as the class clown, not the hall monitor.

Keep this conversational. Nonconfrontational. Catch up like all friends do when they haven't seen each other in a while. Tell her a few stories until I get the big picture—her plan for that stash.

The room shimmers again. *Odd that she hasn't questioned me again on why I'm here.*

I sit next to her on the bed, partly to stop the room from spinning, and run my clammy hands over the fitted sheet. Smooth. Silky. Expensive.

"Yep, here I am," I say. "The fat guy." I launch into my *Tommy*

Boy rendition, and she starts laughing.

"You're outrageous, you know that?" She smiles. "I wish you'd stop thinking of yourself like that."

"Like what?"

"The fat guy."

"Come on, girl." I slap my stomach. "Look at this gut."

She shakes her head. "No. I am not buying it. Look at you. Your blue eyes, your smile . . . both give *me* reason to smile." Her dimples show. "I can't believe you're here."

"Okay, enough." My face is hot. Did she really see me as described? "How've you been?"

She stretches to grab her phone off the table and starts scrolling. "Here it is." She thrusts the phone at me. I'm not the only one wanting to ignore questions. "Remember this?"

It's a picture. The selfie she took at the festival but never sent it to me. No time with all the ruckus once Jacob finally showed up. The photo's not the best. The lighting was bad. But we looked cheery posed outside my tent. Her white cowgirl hat was angled playfully to the side, and my cap of many colors was pulled tight over my head. The brim pointed backward—my normal style.

"You rock the hat, Ginny. I, on the other hand, look crazed."

"Yeah, what's with the bug eyes and the tongue thing?"

"Maybe I was thirsty." I hand the phone to her. "Or maybe I was channeling Georgie."

"Georgie? Your dog?"

I nod. My mind wanders to good ol' itchy, scratchy, happy boy—the name I call him because of his perennial flea problem.

He got into the trash last night and threw up on my area rug. I couldn't stay mad long. He rolled himself beneath his blanket, which undulated as his unseen tail wagged. He is the bright spot in my otherwise directionless life.

I'm worried about him. He doesn't know where I am, and neither do I. *Is this Atlanta? Ginny did say she was moving there, didn't she?*

And what time is it? I check my pockets. No phone.

I glance at the bedroom door and see Uriah. He stands near the bedroom door, beyond the threshold, with his hands shoved in his pockets. He told me things would become clearer as this mission progressed. He was right. No wonder this room shimmers.

Now, the day's events scroll past like movie credits.

Dad took Georgie home with him. We're supposed to watch the hockey championship later. Georgie is probably on the ridge chasing rabbits or driving my mother crazy with his incessant squealing. He usually does that when he wants attention or something to eat. Mom treats him like a human, not a dog. I don't blame her. Not one of us has produced progeny to carry on the family name.

Uriah smiles, and more of the uncertainty dissolves, like stirred sugar in a glass of iced tea. The increased clarity of how and why I'm here results in mixed emotions.

Georgie's in high spirits. Mom and Dad aren't.

Ginny lays the phone next to her on the bed, unaware of my inner turmoil and Uriah's existence. I glance at the doorway. Now Uriah is gone.

"I nearly cried when I found the photo this morning." Ginny looks at me and chews her lip. "I also kept this."

She shows me the rubber memory bracelet on her left wrist. I never regretted giving it to her, only the reason for my getting it. A kid I played with every day of my young life died a few years ago from an inoperable brain cancer. His mother gave it to me after his funeral.

I loved that lady. She was like a second mom. She'd given up her lucrative career as a lobbyist to become a stay-at-home mother, swapping meetings with congressional staff to fix after-school snacks for me and her only child born later in life. I'd visit even when he wasn't around, bombarding her with questions about Capitol Hill. Her observations contributed to my passion for politics and general distain for politicians. Within a year of his death, she and her husband moved away, partly to escape the memories. For her, the grieving had to be done, but it needed to happen in another place.

Until I gave the turquoise-colored band to Ginny, it never left my wrist. Philippians 1:30 was inscribed on it in bold letters. I'm no Bible scholar, so the chapter and verse meant zippo to me—that is, until I looked it up after the funeral. "I thank my God every time I remember you." I almost cried when I read that verse.

"TC, I cherished it," Ginny tells me. "Granny loved the verse. She used to say people are placed in our lives for a reason, even if only for a short amount of time. Without them, we might never live up to our potential or the plan God has for our lives. Didn't I talk about this, or at least something similar, last year?" She rubs her forehead and seems to shiver. "Whatever. She thought we needed to thank God when we thought of these special people."

Ginny goes on to tell me she wore the memory bracelet for weeks before Jacob noticed it while they ate at a fancy restaurant in Atlanta, where diners spoke in hushed voices and waiters stealthily brushed crumbs from the white linen tablecloths. She figured it wouldn't hurt to tell Jacob I'd given it to her. Big mistake. "He went ballistic," she says. "I'd never seen him so mad. His voice got louder and louder, and people at surrounding tables turned to stare. I've never been so uncomfortable in my life."

"Seems a bit over-the-top. Don't you think?"

"I think he was embarrassed more than anything." Ginny's face reddens.

I can't imagine why she would be embarrassed. She didn't act like a jerk. *He* did.

Does she understand what's she dealing with? Because I do. I've experienced people just like Jacob. That's why I should've opened my mouth to begin with.

"He didn't know what Philippians was. I was educating him, and he doesn't like that," Ginny continues. "He started making fun of me and Granny, accused us of being Bible thumpers. He even accused me of having a relationship with you." She stops to let that sink in. "To keep the peace, I took it off, forgot about it and found it today. It's like a sign because here you are." Her eyes widen.

"How did you find me, TC?" She frowns. "I didn't know how to get in touch with you, and boy, did I want to. Kept thinking how I let you slip away. Good grief, we spent hours with each other, and never once did I ask for your phone number or your last name. Typed TC into Facebook and Instagram, even X, but nothing came up. I was so mad at myself."

I was mad at myself too.

"I knew Granny's full name," I tell her. "So, I looked her up. Caught a few breaks. That's how I found you." I keep my tone light and normal while lying through my teeth. She can't handle the truth yet.

And neither can I.

"I actually just went swimming," I say. I still have on my red swim trunks and dirty T-shirt, both damp from my plunge into the river. *Where are my flip-flops?* That's right, they're near the bank where I jumped, and my wallet and phone are in the car. I feel naked without the phone, my lifeline to the world. She hasn't mentioned my bare feet. How would I explain that?

She tilts her head to the side and purses her lips, but oddly she accepts my vague answer without question. I look toward the crib. "You're a mama, Ginny." I comment in my best *Forrest Gump* impersonation, polished from years of watching the movie. The soundtrack and story about two impossibly mismatched people rank high on my list of favorites. Their lopsided love story par- alleled ours—two people who couldn't be more dissimilar in experiences and temperament. But also, strangely alike.

In the end, though, Forrest got the girl. And I did not.

I think of my first love, Chelsey. A girl who dumped me for someone who was rich and good-looking like Jacob. According to the grapevine, Chelsey's a mother now. I'm oddly indifferent to the news now.

"Yes, I'm a mama." Ginny laughs, seeming to forget the *whys* and *wherefores* of my unexpected visit. She doesn't seem curious about my lack of footwear either. Interesting.

The constant shimmering of my surroundings makes me nauseous. Nothing seems real. Nothing except the pills, Ginny's obvious decline, and the chance for redemption. The do-over.

I tiptoe to the crib to peek at the baby. I enjoy babies and kids, but Ginny's never seen this side of me. Might work in my favor later.

"Do you mind?" I ask her.

"Absolutely not. Bring her over here if you'd like."

I lift the baby. She opens her eyes—the same cornflower blue as Ginny's, a definite bonus—and gurgles. "And what's your name, Princess Booger Face?" My clown face—also perfected for kids' entertainment—elicits the expected reaction. She kicks and waves her chubby legs and arms. Bubbles appear on her rosebud-colored lips. She shows me her still toothless gums.

"Hey, I think she likes me." I blow raspberries on her belly. She coos. "How old is she?"

"More than three months. What did you call her? Princess what?"

"All kids love potty talk," I say. "Words like fart, poop, and booger always get them going."

Nestling her in my arms, I rub my nose into the folds of her neck as I step around the clothing. She smells like clean baby, and her pink onesie like a dryer sheet. Ginny never met the original Princess Booger Face, the daughter of a friend. I smile as I remember the annoying kid pranks she'd pull, hoping I'd call her my special name. I always gave in. Her giggle is contagious.

I tell Ginny about that little girl. "She's a ballerina and demanded I see her recital last week. She loved the bouquet of flowers."

"Flowers?" Ginny's mouth drops a little. "Why aren't you married, TC?" She edges closer and looks at my left hand. She sees she's not mistaken. In the year since we parted, no woman has stolen my heart. "You're thirty-three, right? A few years older than me. You should have a passel of kids."

She's probably right, and my parents certainly would've been pleased. But that train's already left the station.

Ginny's mouth quivers, watching me jostle her baby. Her eyes look watery. I can't imagine what's going through her head. Does Jacob, whom I assume is the baby daddy, give his daughter a second look? Stupid question. I saw how he interacted with her earlier. He couldn't wait to get her out of his arms.

I almost blurt out the reason for being single, but I can't go there. I've suppressed my feelings for Ginny, and that's how they'll remain. That's not the point of this visit anyway. I'm supposed to be helping her, being her friend, stopping her from committing suicide, if that's her intention, not acting like a jilted lover.

"What's her name?" I ask.

"Laurel Alma." Ginny's face brightens. "I named her in honor of my sister and Granny."

I sit on the bed and Ginny moves closer, wrapping her arm around my shoulder. It's the first time we've touched since my arrival. We stare at baby Laurel, who stares back at us with her large, banjo-shaped eyes. Ginny caresses the side of Laurel's face.

"I guess I did something right," she says quietly. "A lot has happened since I saw you. I'm not doing well. Can't eat. Yes, you can say it, TC. I noticed the look on your face when you walked into the room. I'm a wreck and wish you didn't see me this way. But you came, unannounced, seeing me at my worst."

"Sorry about that. I don't look great either." I smile. "Got the sense we needed to see each other. Didn't have a chance to give you a heads-up. Fast trip. If you want me to go, I'll go. Some people don't like pop-ins."

She cocks her head to the side. "Oh no. It doesn't matter. You came, and that's all that counts. I needed to see you even if it's for the last time."

I'm not sure how to interpret the remark.

She looks at her lap. The pause feels never-ending. "Have you ever thought that life isn't worth the struggle?"

"Ginny, you know about my ups and downs, my bouts with insecurity and lack of direction. You pointed them out. Remember? But life is always worth living. So, what's going on, girl?" I point to the wine bottles. "You look like you've tied on a good one. And we both know that's not your style. I'm not blind. Something is wrong. Talk to me. I can help. That's why I'm here."

"You wouldn't understand. Granny wouldn't have understood either."

"Try me." *Did she just refer to Granny in the past tense?*

She covers her face with her hands and mumbles. "Why didn't

we meet sooner?"

A question for the ages. One I ask myself often.

And the tears collecting at the corners of her eyes let loose, flowing down her hollowed-out cheeks.

CHAPTER FIVE

Uriah, Today, May 30

I wish I could walk through Ginny's bedroom doorway, but the physics won't allow it. Not under these special circumstances. But that's okay. I'm a behind-the-scenes kind of guy, anyway. I nudge. I deliver messages. I offer encouragement. I've been doing it for eons, most recently for TC. He's my favorite. We could pass as brothers, with our fair coloring, stocky builds, and manner of speaking. Finally, a kindred soul I can protect.

He appealed to me instantly. He's a talker. To him and me—when I'm given the chance—conversation is approached as a full-body sport, a way to amuse people while figuring out what makes them tick. He finds humor in everything and laughs at accents, colloquialisms, and eccentricities, including his own. Of all his attributes, though, I most appreciate how he never puts people or situations into tidy, preconceived boxes. He examines *everything* from all sides. Only then does he form an opinion, which he's all too happy to share. But at least he doesn't jump to conclusions or cling to stereotypes like a lot of other people I've seen. But that's neither here nor there now.

Me? I'm a people watcher too. But I'm also nosey. Snooping around in medicine cabinets and closets isn't beneath me. Neither is eavesdropping. How can I do my job effectively if I don't know the full picture? But right now, hanging around in this expansive hallway, listening to their conversation—that's not cutting it for me. I'm getting antsy. Furthermore, TC and Ginny deserve some privacy. They have a lot of ground to cover and not a lot of time to get it done.

What to do? What to do? I rub my jaw and glance down the hallway. The Big Man knows all, but I do not. The open bedroom doors beckon.

Time to poke around.

My first stop is the nursery to the left. Light is fading, so I flip on the switch. Fancy. Looks like a photo spread in an architectural magazine. A hand-painted mural of a large-leafed tree dominates one pale-pink wall, and stuffed toys line a shelf beneath the window seat. An elaborate dollhouse sits to one side of a white crib and a rocking horse on the other. The room doesn't look used. Will it ever?

Too soon to say.

I back out of the baby's nursery and glance down the hallway, debating whether I should walk back to Ginny's room. *Nah.* I've showered TC with enough atta-boys and go-for-its. He's got it covered.

I head for another room across the hall and peek in. Other than for a rumbled daybed and a wrinkled, button-down dress shirt lying on the bed, it's neat. Excessively so. I wipe my hands on my shorts, check fast to make sure no one is around, and seeing no one, I step in for a closer look. It's amazing what can be learned by analyzing people's belongings.

A wall-sized collection of framed photos is positioned above the daybed, aligned in perfect rows. I lean in to take a closer look. Humph. *What's-his-name sure thinks highly of himself.* Every single photo is of him:

At a golf course.

A grand opening.

The beach.

I spend a minute or two examining a black-and-white of Jacob standing next to an older, imperious-looking man with graying temples and an uplifted chin. *Must be his father. Where is Ginny?* I scan the photos again to make sure I hadn't overlooked one of her, but she doesn't exist in Jacob's perfect pictorial world. *For the life of me, what does she see in him?* I shove my hands into my pockets and step toward a massive glass curio cabinet on the other wall.

The cabinet houses Jacob's trophies, diplomas, and awards and the walk-in closet, its door wide open, displays starched dress shirts and pressed slacks arranged according to color. Shoes of all styles occupy a floor-to-ceiling storage cubby, the toes pointing out. This room is monotonous.

I've gathered all I need to know and am ready to leave when I notice a small, framed photo lying face down on one of the curio shelves. It seems misplaced among the neatly arranged mementos.

I open the glass cabinet door and pick up the frame.

A petite, middle-aged woman wearing stylish slacks and blouse gazes up at Jacob, her arm latched around his waist. Whoever this woman is, Jacob doesn't seem to share her devotion. He leans away from her, his arms folded, as he stares unsmiling into the camera.

I return the framed photo. Other than for the framed photo of Georgie, TC doesn't have photos hanging on the walls or sitting on his mantel. He keeps them in his phone. What gives with Jacob? Does he need to see himself in every room he enters?

Ginny should've met TC sooner. She should've agreed when he offered to drive her home from the music festival last year . . . Oh, the choices people make. Make this right, TC. I'm rooting for you.

CHAPTER SIX

The Festival, One Year Earlier

Ginny and I met by happenstance, like it had been preordained, especially since we were two souls literally among thousands of other festival goers. How else to explain it? I'd never expected meeting someone like her, let alone in a mini-mob of my own creation. But that's exactly what happened.

My only expectation for the long weekend at that backcountry farm was to groove to Phish, one of the headliners. And yes, I did groove because no other word described my dancing to one of the greatest jam bands of all time.

I don't know what Ginny expected. Unlike me, a seasoned festival-goer who digs the laissez-faire vibe, Ginny was a newbie to the outdoor concert world, and her naiveté showed. No one, and I mean *no one*, wore all-white outfits to these events. But she did, and she reminded me of an angel when our paths crossed. Our meeting was just one of those little quirks of fate, orchestrated by Jacob's need to impress a potential client who'd given him a couple of free day passes. Ginny tagged along because Jacob insisted. I guess he didn't want to rub shoulders with the *hoi polloi* alone.

The day had started ordinarily enough. My best friend Bryan and I had arrived a day early to get a primo campsite close to the center of action, a large town square featuring one huge stage for the headliners, a few smaller ones for the up-and-comers, and art exhibits, food tents, and cellphone charging stations. The event planners thought of everything.

So did we. We got our good spot.

Bryan, a tall and skinny dude, set up our yellow-colored four-person tent and matching canopy. He hung the banners and flag that we brought to distinguish our camp from the others. Meanwhile, I humped the cooler and filled it with ice and beer bought earlier at a roadside quickie mart. After positioning the camp chairs within arm's reach of the cooler just inside the tent, I started blasting our playlists through a portable speaker.

We got comfy and the party soon started, all according to plan. That is, until the skies opened the next morning. By early afternoon, when the sun appeared briefly, festivalgoers had thoroughly trampled the grass and weeds, rendering a thick stew of slick red clay that made walking, let alone dancing, quite the challenge.

"Scenery's pretty good this year," Bryan said, pointing to a gorgeous blonde wearing a halter top and a pair of Daisy Dukes. "Like the outfit. Why don't more women dress like that? You should go meet her." He grinned.

I rolled my eyes. *Here we go again.* Bryan, the Jewish matchmaker from hell. "They do," I said. "She's one of thousands. How about that little honey over there?" I grabbed another beer, popped the top and started talking about a former politician on trial for embezzlement. Bryan was used to my constant chatter about pop culture, politics, and religion, and the sudden change in topic didn't faze him. He wasn't listening anyway.

"Women are awesome." Bryan leaned back in his chair and sighed.

"Settle down, amigo," I said. "Don't you have a girlfriend back home?"

"Who says I can't look?"

No one.

For inexplicable reasons, especially given the day's hot, muggy weather, I'd put on a wrinkled suit jacket that had been jammed into my backpack. Impatient to get on the road, Bryan wouldn't wait for me to search my overstuffed closet for my lightweight windbreaker. Other than the coat, I wore my preferred duds: ratty cargo shorts, a sweat-stained Hawaiian-style shirt, hiking boots, and my favorite multi-colored baseball cap.

After a few more minutes of inconsequential chatter, Bryan sat up straight in his chair. "What's that smell? Been smelling it all morning." He leaned over and sniffed my coat. "What's wrong with you, dude? You smell like a dog. No wonder you can't find a girlfriend." He jumped up. "The rain stopped. Let's go. Ditch the coat. Get yourself a woman. We can double date." He laughed.

Though preferring to lounge at the tent, I agreed. Maybe today was the day. The girl of my dreams could be waiting for me just beyond these yellow polyester walls. At the very least, maybe Bryan would get off my case.

I searched my backpack for my ear buds and tossed my baseball cap in the corner because I didn't want to lose it in the crowds. The coat stayed on, partly to annoy Bryan.

Like butterflies freeing themselves from their chrysalises, we emerged from the tent and closed the flaps. "You have more pockets than I do," Bryan said. "Take my keys, would ya? Afraid I'll lose 'em."

I rolled my eyes and pocketed the keys. Now eager to get to the stages where we'd join the hot, smelly masses.

The inimitable Phish wasn't performing until late the following night, and the band taking the stage at that moment didn't interest me. I screwed in my ear buds, found *Tweezer*—my favorite Phish tune on my Android's stored music—and turned up the volume. My feet started moving. My hips swayed and arms flailed as my head rolled in rhythm to the song.

"This party's getting serious now, dawg," I said to Bryan in my boisterous voice.

"Who are you listening to?"

I unleashed my signature laugh and started singing the freezer-tweezer song off-key and at full volume.

People stopped to watch, creating a large circle around me. They whooped and hollered, clapped their hands, egging me on to zanier twists and turns—imbecilic since I'd already compromised my balance with the morning's libations.

Didn't know it then but hidden among the growing crowd was Ginny. At some point, she had joined the circle fest because she was attracted, as she told me later, by the raucous cheers and comments about "how that crazy short dude could dance."

My joy didn't last.

The heavy sludge beneath the soles of my boots had morphed into meat platters. While standing on my left leg and trying to shake off the accumulated mud on my right, Bryan slapped me on the shoulder and asked what was wrong with me. In his opinion, the band on stage deserved a listen. We'd get our Phish fix the following night. Why not broaden our horizons?

His timing couldn't have been worse. I went down, face first, arms and legs splayed, my feet still encased in mud.

Something ripped. My jacket? I tasted blood. My lip? The crowd murmured and the hoots and handclapping stopped.

"Ah man, TC. So sorry, brah," Bryan said. Laughing hysterically, he grabbed my arm and tried to haul me up.

But he lost his balance and fell backwards.

More laughter erupted. But seeing no broken arms or legs, most of the mini mob moved on, leaving me prostrate and Bryan scrambling in the muck. The lyrics to that old Johnny Cash song about drunks crashing through a wall and into the street came to mind.

"Give me your hand."

Still face-down, I turned my head and blinked through the mud caked on my eyes to see who was speaking. That quiet, gentle voice—a melody to my ears since developing a passion for the Southern drawl—didn't come from Bryan. He was nowhere.

Her cowgirl boots came into view first, then two shapely, mud-speckled legs, white shorts, and T-shirt. Bracing my stocky body on my right forearm, I finally saw her face, which was partially hidden by a white cowgirl hat. Her hair was pulled off her neck and into a ponytail. "Come on, let me help you." She took my hand.

Where Bryan failed, Ginny succeeded. She dug her heels into the ground and managed to pull me onto my feet. That surprised me, coming from a woman so small and slender.

"Come on, Ginny, let's go." A man who stood a few feet behind her barked the order. He didn't help her or introduce himself to me. He crossed his arms, tapped his foot, and frowned.

"Wait a sec." She stepped closer to pluck a few blades of grass out of my beard, and then pulled a napkin from her oversized and colorful satchel draped across her torso. She dabbed my bloody mouth and face, then she gently turned my body to search for potential damage on my flipside.

My hands went to my back pockets. I started patting them. Where was my little black book, the book where I jot down my observations and joke ideas? It couldn't be gone.

I got on all fours and started searching the ground.

"What are you looking for?" she asked. "Your wallet?"

"No, my book." I looked up into her face. Though she didn't get on hands and knees, her eyes scanned the trampled grass as she helped me look. "My wallet isn't worth looking for. Not much in it."

"Are you sure you had the book?"

I rubbed my forehead with my muddy hand and laughed. "You

know, I think it might be back at the tent. I'm an idiot."

"No, you're probably just a little distracted. Happens to me too."

Distracted? Not the word I'd chosen. How about slack-jawed and nearly senseless.

I stood, face-to-face with Ginny, and couldn't help but notice how innocent and fresh she looked. She'd not succumbed to covering every square inch of her body with tattoos, and she didn't have tiny holes drilled into her tongue, nose, and ears, then plugged with hoops and studs. She reminded me of a girl from a different era. Where did she grow up?

She had just started wiping the mud smears from my face when we heard a high-pitched squeal.

"Oh my gosh, I can't believe my eyes. Is that you? *Jacob?* What's it been? Years?" A woman pushed her way through the crowd, violating every rule in the festival book of etiquette. She drew glares from those she shoved aside. The statuesque redhead wore a leopard-skin get-up and then flung her arms around Jacob and kissed him on the cheek. He smiled broadly. His chest puffed.

"We need to catch up," she said, pulling on his arm and telling him she'd treat him to a drink. Her orange-painted talons pointed toward the glamp site where the well-heeled took their meals and laid their heads at night. She didn't seem to notice Ginny, my mud-speckled angel in white. How could she? She was smiling rapturously at the man, devouring him with her eyes.

His head swiveled between the two women before he nodded an okay to the redhead. "Ginny, I won't be long. I'll text you later."

He flung his arm around the woman's shoulder, then off they went, blending into the crush of people.

I didn't know what to think or what to do.

"Now what am I supposed to do?" Ginny shook her head in bewilderment.

"Don't know. May as well introduce myself. I'm TC." I wiped my hands on my muddy shorts and extended my hand. "What's your name?"

"Ginny."

We shook hands.

"Jenny?"

"No. Ginny. A diminutive for *Virginia*." She leaned around to take another look at my backside. "I hope you're handy with a needle because that coat of yours is toast."

I twisted my head to assess the wreckage. The back had split up the middle. Why'd I wear that stupid coat anyway? I looked like a tattered sausage. I glanced down at my belly. "Right now, fat guy in a little coat works too, right?"

She smiled uncertainly, and then a lightbulb seemed to go off in her head. "*Tommy Boy*, right?"

Her awareness of the decades-old movie about an overweight underachiever—another mystery given her clean-cut appearance—gave me all the encouragement needed. As people moved around and past us, I reenacted the scene where the Chris Farley character shoved his large self into his buddy's too-small coat and started singing, "Fat guy in a little coat. Fat guy in a little coat. Fat guy in a little cooooaaaat."

Mimicry, like making friends easily, is a skill, and Farley's Midwestern accent and devious giggle had been practiced often.

And right on cue, Ginny deadpanned my favorite line: "Take it off . . ." Her face turned crimson, and she clapped her hand over her mouth. Was she kidding? Everyone said that crude word that evoked the male anatomy. It made the joke. She may be dressed in all white, but could anyone really be that innocent? What was her deal?

Both the weather and Jacob's hasty departure gave me an opportunity to find out.

A towering cumulonimbus cloud had formed high over our heads, and the winds began to blow. *Crackle.* As the sky opened and began dumping buckets, a mustachioed emcee wearing a tie-dyed T-shirt grabbed the microphone from the lead singer and yelled, "Everyone must leave now." Another bolt of lightning lit up the darkening sky.

Ginny bit her lip and watched people rush toward the pavilions and other structures to escape the thunderstorm. "I don't know what to do."

The sky lit up again, followed by another thunderclap. The ground vibrated.

"We need to get under cover. You could run over there to the art tent and risk being stampeded." I pointed. "Or wait out the storm in my tent. Anything's safer than standing out here in the open." I looked at the towering light poles. "Up to you."

Ginny threw up her hands, shrugging. The sky lit up again. Another loud clap. She watched the fleeing crowds, the rapidly filling pavilions. "I guess I have no other choice."

Could today be the day? Had my luck turned? Had the stars aligned? Would Bryan finally get off my case? Who *wouldn't* want to be seen with this gorgeous creature? I tossed all precaution to the wind.

I had to get to know this woman better.

CHAPTER SEVEN

The Festival, One Year Earlier

Sopping wet, Ginny and I reached the tent. I opened the flaps and dove inside, performing a quick, two-step to avoid the two camp chairs and empty beer cans that sat atop the cooler. Looking about the tent, I thanked the boss man living upstairs for the built-in, rainproof floor. At least we wouldn't be wallowing in the slop as we got to know each other better—or at least that was my ambition. Her? Hard to say. I couldn't imagine how she felt having been abandoned by that dude, whoever he was.

But first things first. The ripped coat felt like a second skin and had to go.

I walked to my gear that was stashed in the corner. Embarrassed by my white fish belly and wondering why I didn't take better care of myself, I molted, my back toward Ginny. Didn't want to gross her out. My Hawaiian shirt came off next, and then I tossed both on the ground and changed into a dry shirt—a wrinkled, flamingo-themed, button-down. A quick sniff test confirmed it didn't stink. But my armpits needed attention. I grabbed my deodorant.

"A friend diagnosed me with Dunlop's Disease." I said, buttoning the shirt, thinking a self-deprecating remark would put her at ease. More like it, the self-criticism made me more comfortable. I had no reason not to state the obvious. "It's when your belly done lops over your belt."

No response. *Did she run off?*

I glanced over my shoulder. Ginny stood halfway in the tent, halfway out, watching the hordes headed for their camps. The brim of her hat drooped from the weight of the water, and her T-shirt clung to her body. She crossed her arms, shifted, and fiddled with her satchel strap. Was she having second thoughts? Looking for a quick get-away, a prince charming, someone to rescue her from her impulsiveness?

"Where are my manners? My mom would kill me." I pulled two towels out of a plastic storage bin and handed them to her. At least they'd been laundered. She watched silently as I reordered the tent. The chairs now sat closer to the open flaps so the whole world could see what was happening inside our crib. "Take a load off. This isn't going to end any time soon."

She stood on her toes, her gaze darting as she surveyed festivalgoers heading for their shelters. After a moment, she looked at me for the first time since we slogged to the tent. She tilted her head and caressed the bridge of her nose. "I guess that'd be okay."

With a tiny smile, Ginny accepted the towels, removed her

satchel and hat, and then placed both on the tent floor. She pulled one chair farther away from the other. I watched in silence as she finger-combed her hair before pulling it back into a tidier ponytail. Only then did she ease herself into the chair, one towel draped around her shoulders, held tight at the chest, and then used the other to dry her legs and remove the mud from her boots.

Her meticulous grooming inspired me to do likewise. My beard got a good rub to make sure it didn't harbor grass and clods of mud. Since Ginny had both towels of mine, I used one of Bryan's to mop my mud-splattered legs and shorts. The towel joined the growing heap in the corner. I plopped down.

"Don't know what I'd done had you not shown up." My throat felt like the Great Sahara, made worse by my nervousness. I wanted Ginny to like me, and her white knuckles told me I needed to step up my game to erase any misgivings she might have. She looked a little skittish, ready to bolt. But I didn't blame her. She didn't know me from Adam, and the world is full of creeps. "Want something to drink? I know I need one." I tossed the empties to the side and plunged my hand into the ice to see what we had stocked. "Let's see. We have beer, more beer, and yes, more beer."

She shook her head to the proffered can. "Do you have water?" She hauled her big bag onto her lap and started searching for something. "I don't drink beer, but don't let me stop you." She extracted a pack of soda crackers, ripped the cellophane wrapper open, and took a tiny bite. "I hope this works. My stomach's upset. Want one?"

"Nope. Feeling good. Aside from the busted lip, never felt better." I pulled my hand from the icy water as she leaned over to examine my lip. I could smell her lavender scent and nearly swooned.

"Flesh wound. You'll be fine. Apply some ice, though."

"What are you? A nurse?"

"I am, but maybe not for long. I've been accepted to medical school. I'm excited."

Aha. I was getting somewhere. "What type of medicine?"

"Not sure. Maybe pediatrics. I love kids. But I'm leaning toward child psychiatry. I wish I'd decided sooner. I'll be in my thirties before I can start practicing."

"That's not too old for a career change. I've had several." Truer words were never spoken. In my three-plus decades, I've pinged and ponged from one job to the next, never finding anything that truly gives me a reason to hop out of bed excited in the mornings.

What an interesting creature. My opposite. She was physically flawless and seemed to know what she wanted to do with her life. So far, she wasn't much of a talker, but she was strangely approachable. Sweet. Her scrupulous grooming and embarrassment over saying an off-color word—something most of my female friends do with relish—intrigued me too. She kept clean inside and out.

Vulnerable. A touch naïve. Sheltered.

Ginny reached back into her big bag and extracted a vibrating iPhone. It looked like a little demon, bouncing around, demanding her undivided attention. What did the ringtone sound like? Tormented shrieks from the underworld? She looked at the screen, keyed a response with both thumbs, and tossed the phone back into the bag.

"And what do you do?" she asked politely.

"By day, I'm a down-and-out realtor and property manager. By night, a stand-up comedian." I searched my backpack and found my little black book, the reason for my feverish, somewhat ridiculous search earlier. I opened the book and fanned the pages. "My jokes and observations." I handed the book to her. "I'm a known regular at the open-mic clubs in town."

She glanced at the book. The corners of her mouth turned up, revealing a pair of dimples offset by those gorgeous eyes. "What were you doing when you wrote that down." She pointed to one of the pages, again slaying me with her genteel drawl. My writing had started out legibly enough but had become jumbled and chaotic by the bottom of the page. Drawings of gargoyles ringed the edge. Not one of my more lucid moments.

"Very interesting." She cocked her head to the side and gripped her bag tighter. What was she thinking? Her phone throbbed and buzzed once more, and again she dug it out of her satchel. She looked at the message, pressed her lips together and frowned. She finally responded and then slipped the phone back into her bag.

Who was this mad texter? Was it the man who took off with the other woman? None of my business. Whoever was intruding, I hoped he or she was satisfied. No further interruptions, please. I was on a mission. One of the best-looking women ever to grace this earth sat just inches from me.

"What's very interesting? I asked. "My book? Or the part about the cash-strapped real-estate guy and wanna-be comedian? Neither pays the bills, but things could be worse. At least one job provides material for the other. You can't imagine the people I run into."

"I *can* imagine. You never met my parents." She surveyed the action beyond the tent and offered no more about her pedigree, my line of work, or the book.

People intrigue me. Off-beat characters fill my world and make me wonder if they're drawn to me naturally or if it's the other way around. *Whatever.* They make life interesting, a never-ending source of good times—and if I'm lucky, they inspire joke material dutifully recorded in my little black book. Would she supply material worthy of my joke collection?

I placed the book back where it belonged, inside one of my backpack's zippered pockets. Safe and sound.

Ginny's throw-away comment gnawed at me though. What were her parents like? I wanted to know more. In so many ways, she reminded me of Chelsey, the knockout who had stolen my heart. But Ginny was different. Nicer. Less self-absorbed. There was more to Ginny than what met the eyes. I'd never run across a girl like her.

Taking a gamble, I asked about her parents, wondering if they were as good-looking as she or if they'd been ugly ducklings that somehow created a swan. She seemed oblivious to her good looks, another character trait I found refreshing and a little unusual. Some women couldn't go ten minutes without posturing before a camera.

"I don't want to be rude. You've been very nice." She licked her lips. "But I'm thirsty. Do you have some water?"

"Oh man. My bad. Sorry. Got a little side-tracked."

I dug around in the ice. *"Aha."* She took the bottle as I held the beer briefly to my injured lip and then took a long draw. Since

Ginny ignored my original question, I asked another. "You said you came here with someone else. Who's the other half of we?"

She told me the answer eventually . . . and a whole lot more.

CHAPTER EIGHT

The Festival, One Year Earlier

I don't know if my non-stop chatter unnerved Ginny or something else but getting to know her seemed impossible. We sat by the tent opening, listening to my Phish tunes, and watching the rain fall in torrents. We'd already dispensed with typical conversation starters. I told her I lived three hours northeast in a small burg in East Tennessee. She told me she lived in a small town south of Atlanta with her grandmother, Granny Smith.

"Granny Smith? Too tart. I prefer Pink Ladies," I said.

Ginny didn't get it. She clutched her towel and kept her physical distance, occasionally tapping a text message.

Does she think I'm going to attack her? I'm no axe murderer. I'm the quintessential nice guy, the party boy. How would I get to know her better if she didn't offer more than a few one-word replies to my questions? Never took this long getting a conversation rolling. Was I losing my touch? My nose itched.

Maybe if we played one of those ice-breaker games, the ones popular at seminars and retreats, would get her talking.

Thank God, I didn't have to resort to that. That would've been lame.

"You asked who brought me here. I don't think I told you." She waved her phone. "Jacob. My fiancé."

My heart sank. *So much for finding the woman of my dreams.* That had been Bryan's goal for me when we ventured out into the crowds. Why couldn't I be attracted to someone who wasn't attached or pining over a former love?

"Oh, yeah. Nice." I said this with no enthusiasm. "Is he who you've been texting?"

She nodded. "Didn't you see him?"

"The guy who took off with the tall redhead?" I said with some snark but immediately regretted it. Who was I to point out the obvious? If she didn't think the situation was strange, then why should I? I wanted her to talk, and now that she was, why should I sound rude and risk offending her?

And clearly, she didn't think Jacob's behavior rude. She started clicking off his amazingness on her fingers. I lost count after successful, outgoing, *a winner*. "He's the best thing that's happened to me, and I *thank God* every day for putting Jacob in my life." Her eyes sparkled and her smile revealed her dimples. She then covered her mouth and looked away. To me, her behavior seemed bizarre since he'd just shipwrecked her with me. *How could she be in love with this dude? And why would God hook her up with someone like him, a deserter?*

Jealousy, an emotion I rarely experience, started bubbling within me like a witch's brew. No one ever looks that way when talking about me.

"Wow. That's great." Who was offering the nearly monosyllabic responses now?

I glanced at her left hand for a ring or other symbol of her betrothal. Nothing. So, I asked about wedding plans, figuring it was a safe topic as I struggled to suppress my interest in her. In the love department, she was a lost cause.

A flush crept across her face, and she cleared her throat. "We haven't set a date yet." She sounded a little defensive as she caressed her finger, mentioning something about going to a jeweler and picking out a ring in the very near future. She didn't say anything for a few minutes and stared into the distance, rubbing her finger the whole time, like Aladdin massaging his magic lamp. Was she hoping for a powerful genie to appear and grant her three wishes? And what would those wishes be?

"Anyway," she continued. "We came alone. We were watching you dance when you fell, remember?"

I couldn't help myself. "Who's the redhead?"

"I've never met her." She coughed, looked at her phone, and started reading a text. I could only see the first couple of sentences from where I sat:

"Ginny, stay put. I'm assuming you're still playing the good Samaritan."

She silently read the rest of the message, and then she looked back at me. "He said he'd be back shortly. He's having a drink with the daughter of his dad's former business partner and didn't have a chance to introduce me."

I gave Ginny the thumbs-up.

"I told him that his do-gooder is waiting out the rain inside a bright yellow tent near the bathrooms and food pavilion. He knows to look for the 'Live Free or Die' banners and the big yellow smiley-face flag. I think he can find me."

I knew nothing about Jacob except for Ginny's gushing descriptors, but a strange, visceral dislike took hold of me. Another rare emotion. Who leaves his girlfriend—check, *fiancée*—alone with a stranger? And then sends multiple texts telling her to hang tight while he drinks with another woman?

Not that I minded. She was the best-looking girl for miles around, and I wasn't the only red-blooded male to notice her. I saw the double takes from the men we passed as we slipped and slid to my tent earlier. But I didn't understand Jacob's seeming disregard for her well-being or her nonchalant acceptance of his behavior. Something wasn't right with this situation, and I wondered why the sweet lookers went for clowns like him.

Thoughts of Chelsey, my first love, filled my head. *Forget her. Forget Ginny. Forget them all.*

My rumination ended. Company arrived, giving me another glimpse into Ginny's nature, and the intrigue grew . . . despite myself.

CHAPTER NINE

The Festival, One Year Earlier

As I sat inside the tent with Ginny while rain continued to pelt the roof, I heard Bear's big, booming voice before I saw him. "TC, you there?" Within a nanosecond, he poked his head inside the tent. Rivulets of water ran off his large, hawk-like nose and onto his imposing chest. The tattooed leviathan had nowhere to plant himself, so he hunkered in the demilitarized zone, not completely in or out of the tent, dominating the space between Ginny, myself, and the great outdoors.

"Bear, my man." I stood to shake his hand, but he ignored the gesture and drew me into an enveloping embrace while clapping my back—something he always does when we see each other, a far too rare occurrence to my thinking. I felt like a rag doll as my feet dangled a foot off the ground.

I could've been mistaken, but I thought I heard Ginny gasp.

I returned to my chair and noticed she'd pushed her chair as far away from Bear as possible. She looked like her stomach was tied in knots.

"What's happening?" he asked, oblivious to her changed demeanor.

"Just sitting here with this pretty lady and enjoying the play-list," I said, hoping she'd settle down.

He looked at her and nodded. Now ghostly white, she pulled the towel a little tighter to her body. Other than for saying, "Hey," she said nothing more. Perspiration gathered along her hairline, and her breathing sounded ragged. *What's wrong with her?*

Maybe it was Bear. After all, he could come across as intim-idating with his shaggy hair, long beard, and 275-plus pounds of muscle. Though his size alarms some at first, everyone ends up loving him. He is a sweet, gentle giant who'd give you his last Ben-jamin if you needed it.

"Ah, he won't hurt you." I directed the comment to Ginny. "He's big and lovable. Right, Bear?"

"I am a gentleman." He looked at Ginny and rubbed his chin, making me think he noticed something not quite right about her body language. "Look, I don't have time for idle conversation." Bear talked fast. "Plus, I'm getting even wetter out here. On a mission. Mo's feeding the masses." He pointed in the general direction of Mo and Bear's tent, a good ten-minute walk from us in the camp area designed for groups of twenty or more. "She said to invite you. The whole crew's there."

Over the years, Bryan and I have collected a menagerie of

festival friends—hardcore devotees who, like us, travel the summer festival circuit to hear our favorite bands when the finances and work schedules allow. Though most of these people enjoy some degree of professional success—some even pulling in wads—the term "colorful" defines them better.

Bear and his woman, Mo, are a case in point. He sprinkles his speech with F-bombs and "wicked-bads" and she drapes her large, copper-brown frame in colorful caftan-style blouses or dresses. She bejewels her wrists with bangles, and most of the time she has gold dangling from her ears. Her jewelry makes her jingle every time she moves. But the best thing about Mo is her talent for putting everyone at ease with her ready smile and endearing habit of calling everyone by her favorite moniker—"sugah."

"Sugahbear," as I call the pair, met at a culinary school in California but then moved to Atlanta a few years ago to become top chefs with a restaurant upstart specializing in Southern fusion cooking. With her upbringing in the Mississippi Delta—a region that reveres okra, ham hocks, greens, grits, and biscuits—and his fearlessness having grown up on the mean streets of Boston, they figured they'd put the restaurant on the map. And did. She brings the basics and he the bling. *Southern Living* magazine once featured them as among the South's most creative chefs.

I looked at Ginny. "Are you hungry?"

"I'm good," she said, a little too quickly and as jumpy as a cat. "Don't let me stop you. I'll wait here for Jacob. I'll be okay." She typed a message again on her phone. It took longer than usual because of her shaking hands.

"Bear, I appreciate the invite." I shrugged, now concerned about Ginny's state of mind. "We'll stay here until her friend comes back. I'll catch you later. Tell Mo to expect me."

Before Bear could even answer, she stood abruptly, struggling to disentangle herself from the towel. "No. You go. I need to leave now." Her eyes flittered. She took a step, but she paused, maybe unsure of how she'd get past Bear who was blocking the exit.

"Why?" I asked, getting up to take her arm. I didn't want her to leave. Hadn't I already said I'd catch up with Sugahbear and the gang later? She didn't have to go anywhere.

The ever-insightful Bear saved the day. He glanced over his shoulder and then looked back at me. "It's still raining, and I didn't mean to interrupt. You should probably wait until it calms down anyway." Deep lines formed between his eyebrows. He downed the beer I'd offered and crushed the can, not noticing Ginny flinch at the sound. "I need to get back to help Mo. Bryan is there with some chick, eating his way through the campsite."

He stood from his sumo-wrestling crouch and turned to leave but then he hesitated. He looked directly at Ginny. She studied her cowgirl boots. He paused for a few seconds and cleared his throat. "How about I fix a couple plates and deliver them later? I know Mo's concerned about you getting something to eat, TC. Sometimes I think you guys have a thing going." He winked at me and nodded at Ginny. And then he was gone, leaving a large empty space in the tent.

"Wow." She exhaled and wiped her forehead with her palm as she backed up to retake her camp chair. "I don't know what came over me. I've been feeling puny all day, but nothing like this since . . ." She didn't finish the thought.

"Bear is a good person." I wanted to defend him and his honor, the most generous person I know. If Bear caused the fluster, then she hadn't given him a chance. Before every festival, he and Mo always spend days preparing extravagant chow kept cold in Yeti coolers and offer their culinary concoctions to all takers. Bryan and I never miss taking our meals with Sugahbear when they can make the trip. Their grub and their company are heaven.

I don't know why I continued blabbering about them, but my mouth ran. *You are the average of the five people you spend time with, right?* If she felt uncomfortable around Bear, what did she think of me? I wanted Ginny to appreciate his success, both professionally and personally. I wanted her to recognize his goodness. A day doesn't pass without me texting either him or Mo, getting their opinions on potential joke material or their take on some world calamity.

"I love Mo, Bear's girlfriend. We're honeys." I jabbered on. "Yeah, I once told Mo I was in love with her and that she should leave Bear and move in with me. Do know what she said?"

Ginny shrugged. Her breathing had returned to normal.

"She told me my offer was enticing but she liked her men big. And to quote her, 'And you, little big man, ain't big.' She planted a big kiss on the top of my head." That's when I became known as "Little Big Man," an apt nickname given my ridiculously short stature and loud, attention-getting manner.

Ginny smiled but made no comment about Mo.

"Who's the skinny guy?" She asked. A random question, considering how long it had been since we'd seen Bryan. "He took off with a tiny brunette after I pulled you from the mud." She finished her bottle of water, looked around for a trash bag, and seeing none, she handed the empty bottle to me. The bottle, along with Bear's smashed beer can, got tossed to the corner.

"Bryan, my best friend. The woman? Maybe the chick camping over there." I pointed to a red pup tent a couple of campsites away. I wondered what Ginny would think of Bryan. Certainly, his scrawniness wouldn't ignite a panic attack.

Ginny scooched her chair closer to mine and started folding the towel she dropped. She laid it next to her chair and stretched out her legs. All thoughts of leaving must have vanished, or maybe she figured she could handle me. I mentally crossed my fingers, hoping she'd stay for the long haul. That she might take a hankering for me. Fiancé or no fiancé.

"Where did you say the big guy worked?"

"Bear? Delta Dawn," I said, pleased she'd asked. Maybe her upset stomach had caused the sweating, difficult breathing, and shaking hands. "Not sure I dig the name, but the food and service are outstanding. Don't tell Mo I said that about the name. She suggested it. Her mama loved the song." That bit inspired me to sing the first few stanzas loudly and off-key.

Ginny grimaced but seemed amused by the caterwauling. A little smile formed, and then she changed the subject. "I'm moving to Atlanta myself. Jacob bought a place there, an easy commute to the medical school where I've been accepted. He wants me to move in before we get married, and I start classes."

That tidbit threw me a little. She didn't seem the type to shack up with a man, engaged or not. I let it slide. I didn't have the big picture. "You should check out Sugahbear's restaurant."

But before the budding conversation had time to bloom, Aimee, another friend, blew in with her posse. Probably the biggest favor that redheaded wild thing ever did for me.

CHAPTER TEN

Today, May 30

Seated on the edge of Ginny's king-sized bed, Laurel lies in my arms. I don't know how to comfort her mother. She's hunched over, sobbing into her hands after confessing life might not be worth living. But I didn't cause her misery. She did. She made her bed when she took up with Jacob, choosing him over me. Just like Chelsey did. I wasn't good enough for her either.

And now I'm supposed to make this right? What was the Big Man thinking when he sent me here?

The room feels like it's closing in around me. My chest feels tight, and my head feels like it's ready to explode. I want to remind her of a few inconvenient facts. *Who, after all, painted those pretty pictures of rainbows and unicorns while Jacob gallivanted with that redhead, doing God knows what? Cry away, girl. You deserve everything you got.*

That's when I hear it. The small voice. *Who do you think you are?* I stare at the top of Ginny's head and am filled with self-reproach. She'd made a mistake—one I'd made—and now needs help seeing her way out. She hadn't led me on and didn't cause my angst. *I* did that all by myself.

I glance at the threshold. Uriah is gone, but his words ring in my head. This could be a mountaintop moment for me . . . and possibly her. I draw Ginny close in a one-armed embrace. Little Laurel sandwiched between us. The resentment has evaporated, replaced by an overwhelming sense of peace. It's the best high ever.

"Please give her to me." Ginny sniffles and wipes her eyes and nose with the back of her hand. "Didn't I just feed her?"

I shrug. How would I know? I just got here, not quite sure how to open her eyes, and knowing from experience and research that this might be tricky.

I look at the baby. Laurel's head moves from side to side. Her mouth is open. Ginny sighs, reaches under her T-shirt, and unsnaps her bra. She barely musters the strength to take her daughter.

Nursing mothers make me uncomfortable. I scratch my nose and glance at the empty bottles lying on the floor. Has she anesthetized her baby with her drinking? The little one hasn't squawked since my arrival. Ginny's a nurse. Shouldn't she know better? I need to get to the bottom of this. Get specifics. Look at all angles.

Ginny notices my gaze and blushes, subtly checking to make sure the bag remains hidden beneath her pillow. "I guess I could fix a bottle. I'm weaning her, but that means I'd have to go to the kitchen and I'm afraid you won't be here when I get back."

Given the circumstances that landed me here, I doubt I'd be here either, in this dream-like room. I'm not sure where I'd be. I peek at the doorway. Uriah is still gone. Where is that guy?

Ginny asks me to grab the nursing blanket draped over an upholstered chair next to the crib. She covers Laurel and herself, and I immediately hear the baby's sucking noises. The blanket moves with her happy kicks. I want to give them some privacy, so I tour the room. My legs feel heavy, like wading through knee-high water. The room shimmers.

Again, I take in the bedroom's tastefulness, the choice of neutral shades of cream and gray, complemented by expensive artwork. But it lacks warmth and personality. Did Ginny have a say in any of this? Nothing of hers seems to be in the room, aside from the untidy piles of clothes, books, and bottles. No photos of Granny or Laurel. Just decorations obviously chosen by a decorator. Ginny seems to simply occupy the space.

I wander over to the window and adjust the wooden slats to see better. By the look of things, Ginny is in "deep cotton," as her Granny might say. The estate-like homes sit back from a tree-lined street, flanked by carpets of manicured grass that look soft enough to sleep on. Ginny once told me that Jacob's home in Atlanta was nice. An understatement. Only people with serious money live here.

"What's the name of this neighborhood?"

"Tuxedo Park."

"That's what I thought." Location confirmed. Though not an Atlantan, my career in real estate has introduced me to some of the nation's more exclusive neighborhoods. This one ranks with

Belle Meade in Nashville or Beverly Hills. But the latter is just a guess. I've never spent time in California but have a pretty good idea from watching movies.

In stark contrast, home for me is a Depression-era, two-bedroom, clapboard-style house with a postage-stamp-sized yard filled with clover and broadleaf weeds. Like the others on my street, a front porch spans the front, held up by Craftsman-style posts. I spend my leisure hours there, sitting beneath the ceiling fan on one of two plastic Adirondack chairs. From this spot, I do my best thinking and people watching. Joke telling too, especially when friends pop in, a daily occurrence when the weather cooperates. My porch, I can say unconditionally, is the best space in my house.

I drop the slats and walk back to the chair. Uriah said something earlier about time being short. I shut my eyes and draw in a deep breath. I'm entering uncharted waters where I might have to do and say things against my nature, further upset by my earlier pique toward Ginny. But I learned a truth about myself, didn't I? I'd allowed the resentment to fester. No doubt, I'll be learning other lessons during my visit with Ginny.

"I'm tired of talking about me." Ginny speaks, interrupting my thoughts. "What have you been up to? Tell me a story. I need a laugh."

Maybe a story would get her mind off her pain and whatever she planned to do with those pills. After all, my stories about the colorful people in my life seemed to charm her last year.

Before thinking things through properly, though, I start talking about Sloth. That's not his real name, just the nickname I coined because of his turned-down eyes and matted hair. He lived across the street from me in a ramshackle house with his mentally challenged wife and two daughters. Given Ginny's childhood experiences, that was a bad choice. But I'd always gotten laughs at the bar or on my porch when telling stories about him.

"Sloth is in the slammer," I say. "He took a shot at his cousin living in a camper in his backyard. Within seconds, the hood woke up. Someone called the cops on him."

Ginny looks up and smiles. "This should be good."

I nod. "It is."

At first, when this happened, I had stayed in bed and pulled the covers over my head. But with blue lights flashing and radios crackling outside my window, I couldn't sleep. So, I got up to watch the action unfold from my front porch. "Guess who showed up?"

"Bud." She grins, giving me hope she's forgotten life has become intolerable.

She looks under the blanket and sighs. "Will you ever be done?" She raises her head. "Not you, her. You've a real talent for collecting misfits and telling stories about them." Ginny pats the blanketed bundle and smiles. Her bloodshot eyes look painful after her crying jag, but at least her dimples show. The corners of her eyes crinkle.

Good. I continue the story.

Lured from his lair by the gunshots, Bud had seen me sitting on the porch and made a beeline for my place. His gravelly voice carried across the neighborhood as he clutched his busted back. He wore plaid pajama bottoms and a grungy T-shirt. He stepped up on the curb in front of my house, and he started asking questions in his mongrel dialect—a merging of standard Midwestern with Appalachian twang. Bud, who'd spent time in a federal prison, eyed the police cars suspiciously and scurried up the short walkway to my porch.

Bud can be amusing when he talks about his man cave, a four-by-four space off the kitchen where his Barcalounger sits in front of a massive TV hung on the wall. But at three in the morning, I wasn't in the mood for his company or his constant harangue about my dog-training skills. At least Georgie sprays the bushes and trees. His hyperactive grandson pees on the sidewalk.

"Did he ask for a beer?" Ginny asks.

"Of course. That's standard."

As Bud took the other porch chair, I told him it was against the law to drink beer at three in the morning. The city just passed the ordinance. Not a smooth move with the cops congregated at the Sloth's, I told him. "Good old Bud told me the new law made as much sense as teats on a bull."

She laughs out loud, and for a moment, I feel confident. I want my stories to act as a soothing aloe for both of us. I'm going to miss Bud and his beer mooching.

"For a former inmate, he's gullible. But when I busted out laughing, he got wise and told me I was as windy as a sack full of farts. He didn't know why he bothered being my friend. I told him we weren't. If he didn't like my dog, I didn't like him."

Ginny hoots, just like she did a year ago when I first introduced her to the characters in my neighborhood. "How do you find these people?"

Getting jazzed that I might be distracting her from her dark thoughts, which would certainly prevent an ugly confrontation, I jump from the chair and do a little dance. And that's when I realize I can't tell her the whole story. I ease back into the chair. *How could I be so unwise?*

What happened after Sloth's arrest still unsettles me.

With Sloth jailed, the burden fell on the missus—and she didn't have much going on upstairs. A few days after Sloth's arrest, she fell and shattered her leg. She ended up in the hospital, leaving her two equally challenged daughters alone in the house. The neighbors and I noticed the girls sitting on their front porch, but no one bothered asking where their mother was or who was taking care of them.

They eventually sought help from a teacher, who learned of Sloth's years-long sexual abuse of both mother and daughters. The revelation initiated a Department of Child Services investigation, and the girls were removed and placed in a foster home. I haven't seen them since.

What bothers me more than anything is that I suspected another of taking advantage of those girls. A teenage boy living in one of my parent's apartment units next door would invite them over after his dad left for work. I'd watch the girls creeping home later, speaking in hushed tones, furtively looking to see if anyone was watching. Little did they know . . . I was doing just that.

Though their clothing didn't appear disheveled, something seemed off. Having no use for busybodies who indict others on first appearances, I decided to keep my mouth shut. Why meddle? They didn't appear hurt. But now I realize I'd been wrong. Even if they'd only been watching television or playing video games, the boy had no business entertaining those girls without an adult being around. They had the maturity of small children and could've been easily manipulated, abused, just as I learned later that their father had done to them. *Why hadn't I said something to the boy's dad, a stand-up guy, a good tenant?*

And why did I bring up this story? Sloth's incarceration was the only bright spot in that messed-up story. Ginny didn't need to hear about the abuse. It was too close to home.

"Well, aren't you going to finish the story?" Ginny stares at me, maybe wondering why I stopped talking.

So, I wing it and describe Sloth's cussing and carrying on as deputies crab walked him to one cruiser and his cousin to the other.

"That's my neighborhood in a nutshell," I say, slapping my thighs.

"I almost forgot how much fun you are." Ginny's mouth smiles, but her eyes don't.

Chelsey, my first love, said the same once. And look where that got me. No point in reopening that wound, or the one I'd blamed Ginny for inflicting. No point in getting caught up in the why-me questions. I need to stay focused on what Uriah said. Ginny is in trouble, and this could be my finest hour.

But I can't help but wonder . . . Why hadn't we reunited under happier, less otherworldly circumstances? Why did Ginny stay with Jacob? Why couldn't she see he had obvious issues? Why hadn't I opened my mouth? If I had, I probably wouldn't be sitting here now, wondering how I would make a difference in Ginny's life.

CHAPTER ELEVEN

Today, May 30

The memory of Sloth's girls troubles me. I drum the arms of the chair and decide another circuit around the room would ease my disquiet. The window offers a good diversion. Peering through the slats, nothing catches my interest. My thoughts return to the girls and the rest of my neighbors. They may come from a different social class than Ginny's neighbors, but money and prestige don't protect people from sadness and despair. Bad things happen everywhere.

I head for the chair, relieved Ginny hasn't questioned me further about my random, out-of-the-blue appearance. Uriah said things would start making sense and they are . . . sort of. I understand how I got here, but not the details contributing to her downward slide. She stood up to Jacob last year. Why does she put up with his crap now? Something else must have happened . . .

Wait, hadn't she mentioned Granny in the past tense just a little while ago? *Where's Granny?* She needs to tell me more.

"How's medical school?" I ask, thinking this a good launching point.

Ginny peeks underneath the blanket. "Out like a light." She says this more to herself than to me. She dabs the little one's mouth with the blanket and adjusts her clothing. "Ugh, I hate to wake you, sweet pea, but you need a burp and a diaper change." She may not care about herself, but she seems to take good care of the baby, aside from the drinking. A one-off? I can only hope.

She pats Laurel's back and looks blank-eyed at the wall. I noticed the look earlier when lingering with Uriah at her bedroom door. My stories haven't taken her mind off things.

I run both hands through my hair and wait, watching as she lays Laurel on the bed before retrieving both a diaper and the wipes from the hanging hamper. She trudges back, changes her drowsy baby, drops the dirty diaper on the floor, and scoops Laurel up for a return trip to the crib. One year ago, she would've never dropped a wet diaper on the floor. This is so out of character.

"Don't make too much noise," Ginny says. "I need her to sleep. She was a terror last night. Nothing made her happy."

"What do you think I'm going to do? Rattle her crib?"

"I guess not. I'm exhausted and can't think straight." She walks past me, feet shuffling. She sits and fiddles with the memory bracelet. "What were we talking about?"

"I asked you about medical school."

"That's right. I got in but withdrew for obvious reasons," Ginny glances at the crib and then at me. "I'm an emergency room nurse at the university hospital. I'm not sure if becoming a doctor was *my* dream or Jacob's," she says, and then continues to share more. About how he liked bragging about her smarts and ambitions. Made him proud.

That is, until she dropped the mother of all bombs on his head. "Boy, I didn't see that one coming," she says. "I thought he'd be happy when I told him we were pregnant." She shakes her head. "He said I got knocked up—his words, not mine—to spite him, that he wasn't the one responsible."

I can't imagine someone not taking responsibility for this little life. Who *wouldn't* be proud to be Laurel's daddy? No one, including myself.

I keep the sentiment to myself. Why burden Ginny with my feelings, the fantasies about spending the rest of my life with someone like her? When I got home after meeting her, my imagination did go there. Not the physical stuff, although that did cross my mind—I'm a guy after all—but the intimacy of two people living together and sharing their lives. My parents would have loved Ginny and appreciated her positive effect on me. Around her, I had curbed some off my more obnoxious habits. I had done better.

Nope, Ginny doesn't need to know my daydreams. Not the reason for my visit.

"TC, he nearly convinced me to abort her," Ginny says, interrupting my reverie. "I almost gave in." She goes on to explain how she went to the clinic, met with the counselor, and returned the next day for the procedure. But she couldn't go through with it and left. "He went nuts. I guess that's when things started going downhill. Fast. Maybe they were already bad, and I didn't want to see it."

Nothing she said surprises me. Is she ready to accept the truth now? She thought Jacob walked on water a year ago.

"You were pregnant when we met, weren't you?" I ask, remembering when she ate crackers and complained of feeling puny.

She bobs her head. "Didn't know at the time."

"Why didn't you go through with the abortion?"

"You know, Granny never liked him." Ginny's shoulders sag as she tells me her grandmother's opinions. Ginny had alluded to Granny Smith's distaste for Jacob when we chatted a year ago but left out details. She's laying the particulars out like a picnic lunch now. Granny thought Jacob was self-absorbed. Satan himself. A charmer who'd eventually show his true colors.

Ginny rubs her arms and shutters. "A few months after we started dating, I asked him to drive down to meet her. He poured on the charm. Solicitous to me, polite to Granny. He escorted Granny to the kitchen table and told her to stay seated as he helped clear the dishes and scrubbed the pots and pans after dinner—things Granny usually noticed and appreciated. When he left, I couldn't wait to get her opinion. Do you know what she said?"

"Tell me."

"'He thinks the sun comes up just to hear him crow. Somethin' ain't right about that boy. He's gonna tear you apart, baby girl.' Those were her exact words."

I never met Ginny's firebrand of a grandmother, a woman of great faith. Last year, Ginny had described her as tough, determined, a force to reckon with—especially where her grand-daughter was concerned, the one she had raised, nurtured, and protected.

Now that she fills in the blanks for me, my estimation of Granny's good judgment raises exponentially. I wish I could have met her. What would she do if she were sitting in this room? Failure, as it seemed to me then, wasn't an option for Granny. And it can't be one for me either. Too much is at stake.

"When I told her that Jacob was insisting I end the pregnancy, she begged me to move back with her." Ginny falls back onto the bed and covers her face with her forearm. Her chest rises and falls. Quiet fills the room. She starts again, and her voice quavers. "My sweet Granny. She told me I shouldn't have had relations with him, but what was done was done. The good Lord created my child, and it behooved me to see the pregnancy through. Like everyone else on the planet, my child had a job to do. Nothing good came from killing one of God's creations."

She sits up but doesn't say anything for a few seconds. I wait her out, as she examines the chipped polish on her fingernails, hair falling into her eyes.

"You know . . ." She glances at me. "He abandoned me at the hospital. Granny was right. I lost everything because of him—my grandmother, friends, and a job I loved when I lived with her, long before I considered medical school. And why? I am ashamed to admit this. I wanted to impress his family. His mother and father have power, influence, and money. Jacob could buy me nice things, take me to fancy parties. Didn't I tell you money didn't impress me?"

"Something to that effect."

"Well, I wasn't honest." She tells me about Granny's modest means, which I'd already surmised. The coupon clipping. The old truck. The frayed furniture and worn kitchen linoleum. Granny refused to waste money on fast food, let alone expensive entrées at five-star restaurants. That changed when Jacob entered her world.

From the jump, he took her to black-tie parties, the theater, sporting events watched from his family's skybox. He'd whip out his credit card and assure her not to worry about money as she tried on designer clothing and shoes. He had plenty and didn't think twice about flying first class when they traveled to his parent's vacation place in the Caribbean. Seeing that she'd struggled with small talk, he'd coach her on what to say to the bigwigs in his circle, and not to worry if conversation eluded her. "He seemed so happy when others told me I was pretty . . . elegant." Her hands flutter about her face. "TC, he showed me a lifestyle I'd only seen in movies or read about in novels. I could barely believe my luck."

She shakes her head. "My luck has run out. Sometimes I think *he* wants me dead."

That gets my attention. I glance at the pillow hiding the pills. Does she suspect him of trying to kill her? I don't get a chance to ask.

"So now you have the whole story. I'm living with a wealthy man who refuses to marry me or acknowledge his daughter. Laurel and I have a roof over our heads only because of his generosity. He's right. I am worthless." She buries her face in her hands.

"You need to leave, Ginny. Now. Granny's right. Jacob has torn you apart. He's bad news and it won't get better."

"Where would I go?"

"What about Granny's? And don't you have an aunt? Adele?"

"Granny died, and I'm not burdening my aunt with my problems. Can you imagine? Good old Ginny is a chip off her mother's block. Aunt Adele doesn't need the reminder."

The heaviness in my legs travels to my core. She's been delivered a double-whammy and doesn't know where to turn. The defeated attitude makes sense, and so does the drinking. Those pills are a worry—a big one.

I struggle as I move from the chair to sit next to her on the bed. I take her hand, which lies limply in mine. She doesn't cry, but squeezes her eyes shut.

"Ginny, I'm so sorry. I know Granny meant everything to you. What happened to her?"

In a monotone voice, she tells me the story.

CHAPTER TWELVE

Uriah, Today, May 30

I walk back to Ginny's room to check on TC. He looks up and sees me standing in the doorway. The scared, deer-in-the-headlights look is gone, replaced by . . . what? Determination? TC gives me a curt nod as he presses his lips together. *Good.* No reason to hang here. He's got this.

I stroll past the nursery and Jacob's shrine to himself. Creeping down the curved stairway, I notice a couple of doors in the foyer. I try one. A powder room. The other is locked.

Interesting. Wonder what's hiding in there?

A gigantic room with a tray ceiling takes up the back of the house. This place is a palace, so unlike TC's bungalow, which he decorated with hand-me-down furniture. The differences in lifestyle couldn't be clearer. Expensive-looking, overstuffed, down-filled sofas and club chairs are arranged around a large fireplace flanked by built-in bookshelves. My gaze is drawn to a large abstract painting positioned above the mantel. The splashes of red and black, accented by small strokes of yellow, offer the room's only color.

A noise comes from the kitchen. I turn my head. Jacob, with his back toward me, sits on a bar stool. He talks into his iPhone and flips through a glossy magazine.

"Hey, darlin'."

I know it's not necessary, but I'm not taking any chances. I hide behind a massive potted tree positioned near a column separating the two rooms. A good place to listen and watch.

"I'll be over in a few. Can't wait." Jacob listens and shakes his head in agreement. "Wear that sexy little red dress and stiletto heels I bought you. Hear? Ahh, don't worry about her. Told her I had a business trip. Flying out tonight."

I know a lot—more than TC right now—but not all. The Big Man only gave me generalities. I shouldn't be surprised by Jacob's lies that drip off his tongue like honey. But I am.

I close my eyes and hear Jacob laugh.

"Ginny's upstairs. Thinks I left. Not gonna think about her until we get back." He closes the magazine. "Honey, I told you. It's over, but it's complicated. Just need to figure out how to handle it. Need to talk to my father. Hire an attorney. You're right. My mother isn't going to like it, but she'll come around. She always does."

Jacob stands. "Now, why would I want to hurt Ginny? You know me better than that. But I don't like being lied to. She's taken advantage of me and my family." He rolls his head from side to side.

"I did a little checking into her past. I know my father won't want to be associated with that train wreck. Neither will my mother." Jacob taps his fingers on the granite counter. "Yep, he's thinking about running for office. Would you please stop worrying. Everything will work out. I promise."

Trying to get a better view, I lean too far into the plant and the pot moves. Sometimes I forget my own strength and chastise myself for not being more careful. The scraping sound echoes across the living room. I hold my breath.

"Hold on."

Jacob pushes the stool aside. He frowns as he walks across the hardwood floor toward the foyer. I squat behind the cauldron-sized pot and peek through the low-hanging branches, not wanting Jacob to sense my presence.

Jacob walks to the staircase and looks up. He doesn't seem to know what to do. He grabs the newel post and starts climbing.

No. No. No. I need to come up with a good distraction. Maybe I'll knock over the plant. Throw fistfuls of dirt. Beat one of the copper pots hanging over the kitchen island. But the sound of Jacob's approaching footsteps draws closer, and I slump in relief. *Too close.* Not good. I can't be the reason for a disruption. I couldn't live with myself.

"Sorry about that." Jacob picks up his conversation as he takes his seat on the barstool. "Thought I heard something. She could be stumbling around or flat on her face for all I know. She's blind drunk. What do you mean? I've been sympathetic. Whose side are you on anyway? I can't bring her Granny back."

Jacob continues the finger tapping. His leg jingles. "I didn't encourage her drinking. That's her choice. Saw her stash of pills too. Not sure where she got them or what she plans to do with them. Maybe she'll take matters into her own hands and spare me the trouble of a fight."

He laughs. "It's a joke, for crying out loud. Get a sense of humor, girl." He shrugs. "Divorce? What are you talking about? Ginny and I aren't married. Who told you that? I got her pregnant and now she's living with me, eating my food, and drinking my wine. She may have grown up on biscuits and sweet tea but likes the good stuff now."

Jacob adjusts himself in the stool to sit taller. "Honey don't pull a Ginny on me. I never said anything about being married to her." He slaps the countertop with an open palm. "We can talk about this later. Just want you to understand why I'm in limbo, why this is taking so long. She has custody. I don't, and it will take a killer lawyer and a sympathetic judge to reverse that."

Jacob rests his head on his palm, listening. "No, I can't just kick her out and let her take the baby. It's my duty to protect *my* child. Good grief, you're the one who mentioned it to me. Are you with me?"

I can't stomach anymore of Jacob's conversation. I slip out the French doors and sit on the stoop that leads down to a flagstone patio and kidney-shaped built-in pool, secluded by mature trees.

This isn't a home. It's an inferno on earth. How could anyone want to spend time with Jacob? Obviously some people could. Ginny took up with him, and apparently, he has another woman dangling on his treacherous hook. Does that poor woman know what she's getting into, or is she as bad as he is?

I look skyward. It's getting darker now. Time to check out the neighborhood. I know the Big Man knows what he's doing. The question is, does TC? Can he turn this situation around before it's too late? Will Ginny tell him more about Jacob?

Maybe I should tell him. He needs this information.

What am I thinking? I can't tell TC anything. I'm not allowed to pass through Ginny's bedroom threshold.

TC is on his own.

CHAPTER THIRTEEN

The Festival, One Year Earlier

Except for Ginny's strange reaction to Bear, I was feeling pretty good about how my day was unfolding. The redheaded whirlwind, Aimee—my favorite gal pal—showed up with her gang of misfits and I knew I'd be amused. Would Ginny? I'd never encountered anyone quite so reserved in behavior and speech. No slang. No cursing. Full sentences, spoken in a beautiful Southern drawl.

As it turned out, Aimee's arrival and her stories worked their charm. Maybe Bear scared the bejeebers out of her, but Aimee put Ginny at ease, loosened her up a bit. Before long, Ginny was even sharing her own funny stories about Granny when she could get a word in edgewise. To my surprise, she had a gift, like us, for telling a good yarn.

As Aimee gabbed about me and our adventures together, though, I did notice Ginny's heavy sighs. How she'd stare down at her feet. *Was she thinking she'd missed something along the way?* That made me wonder about the friends in her life. How she spent her time. What motivated her. Eventually she would tell me the nitty-gritty, but that was hours away.

With Aimee as the ringmaster, the tent quickly turned into a three-ring circus. Elfin-sized, she wore cut-off, blue-jean overalls, a tank top, and a pair of lethal Doc Martens boots that made her skinny legs look skinnier. She pushed her way inside and stamped on my booted foot and nearly tripped. That elicited a string of insults directed at me. Had I been barefoot, my toes would have looked like roadkill.

Meanwhile, Aimee's gang—a couple of guys with long beards and a twenty-something red-haired woman, maybe a cousin— milled around on the muddy, blue tarp below the canopy.

She calmed down once she found a place to stand between Ginny and me and wasted no time introducing us to her cohorts. They refused a beer when offered and mumbled something about visiting another campsite. Aimee ignored them, apparently more interested in bombarding me with questions as she cooled herself with an ancient, well-used hand fan compliments of a funeral home. Her short, spiky hair laid matted to her forehead.

"Why y'all sittin' in the tent instead of that nice veranda out front?" She pointed. "I'm not staying long. Thought we'd stop by to say hey. It's hotter'n blue blazes in here. I'm glistenin' all over."

"Then stay outside underneath the nice veranda." Someone else may think this rude, but that's how we've always interacted since deciding to keep the relationship platonic.

"Go to H-E double-L, fool." Aimee didn't miss a beat. Fanning her underarms and face, she looked around for somewhere to sit.

I pushed the cooler closer to the tent opening and told her to behave herself. "Wish we had more chairs," I said to her escorts. They looked at one another and informed Aimee they were taking off.

"Catch y'all later." Aimee shouted at them as they headed toward the central plaza, weaving past girls wearing bikini tops and short shorts, oblivious to the drizzle.

Aimee plopped down and started scratching her freckled legs.

"Do you have chigger bites?" I asked.

"These bugs are tearing me up." Large welts covered her arms and legs.

I rifled through my backpack and found the bug spray. She grabbed the can, without even a *thanks*, and started spraying her welts with its contents.

Once she was done, she looked at Ginny. "I'm Aimee. Must introduce myself since this fool won't."

Ginny smiled broadly and extended her hand, eyes twinkling.

"What's on your face, Aimee?" I asked. "Glitter?"

"Whaddya think?" She stood within inches of my face and pointed to the tiny hearts and glitter paint that wrapped from her freckled cheek bones to her eyes.

"Bad choice for you," I said. "Looks a bit girly-girl. Skulls and crossbones better suit you."

Aimee punched my arm before sitting down on the cooler and launching into a story about her maternal grandmother—a sweet, white-haired lady who lives in a log cabin in the woods with Aimee's grandfather, Pappaw MacDonald, a heavily wrinkled, curmudgeonly sort.

I could have hugged Aimee. The story put me in a positive light and demonstrated my talent at striking up conversations with anyone. Even my first love's folks liked me and my prattle, but their good opinion didn't dissuade their daughter from kicking me to the curb.

Seeing Ginny's relaxed and happy facial expressions, I muscled into Aimee's monologue. "Aimee here isn't much in the way of housekeeping and cooking. She sure didn't take after her grandmother. Now she's a domestic goddess."

Aimee nodded as I described Memaw's talent in the kitchen. I never turn down an invitation to supper, especially if the menu includes her specialties: cornbread, mac 'n' cheese, slaw, and pork butt smoked inside a barrel, a Pappaw-built contraption.

"Pappaw enjoys my company too," I said. "Remember the first time you brought me around, Aimee?"

"You showed him good."

Ginny sat on the edge of the camp chair and grinned.

We had driven over one Saturday afternoon in her Jeep. Pappaw was outside, fiddling with a pile of firewood that was stacked next to the foundation. Aimee dashed up the wooden front porch steps, leaving me alone with this grumpy-looking old man, who sized me up through narrowed eyes. And then he challenged me to a target-shooting contest with a .22 pistol and rifle. Cans of various sizes were set up on sawhorses at the edge of a small clearing. An old pie pan hung from a tree.

I took my firing stance, sighted the bullseye painted at the center of the pan, and fired. *Clink.* Right through the middle.

Pappaw looked at me with a sideways glance. "*Humph.*" He handed the pistol to me and stood in silence as I drew a bead. Same result. The victorious sound of clanked metal filled me with pride.

"Where'd you learn to shoot?" he asked.

"My grandfather, sir. He's a lot like you. A mountain man. Likes hunting and fishing."

A small smile formed on Pappaw's lips as he clapped me on the back. "Had you figured wrong, son." He slung his arm over my shoulder, and we headed back to the cabin.

Aimee guffawed at my story. "Did he ask if we were an item? How I'd never find a man because I'm no good at cookin'?"

Pappaw had mentioned it that afternoon. But I spared him the details of our abandoned attempt at romance. Furthermore, I'd gotten into his good graces that day with my steely-eyed precision on the shooting range. Why mess things up? Plus, he had promised to take me fishing.

Ginny's blue eyes shined.

"I don't know why she and Pappaw like you." Aimee shook her head. "Their bull crap meter must be broke."

"They like me because I'm lovable." I showed her my full set of pearly-whites and opened my arms wide. "What's there not to love?"

But before Aimee could react, Ginny spoke up. "I think my Granny would love TC too. Maybe I can introduce you one day." She directed that comment to me, and my spirits soared like the mythological Icarus. The moral about flying too high forgotten.

She had said nary a word in the presence of Bear, and until then, she had kept her opinions of me quiet.

I could've hugged Aimee. She'd turned me into a hero in front of the woman I most wanted to impress.

Ginny reached for her bag, withdrew a spiral notebook, and fanned herself with it. "I'm wilting."

"I told ya it was hot," Aimee said to me. "This girl has some sense."

"Let's move this party outside." Ginny clapped her hands together. "The rain has stopped. Time to stretch our legs and get some air."

"No joke. Smells bad in here, like wet dog. Did you bring Georgie?" Aimee looked at me, pocketed the fan, and pinched her nose. "You're a hog wherever you go." Her cheek bones sparkled.

CHAPTER FOURTEEN

The Festival, One Year Earlier

At Ginny's suggestion, we moved the party outside. I used Bryan's towel to clean up most of the muddy footprints on the tarp, while Ginny and Aimee positioned the two camp chairs, cooler, and speaker for conversation and convenience beneath the lemon-colored canopy. The camp was shipshape, and we settled in.

The party ripped. I'd come to see Phish, Sugahbear, and the gang, never imaging this. A fetching blonde on one side and the red-headed dervish on the other. Life couldn't be better.

"How'd you two meet," Ginny asked. Her look of wistfulness had returned. Again, I wondered about her upbringing, her parents, and her interests other than for Jacob, who hadn't texted in a while. *Why doesn't she talk about her past or present?*

"We met at a bar," I said. "Where else?"

"The floor's yours," Aimee said. "You can't go two seconds

without flappin' your lips."

Despite our bickering, Aimee is a very close friend. A confidante. We met a week or two after I left the Washington, DC, area, and my job selling plumbing parts to contractors. Chelsey had dumped me months earlier and I needed a shake-up. I was weary of going through the motions and had made a habit of trying to forget my troubles by drinking, which resulted in throbbing hangovers.

My job was on the line. But before my employer could fire me, I quit. My parents had relocated to East Tennessee, and with nothing better on deck, I agreed to manage their rental properties and get a real-estate license. Not a bad gig since I could keep my own hours. Plus, I was hundreds of miles from Chelsey. *Out of sight, out of mind.*

The night Aimee and I had met at Brady's—one of those dive bars with ripped, fake leather stools—the place was packed, but I'd lucked out. Two barstools became available as soon as I introduced myself to the bartender and ordered my Pabst Blue Ribbon, the only brand I could afford. I had lifted the bottle to my mouth when a wisp of a girl, one who had a milky-white complexion, rushed to the last open seat next to me.

She ordered a locally brewed IPA and then twirled around to introduce herself. Her blue eyes danced in merriment. Little did I know, she was qualifying me as a potential client. Before I could tell her my name, rowdy whoops erupted from the general direction of the dance floor. A woman, clad in a pair of cut-off shorts that barely covered her ample rear-end and tramp-stamp tattoo, had parked herself in front of the stage. She performed a lascivious move—*minus* the dance pole.

Woo-wee. These folks knew how to party. And so did Aimee.

Though my adopted town has lost some of its regional sleepiness and distinctive dialect, Aimee clings to her heritage and makes no apologies for it. Her Scots-Irish ancestors had braved forbidding terrain, rocky soil, and other perils to plant their roots in what would become the state of Tennessee. She's never lived anywhere else and spent her childhood exploring the surrounding mountains.

Becoming a hired mountain guide for rich outdoorsy types, many from the North, is a fitting occupation. "Twang is my thang." Aimee tells me often. "If hillbilly is what those *Yankees* want, hillbilly is what they'll get." For them, she pours the accent on thicker.

"I remember that chick," Aimee said, referring to the dancing lady on the that wild and crazy night we had met.

"And do you remember what you said, Aimee?"

She planted her hands on her narrow hips, all *big and bad* like. She paused for comedic timing, and together, we shouted, *"Law, that girl better pull her drawers down! We kin see clear to the promised land."*

I don't know if it was Aimee's accent or the words themselves, but Ginny started howling and her eyes filled with tears. "You two are a riot. I can't remember when I laughed so much."

Aimee seemed pleased with herself and her role in bringing Ginny out of her shell. And honestly, I could have kissed her for that. Despite her bravado, Aimee is a sweetie.

Of all my female friends, she understands me best. She shares my passion for low-brow humor and politics. Whatever the world has to offer. We both suffer from a smorgasbord of insecurities, brought on, among other things, by love gone bad. Not even Bryan understands the depths of my heartbreak. But Aimee does. She experienced it herself, and like me, she's built walls to protect herself. She is my security blanket, and I am hers. We are inseparable.

If we aren't swimming in the Little River, we're floating on it or hiking along its banks. We spend hours exploring the trails that snake through the hundreds of thousands of acres comprising the Smoky Mountain National Park.

Under Aimee's tutelage, I've discovered an aspect of my personality I never knew. Aside from the biannual trips to visit my mountain-living grandfather in Pennsylvania, my only exposure to the great outdoors as a suburban kid had involved sneaking out at night and rolling toilet paper across the neighbors' trees and bushes or egging a few cars.

The first time Aimee and I climbed Mt. LeConte and summitted thousands of feet above sea level, I experienced a rush that I'd never felt before. With the majesty of nature spread out before us, I'd forgotten the world and contemplated the divine, putting all thoughts of Chelsey and my inadequacies aside.

Somewhere along the way, the conversation that had Ginny clutching her sides and dabbing her eyes had stalled. I started babbling, desperate to keep the party going.

I looked at Aimee. *Challenge me to an arm-wrestling competition. Anything.* Aimee's furrowed brow spoke volumes. She seemed to be giving me unspoken advice—and I knew exactly what it was:

Guard your heart, big boy.

CHAPTER FIFTEEN

The Festival, One Year Earlier

The mood beneath the canopy took an imperceptible turn. Having just met Aimee, Ginny had no clue of Aimee's changed demeanor.

Aimee had transitioned into mama-bear mode.

"Hey Ginny, how do you know TC?" Aimee gave a small turned-up smile. I'd seen the expression before when she wanted information and didn't want to come off as too pushy or obnoxious. Yes, she could be pushy and obnoxious, but she's also a Southerner. Good manners counted.

Ginny coughed. "That's a long story, isn't it TC?"

I shrugged. It wasn't my place to explain.

Ginny slapped her thighs and stood. "I need the bathroom. How about you?" She looked at Aimee. Must be a girl thing. Men never traveled in packs to do their business.

"Sorry. Doin' good in that department," Aimee said. "Need to talk to TC about something . . . private."

"Of course," Ginny said, nodding quickly. "I'll be back in a few minutes. Would you please keep an eye out for Jacob, TC, and tell him to wait until I get back."

Ginny scampered off with her satchel draped over her torso.

"Who's Jacob?" Aimee demanded, scooching to the edge of the cooler, closer to me. Her eyes narrowed. "How did you meet her?"

I lifted my hands in the air. Her aggressiveness surprised me. Aimee shelled me with a few more questions as I explained how Ginny and I met and why she agreed to join me at the tent.

"Why on God's green earth would you be making goo-goo eyes to someone you can't have? Dude, what's wrong with you? Didn't you say she's engaged?" Aimee nearly shouted. "You're setting yourself up for another let down, and then I'll have to listen to you crying like a dang baby. Not in the mood."

"Are you jealous?"

Aimee's eyes narrowed, and she ran her hands through her matted-down hair. It stood on end, like normal. "Jealous? Every time you open that trap of yours, stupid falls out. No, I'm not jealous. Just worried. What else do you know about her?"

I had to admit that I knew little. Until Aimee had showed up, Ginny kept her counsel, watchful and reserved. The stroll we took down memory lane, and especially that story about the lascivious dancer, seemed to remove any misgivings Ginny might have had about spending time with me. If Aimee liked me, maybe Ginny figured I wasn't a bad bloke after all.

"Don't you like her?" I asked.

"Yeah. She's lots of fun," Aimee said. "Seems to love her Granny and your stupid stories, that's for sure." Aimee's only concern was the big elephant plopped in the middle of the campsite. "You're attracted to her. Aren't you? Are you hoping she'll dump the boyfriend? For crying out loud, genius, she's engaged. She lives in another state. Are you planning a long-distance romance if you somehow slay her with your charm?" Aimee was full of righteous indignation, but I understood why. She only wanted to protect me.

Thank God, Ginny announced her return as she stepped onto the tarp. We were so caught up in our conversation that we would've never seen her coming.

"Did Jacob come?" Ginny said this in a loud voice. We looked up and shook our heads and Ginny's shoulders sagged. Aimee gave me her special "I-told-you-so" look.

"Have I interrupted your conversation?" Ginny clutched her satchel as she moved closer to her camp chair. "I'm happy to take a walk if you need more time to talk." She gave us an uncertain smile.

Aimee was fast on her feet. "You didn't interrupt a dang thing," Aimee said, smacking her thighs. "Just telling TC how Yankees make my butt itch. That big party coming in from New York canceled last night. No friggin' manners. Fixin' to charge 'em anyway." Aimee waved her hand in dismissal. "Since I had nothing else cookin' this weekend, I thought what the heck. May as well take the freebie festival ticket and check in on TC, here. He needs babysitting."

CHAPTER SIXTEEN

The Festival, One Year Earlier

I didn't trust leaving Aimee alone with Ginny and scaring her off with too many probing questions, but I had no other choice. My eyes were swimming inside their sockets. At my parents' place, my physical discomfort is relieved by standing on their back deck facing the woods. Not a wise move here. I didn't want someone accusing me of indecent exposure and having me thrown into the slammer.

Ginny wouldn't be impressed.

I stood. "Hold the fort."

Aimee had lost some of her earlier intensity and turned on the big persona. Her over-the-top conversational style had made Ginny comfortable, and I suppose Aimee figured she'd find out more by acting like a loon rather than a prosecutor.

Aimee nabbed my seat, saying something about striking while the iron's hot. The girl was nimble. Had to give her that.

"Well, you ain't sittin' now." She winked a ghoulish, cringe-worthy gesture that caused her eyes and mouth to operate out of sync with each other.

Ginny laughed. "You two are a mess."

I checked the charge on my phone, still rocking my playlist, and stepped inside the tent for a wireless charger. "Leaving the phone here. Needs some juice." I checked my still-damp cargo shorts for my wallet. My tastebuds had grown tired of beer and screamed for something sweet and fizzy. "Do you girls want anything?"

"Get me a Coke," Aimee said in that demanding, twangy voice of hers.

"What kind? Mountain Dew? Dr. Pepper? Orange Fanta?" Southerners have a quirky habit of calling all soft drinks "Coke," making follow-up questions necessary.

"Stupid question. What do you think? Dew, of course." Aimee's passion for the neon-colored, highly caffeinated drink had no bounds. She defended it and her right to drink as much as she wanted. Dental decay—referred to as Mountain Dew Mouth—be damned. "I need some caffeine."

"No, you don't," I said. "You need a tranquilizer."

I looked at Ginny. Her fingers tapped along her phone's screen as she wrote a text message. Frown lines formed between her eyebrows. She hadn't gotten a text from Jacob in a while. A long while. Was she worried? "Ginny, want a drink?"

She looked at me. "Uh, yes. A Coke, a real one, please."

"Got it. Hey, if you need to recharge your phone, Ginny, you can use my charger."

"Thanks. I'm good." She looked down at the phone and continued tapping away.

With the long lines at the bathrooms and concession area, it took nearly an hour to take care of business. When I got back, Aimee had already left. Ginny watched the campers across from our campsite having a tug-of-war contest with a mud-covered bedsheet. She wore a lopsided grin and her eyes twinkled. She looked relaxed. Happy. *Good old Aimee. I owed her a beer.*

"Where's the redhead?" I handed Ginny her Coke and emptied my pockets, not sure of what would happen next. Aimee always adds flavor to parties, and I wasn't sure I alone could keep Ginny rooted to the campsite.

"Gone. She took off with her friends. Not sure where they're going, but she didn't want to go. I didn't want her to go either."

I frowned. "You don't need a chaperone around me. Haven't attacked you yet, have I?"

"Oh, I know that. But she's entertaining. She reminds me of Granny. Spunky."

"You don't know the half of it."

"You're lucky." Ginny paused before continuing. "She may not show it, but she adores you. She said she'd trust you with her life." *What else did Aimee tell her about me?* "She also said you're the only Yankee who doesn't make her backside itch. Does she mean these things?" Ginny gave me a quizzical look. "I know the old-timers in my hometown sometimes speak disparagingly of Northerners, but no one my age."

"She's only happy when she's shocking or offending someone."

At first, her in-your-face comments had thrown me before I got her number. "Aimee has an act, part of her branding—the hillbilly woman who offers authentic experiences and colorful stories about her moonshining relations," I said. "She doesn't fool me anymore."

How can she? We're Frick and Frack.

"Do you know that she graduated summa cum laude?" Ginny asked.

I nodded. "She's quick. No doubt. She knows what's she doing. And I'd bet my last dollar she didn't say backside either." Cussing is another habit I share with Aimee. Off-color words slip out as stealthily as Georgie dashing through an open door.

"I cleaned it up." Ginny opened her bottle and took a dainty sip. "Granny doesn't curse. She's rubbed off on me."

I processed that tidbit, pleased I'd kept my cussing to a minimum. If I spent more time with Ginny, no one would recognize me.

Two foil-wrapped disposable plates sat near her feet. *Is that what I think it is?* Bear did bring us vittles. I rubbed my hands together, my mouth watered. I'd starve had it not been for my big generous friend. I put Aimee's Dew in the cooler, unscrewed the top of my Orange Fanta, and sat. I offered a plate to Ginny, but she shook her head.

"One sec." She retrieved her spiral-ring notebook—the one she had used as a fan earlier—from the cupholder and flipped to a page. So, she recorded musings in a notebook too. Maybe I would add to my jottings later.

I got up to check my backpack inside the tent. *Good.* The book was safe inside the pocket.

"Bryan delivered the plates." Ginny raised her voice, so I'd hear. "You missed him. He came back to change his clothes."

I returned to the camp chair.

"People kept stopping by and asking where you were." She ran her finger down the page and looked up. "Got so busy, I had to take notes. Some people insisted I pass along messages."

I was in disbelief. Not by the number of people who dropped by to visit, but the fact she recorded the names and messages like a receptionist dutifully writing down messages on a pink pad. Why didn't she just tap reminders into her phone like everybody else our age? *Wait a minute. I can't judge. I go nowhere without my little black book.*

"What?" Ginny laughed at herself and flapped the notebook in the air. "Okay, I may be weird, but at least I'm organized."

"That you are."

She ripped the page out and handed it to me.

"Did Bryan say anything?" I asked.

"Well, he thanked me for cleaning."

"You cleaned?" I looked around the camp and noticed the improvement.

"If you haven't noticed, I'm a bit of a clean freak." While I was gone, she borrowed a trash bag from people at a nearby tent and busied herself picking up beer cans and other trash. That was when Bryan walked inside. I wished I'd been there to see the look on his face. He must have yelped, not expecting to see the angel in white tending to our mess.

She said they chatted a bit about this and that, and then he left. I knew exactly what was going on inside his head. I've known Bryan since middle school. A couple of years ago, he moved to Baltimore with Mooches, his twenty-pound alley cat that dines on rats when allowed to roam. Bryan visits often, sometimes alone, sometimes with his girlfriend. Never with Mooches. He'd eat Georgie whole.

Wherever he was, Bryan, no doubt, was mentally preparing his interrogation for the ride home. My spending time with a blonde-haired hottie would only arouse his curiosity and questions. He's made my personal love life his business . . . "Chelsey isn't the only fish in the sea," he tells me. "Put yourself out there."

I sometimes approach the women he thinks I should flirt with, and sometimes I don't. Doesn't matter. Nothing changes. My conversations all end the same way. I have a new buddy. I don't mind, especially after the debacle with Chelsey. Or at least that's what I tell myself.

But at that moment, I wasn't so sure. I felt good around Ginny. Felt good about myself.

"I've made plenty of mistakes in my life," I said, throwing all caution to the wind, "but choosing the people I hang with isn't one of them. That includes you."

I leaned back in my chair and shoved the list into my pocket, hiding my face. Why did I open my mouth? I didn't want her thinking I was coming on to her. She'd probably heard her share of BS from drooling, lovesick males. Thanks in large part to Aimee, we'd come a long way since arriving at the tent, and I didn't want to blow it.

"Yep, Ginny, you're okay. You like my stories. You clean my crib. Maybe I'll hire you as my personal secretary."

I said this in one breathe and gave a quick glance to make sure she wasn't unnerved as I wiped my sweaty palms on my shorts.

She pushed aside a few strands of hair and bit the inside of her lower lip.

Uh-oh. Did she infer my compliment as a hackneyed pick-up line? Frankly, I don't think she was even paying close attention. She seemed lost in thought.

"You know, TC, I'm surprised I'm here . . . with you," she said after a bit. "I don't have a lot of friends. Big crowds drain me. And I know I'd never be caught dead dancing the way you were. You were so into it, and you didn't seem to care what people thought." She shook her head. "People were laughing. Not *at* you, but with you. I think they appreciated the lack self-consciousness. The way you were being yourself. I sure appreciated it myself. Sometimes I wish I could just let my hair down."

I shrugged. "That's what I do." It hadn't been the first time I'd made a scene. Bryan always says he loves hanging back and watching other people watch me. Maybe that's why I do it.

She didn't say anything for another second or two. "Two of my closest friends are upset with me now." Her voice was quiet. She glanced at me. "They say I no longer make time for them. And they're right."

She told me that since she started dating Jacob, she had little free time for anything or anyone. Even Granny. Jacob always planned their weekends, never asking if she'd be interested in his plans. He hadn't even told her about the festival tickets until last night, several hours after she'd arrived in Atlanta. She had looked forward to a quiet weekend with him, streaming movies in his theater room, making dinner, sitting out at the patio fire pit, taking a swim. Talking.

"I was a little annoyed but got over it," she said. "He'd gotten the tickets from someone he wants to do business with and didn't want to come off as a stick-in-the-mud by turning them down. He doesn't normally go to events like this." She said this as an aside. "Just wish I hadn't felt so horrible this morning."

Until that moment, Ginny hadn't shared much about Jacob or her social life outside of her life with Granny.

"Now that I'm moving to Atlanta, I guess it'll be even harder getting together with my friends."

I grabbed a plate and again offered the other to her, along with the plastic-wrapped disposable cutlery Sugahbear included in the care package. I was starving. "I know you haven't asked for my advice, but here it is anyway: maintain those relationships." I took a bite of Bear's barbecued Asian-spiced baby back ribs and Mo's special cornbread. "Mmm." I put the conversation on hold and savored the food. "You need your friends," I said between bites of the vegetable skewers and grilled potatoes. "You need your Granny. I don't know what I'd do without my people. Case in point: this chow."

I took another mouthful. Some of the sauce dribbled down my shirt. One of the flamingos wore a hat. I examined the stain closer and wiped it off.

Ginny stared absently at the neighbors sprawled on their tarp, apparently tuckered out from their earlier tug-of-war, her plate balanced on her lap.

She nodded. "You're probably right about needing your friends and family. Or in my case, Granny." She sampled the fare. "Ooh, this is good. This cornbread may be better than Granny's, and that's saying something. Please thank Bear and Mo for me. He is a sweetheart."

What did she just say? *Bear's a sweetheart?* Since when? She seemed to be having a panic attack in his presence just a few hours ago.

"No problem," I said. "I think I'll wander over there after you leave. Or you can join me and tell him yourself."

Now what did I do?

She stood and looked about. "I'm holding you up, aren't I? This is so embarrassing."

"Where are you going? Sit down."

"Are you sure?" She bit her lip, but eventually did as I said.

I gestured to the people moving past us. "I'm the winner in this deal. If Jacob hadn't ditched you, we'd never have met. I'll tell you when you start getting on my nerves."

Though I wiggled my eyebrows and made a goofy face, my comment must have opened a wound because she flinched a little and covered her face with both hands. What was she doing? Warding off a nagging truth not ready to accept?

CHAPTER SEVENTEEN

The Festival, One Year Earlier

My mouth was always getting me into trouble. I shouldn't have said anything about her being ditched even though it looked that way to me. I touched her arm, moved closer, and tried to assure her that Jacob was fine. Not to worry. If she wanted, she could stay here, or I would drive her home to Granny's. Didn't Ginny say I'd get on with her grandmother? Didn't she say Granny made a mean cornbread?

I pulled Bryan's car keys from my pocket. "Let's roll." Bryan wouldn't have minded. After all, an impromptu road trip would give me more time with Ginny. Regardless of Aimee's doubts, maybe I could convince Ginny to stop wasting her time with Jacob. I loved the way she smiled at me. "I'm ready whenever you are."

"Absolutely not." She shook her head. "You're not leaving your friends because of me. Furthermore, I can't just leave Jacob."

Why not? He had no problem leaving her.

"Okay, suit yourself." I pocketed the keys. Disappointed. "Let me know if you change your mind."

She tapped another message into her phone, and this worried me. We needed to get off the topic of Jacob . . . before she changed her mind and went out searching for him. I didn't want her to leave.

I started babbling about the movies I'd seen, the books I'd read. She put her phone down. "I love movies." She grinned and then rattled off a few romcoms . . . flicks that only chicks watched.

"Have you ever seen the *Addams Family*?"

Ginny nodded.

"Remember Uncle Fester?"

"I do."

I told her about the time my high school buddies shaved my eyebrows and hair after I'd passed out in someone's basement one Saturday night. "Well, that's who I looked like when I woke up the next morning. I looked like a freak and felt even worse."

Ginny couldn't relate to hangovers since she'd never imbibe, let alone over imbibe like me, especially after Chelsey ended our relationship and I went a little crazy, gaining twenty-five pounds.

Ginny had already told me of her discomfort attending big parties where kids drank, smoked weed, and hooked up. She wasn't a snob or anything. And I believed her. She just didn't feel comfortable in those situations. But she did like to laugh. And that's what she was doing then, enjoying me, and not thinking about her wayward fiancé.

I set up the scene, the fact I had to go to church that morning, with or without eyebrows and dark circles. One of my brothers, Cameron, was supposed to be getting confirmed. Command performance. We were already running late when I came downstairs in my Sunday best, looking like a corpse in funeral attire.

Though I'd told a few psycho-mom stories earlier, Ginny hadn't gotten the full picture. My mother is Atilla the Hun. She studied my face, and I could tell she couldn't figure out the countenance before her. She looked like she was studying a Picasso and not understanding the skewed and out-of-whack facial features.

When she'd realized I'd been shorn, she went nuts. She yelled that I looked like Uncle Fester, a dad-blamed freak. And why? For the forty-millionth time she asked what was wrong with me.

"What did you say?" Ginny laughed, inching herself to the edge of her chair.

"I told her to be thankful I didn't look like Cousin Itt."

Mom didn't talk to me for the rest of the day, which was A-okay with me. My head hurt from my hangover and from trying to figure out how I'd fix my hairless visage. I had even considered asking for her eyebrow pencil but scrapped the idea. Too metro-sexual. I'd rather take the slings and arrows. And that's what I did.

"My brother couldn't have cared less when the stunt happened, but now he likes to take cheap shots whenever our clan assembles."

"Cheap shots?"

"Yeah, brotherly ribbing. I guess you don't have brothers."

Ginny didn't answer. "I don't blame your mother. I don't know what Granny would have done with you." She displayed that pretty smile of hers. "You must have plucked your mother's nerves."

I ignored Ginny's stealthy change in topics. She was saying *nada* about family members, aside from Granny, and I wasn't about to cry for my mother. Then and now, she can hold her own. Raising three rowdy boys offered her a choice. She'd get tough or spend her days locked inside a padded cell, banging her head against the wall and drooling. She chose the former.

I leaned back in my chair, stroked my beard.

Ginny's comment made me think. Now an adult, I can understand why my partying and general lack of direction concerned my parents. They worried. And maybe they still do. In their middle-class world, kids grow up, move away, start families, and contribute to society. Tumbleweed offspring who bounce from job to job confuse them.

I pushed the thoughts aside. "Like I said, all's good. Don't feel like you need to go."

Ginny nodded, but she tapped her fingers on the arms of the chair and bit her lip—a tell I was beginning to deduce—that indicated discomfort and uncertainty, like my nose scratching. "You know, Jacob has never done anything like this before. Disappearing. He usually doesn't let me out of his sight. He texts me a million times a day, almost to the point of being annoying. I'm worried something has happened. Do you think I should check with security?"

"Not yet. What's it been? Three hours? Didn't he run off with a family friend? As you may have noticed, I can get carried away too, when it comes to a good party." I grinned and didn't tell her what really rolled through my head. That, unlike Jacob, I had no one to answer to. He did, and he had no excuses for leaving Ginny with a stranger. This entire situation was getting curiouser and curiouser. I almost blurted this out, which would've violated my sacrosanct tenet that people should mind their business. I kept my thoughts quiet. *Why did she put up with this?*

Her phone buzzed. She read the message, sagged against the back of her chair, and typed her response. "I can relax now. He asked me not to be mad. He's having a great time catching up with his friend." Was she trying to convince me of Jacob's remorse and honest intentions? She exhaled. "I'm so relieved. I was getting worried."

"For your sake, I am too." I watched a guy guzzle a beer to the cheers of his drunken comrades. "Did he ask how *you're* doing?"

"Why would he ask that?" A red blush spread over her face. She straightened.

My attitude toward this guy went from a nagging dislike to a pants-on-fire, five-alarm warning inside my head—*ding, ding, ding*, pay attention here. I knew I was glowering. If Ginny noticed, she didn't say.

Give him the benefit of the doubt, I told myself. I hadn't been privy to their text messages. Maybe his hours-long disappearance was perfectly innocent and normal. Maybe he simply knew Ginny could take care of herself.

As I rolled these scenarios over in my mind, I couldn't think of a single female friend who would've tolerated being abandoned, let alone by someone she loved and intended to marry. These women would have bailed, called an Uber—or even better, they would've called me. I'd driven many a long distance to rescue friends from disagreeable situations. And I was willing to do the same for her.

I couldn't figure Ginny out. She seemed bright and level-headed. Insightful. Decent. Caring. Fun to be around—characteristics I wanted in a girl. Who saved me from the mud, after all?

But where Jacob was concerned, she seemed to lose perspective. Didn't she know that his behavior was rude? Odd?

I needed to peel away her layers before I could grasp the full measure of this woman who'd dropped into my life. My lucky day or not, I was determined to get closer to her and sensed she needed my protection. My emotions were certainly running contrary to my live-and-let-live approach to life.

Despite Aimee's warning, this girl was getting under my skin.

But sometimes, the heart won't listen to the head.

CHAPTER EIGHTEEN

The Festival, One Year Earlier

Even though she was marooned with me, Ginny seemed to take it in stride. Now that she knew Jacob hadn't been trampled or kidnapped, she seemed unconcerned about his now hours-long disappearance with a woman she didn't know. *Fine by me.* I thought I still had time to turn her around. To start taking an interest in me. We sat in a companionable silence beneath the canopy, listening to music and watching festival goers navigate the mud. Strangers might have thought we were a couple.

"I've been so distracted," she said, touching my arm. "Thank you for letting me stay with you until Jacob gets back. I know you have other things to do, and I appreciate you keeping me company."

"Don't mention it. We've had fun. I can hang out with Bryan any old time." Little did she know, I didn't care if Jacob ever came back. But I couldn't stop thinking about how selfish he appeared to be. Why she thought him so special. Normally, I don't bombard people with questions, preferring to observe instead, figuring people will share their stuff when they're good and ready. But the questions pestered. Nothing ventured, nothing gained. So, I decided to ask a few, conversationally, careful not to come on too strong. She was happy to share, and at times, I wished I'd just kept my questions to myself. Her descriptions of Jacob annoyed me and reminded me of someone I once knew. Someone I hoped to never see again.

"Hey, how'd you and Jacob meet?" I tilted my head to the side and got comfortable in my chair. "What does he do for a living? Where does he live? I don't think you've told me."

Ginny gave me a wide grin. "I'll start at the beginning," she said in a bubbly voice. Her hands fluttered about her face, and she moved closer to the edge of her camp chair. "Best place to start."

I nodded and made a point of pocketing my phone.

Ginny explained that Jacob is an only child, the presumed heir to a large and very successful Atlanta-based land development firm that his father started a couple of decades ago. He had been inspecting potential properties along the Georgia coast and was headed back to Atlanta when he upended his motorcycle, swerving to avoid a collision.

"What kind of motorcycle?" I asked.

"A BMW, his pride and joy." She pretended to grasp a pair of handlebars and imitated a revving engine. That made me laugh.

"You've been hanging out with me too long."

She jabbed my chest. "No doubt."

An old man driving a big Buick hadn't seen Jacob when he pulled out into traffic and didn't realize something had happened until he glanced at his rearview mirror and saw Jacob sprawled on the road behind him. Ginny worked in the emergency room where the ambulance brought him.

"That's how we met." Her eyes danced. She loved telling the meet-cute story.

What fascinated me were the details. She wasn't there so how did she know the blow-by-blow? Did she read the accident report? Talk to the cops? Her recounting of what happened transported me into the scene. I could feel the slight temperature change after the rainstorm. Smell the ozone. See shimmering motor oil and cigarette butts floating in the puddles. I could see the old man, his hands shaking, putting his land yacht into reverse, pulling along-side of Jacob as he writhed in pain, and shakily dialing 911 on his flip phone.

"Jacob told me that he was glad he hadn't hit the old man. He couldn't have lived with himself. Thank God, neither of them was going fast." Ginny looked serene, confident that she'd made the right choice for a life partner. She continued the story. Other than for a few dents and scratches, the bike wasn't ruined, but Jacob fractured his arm and sprained a couple fingers while he tried to break the fall. Cuts and bruises covered his legs and arms and one laceration required stitches.

Jacob didn't complain of numbness, tingling, blurred vision, or any other symptoms associated with a neck injury. But the paramedic and EMT—guys Ginny knew well—played it safe and strapped a brace around his neck because he seemed confused.

"They carried him to the hospital. My luck." She smiled at the memory, as if it were enshrined inside her head like a holy day. "He wouldn't let go of my hand. As the docs cut off his jacket, he told me that he must have died because he thought he was seeing an angel. How I was the most beautiful girl he ever saw." She glanced at me to make sure I was listening.

I smiled, probably somewhat skeptically, because the whole thing sounded schmaltzy to me, like a scene from one of those romance novels my great-grandmother used to read. But I wasn't about to burst her bubble or reveal my attraction to her. In no way did I want her running off and looking for Jacob. *Play it cool. Play it cool.* A chant inside my head.

She sat upright in the chair and wrapped her arms around her knees.

"Jacob is very handsome and charming." She looked contented. As she explained, the old man was clearly at fault and was upset he hadn't seen Jacob. He kept saying he better get his eyesight checked, and he wouldn't leave the hospital even though Ginny and others assured him that Jacob wasn't hurt badly. According to Ginny, Jacob had everyone under his spell by the time he left.

"I wonder if the old man ended up paying for the repairs and a new jacket?" Ginny tapped her mouth with her finger.

"What do you mean?" I wasn't tracking. The question had no context.

Ginny furrowed her brow. "Oh, I guess I'm being silly, but I've often wondered if Jacob followed through on his promise."

She noticed my confusion. "Let me explain. When I wheeled Jacob into the waiting room, the old man was still there. He got up and hobbled over. Poor guy weighed no more than a hundred pounds and his clothing looked frayed." She leaned back in her chair and crossed her ankles. "Jacob noticed his appearance and told the man not to worry about anything. He didn't want him saddled with higher insurance rates or repair costs. He took the man's phone number but refused his insurance information. That's what impressed me."

Ginny fiddled with her ponytail. "I just wonder if Jacob ever spoke with him again." She didn't say anything for a couple of beats, and then started bobbing her head. She sighed as she drew in her legs, wrapping her arms around her knees. "Of course, he spared the old man," she said. "Why would I think otherwise?" She turned to me. "I love telling people about Jacob."

I bet he was on the horn the next day demanding money. I suppressed the thought. "How did he get home?" When did you start seeing each other?"

"I called his father first, but he and Jacob's mother were attending a gala and couldn't get away, so I called an Uber."

I sat up straighter. In that moment, I felt a twinge of sadness for Jacob. My parents would've never chosen a party over me or both my brothers—Cameron and Scott. What had his childhood been like?

"What are his parents like?" My curiosity wouldn't be sated.

Ginny didn't know them well. She saw them at company functions, that type of thing. His mom didn't say much—especially around Jacob's dad—and seemed devoted to both, always smiling when they entered a room. Jacob's dad was her opposite. He had a big personality and liked to be in the spotlight. "In his youth, he must have been quite the ladies' man. Jacob takes after him." Ginny mentioned this as an aside.

"What? Jacob is a lady's man?" I couldn't hold back my sarcastic question.

"No. Jacob's charming, like his father." She cupped her face with both hands and smiled. *Didn't she wonder what he was doing with that redhead?* "Jacob works very hard, talks to his dad every day. I know he wants his father's approval. He gets frustrated every time he disappoints his dad."

I let that marinate for a second or two. "He disappoints his dad? How?"

"Are you going to let me finish my story?" She chirped.

"Of course. Sorry." I waved my hand in the air. "You have the floor. Don't let me stop you."

She looked at me through narrowed eyes but continued. "He was in no condition to drive. Plus, he had no transportation. Someone, maybe Jacob . . . I don't know . . . called to have his motorcycle towed." Ginny leaned in closer to me. "He asked me to drive him home, but, of course, I said no."

"Smart move, Ginny. Didn't Granny warn you about strangers?" My snark was showing, and I needed to tone it down.

"Of course, she warned me about strangers," she said, moving away, crossing her arms. "I'm sure Granny wouldn't have wanted me taking off with you either. But I did."

At that moment, I wished I'd been more circumspect. *Why remind her of her out-of-character behavior?*

"How long ago did you meet Jacob?" I asked this quickly.

"About twelve months ago."

"What? You met him last spring and you're already engaged? Don't you think you're being a little hasty?" *Please, please don't marry that guy.*

"Granny thinks I should wait and get to know him better. When she hears I'm moving to Atlanta, I know she'll be disappointed. I wish she saw what I see in him." I filed that morsel and wondered what Granny did see. The same thing as I?

With little prodding from me, Ginny then offered details about their courtship. A few days after the accident, Jacob brought flowers to the hospital and asked Ginny for a date. He said he couldn't get her out of his mind and was going crazy thinking about her. Ginny took a small bouquet of rosebuds home, but the larger arrangements stayed at the nurse's station for everyone to enjoy.

"Why? Doesn't Granny like flowers?"

"They were huge. My goodness, I'm sure they wouldn't have fit inside my car." She paused, absently rubbing her chin. "Granny was suspicious too when I told her about all the other arrangements. She thought the first bouquet sufficed."

At first, Ginny was skeptical too. She didn't date much growing up, and she usually spent her weekends studying, working part-time at a walk-in medical clinic, or going to the movies with girls from her Christian school. But she did have a few love interests, all of whom Granny thoroughly vetted before Ginny could go out with them. Nice boys, Ginny said. Quiet like her. None behaved like Jacob.

At Granny's urging, she had tried to slow things down. She'd meet him for lunch and an occasional movie, but he wouldn't take no for an answer. He wore her down, inviting her to grand openings, chic restaurants, and parties in Atlanta and elsewhere. At these events, he'd never leave her side as he introduced her to his business associates and the occasional politician and judge. He enjoyed showing her off, and always made sure she looked perfect. She wore the clothes and jewelry he bought, felt special and pampered. She said she felt like a princess.

"Where I'm concerned, he spares nothing. He says he loves that others envy him."

Envy? That was his motivation? I was instantly reminded of someone I once knew. No wonder Granny worried. Again, I kept my mouth shut, tried to keep my face neutral.

"I told him I wasn't impressed with his money." Ginny gave me a quick nod, making me think she was trying to convince herself as much as me. "I appreciate thoughtfulness, compassion, and encouragement. The world is a tough place, TC, and I want my boyfriend, husband—whoever—to be there for me."

This set my teeth on edge. Abandoning her at a music festival was how he showed his concern? What was his con? I had my suspicions but didn't know what to do. Should I warn her or keep my nose out of it?

By this time, a war had erupted between the battling voices inside my head. The dominant voice—the one that usually has my ear—urged me to think rationally. Avoid a rush to judgment.

Give Jacob the benefit of the doubt. My attraction to Ginny had muddied my thinking, and it was foolhardy to think she'd ever be interested in me, an overweight underachiever like that Chris Farley character in *Tommy Boy*.

The other voice, my better angel, the still-small voice, my gut, whatever, counseled otherwise. I *should* share my suspicions about Jacob regardless of Ginny's feelings for me. I'd be doing her a favor since I had experience with toxic personalities. Of course, this voice was ignored. The other had argued more effectively. I hadn't met Jacob, didn't know all the facts, so how could I think the worst of him?

So caught up in the self-talk, I nearly missed Ginny's question.

"You know what he said then?"

I shrugged.

"He took my hands and confessed I was the first woman he ever truly loved."

Hadn't I heard that line before, or something similar?

Jacob had his act down—and Ginny was oblivious.

CHAPTER NINETEEN

The Festival, A Year Earlier

I may have looked like I was paying attention to Ginny's love story—nodding and making agreeable noises at proper times—but my mind wandered. I thought about Chelsey, my adolescent crush who took up with me several years after we graduated from college. We got together at a party.

She was on the rebound. Her boyfriend, a prep-school guy with polished manners, wanted to play the field before settling down with Chelsey. Everyone assumed they'd get married, including me. Both wanted the same things in life. Money. The McMansion. Glittering dinner parties. Kids who would attend expensive private schools.

With her, I couldn't believe my luck. And for the first time since childhood, I felt secure, like I was on the right track. I worked harder at my job, even imagining a long-term career in sales, knowing the money might please Chelsey.

This was a delusion.

Behind my back, she'd resumed her relationship with her true love and confessed only after the rumors had started. She apologized for hurting me, but our relationship was going nowhere. She couldn't imagine a life with someone who was as unfocused and unserious as I was. She loved hanging out with me because I made her laugh, but we were better off being friends, she had said. The wedding invitation arrived a few months after our break-up—an incident my most trusted inner voice cited as *prima facie* evidence for avoiding women at all costs.

My insecurities worsened. The walls went up. No one would break my heart again.

But after meeting Ginny, I felt a smidgeon of hope. Maybe it was time to put myself out there, as Bryan advised. Ginny seemed to like me, despite her engagement to Jacob. *Why did she keep touching my arm?*

I shook off the thoughts, shifted in my chair, and made more effort to listen. After all, I had encouraged the details. But the more she shared, the more my inner voice chattered: *What are you doing? Setting yourself up for another letdown, just like with Chelsey?* I swung from one emotion to the other, optimistic then defeated, back, and forth . . . until I was more confused than ever.

"He tells me we complement one another," Ginny said. "Where he's outgoing, I'm more reserved. He likes that. He says it makes us interesting. You know, I used to feel bad about that."

"What?" My mind had wandered.

"About being a little detached." Ginny stopped. "Are you

listening? Is this boring you? Because we can talk about something else."

"Not bored at all," I said. "What's this about being . . ."

"Detached." She picked up where she'd left off. "I was shy growing up, and certainly wasn't one of the popular girls. I did not go to parties and dances, that type of thing. Some kids my age even called me a snob, but they didn't understand. I'm watchful."

She studied her manicured fingernails, further describing Jacob's flattery and attention. She began spending most of her free time with him. For the first time, she said she felt special, even confident of meeting new people. And yes, she was getting better at small talk, especially in small, more intimate settings. "It takes me a while to warm up, but I am getting better. Don't you think?"

Yeah, I supposed she was getting better. She'd certainly kept her counsel when we made our acquaintance a few hours ago. Now, she was a regular chatterbox. Not in the same league with me, but few were.

"There's nothing wrong with that," she said. "Is there?"

"What?"

"Being reserved, watchful?"

"I guess not. Unless there's a reason for holding back and not letting people know you better." I looked directly into her face.

She blanched and scratched a spot above her left eyebrow. "Anyway, he says we'll make a good team."

A team? What is this? A football game? A competition? What an asshat.

Ginny then told me that Jacob had encouraged her to go to

medical school, and he even offered to pay for tuition and books. My gut reared up. *How generous of him . . . and conniving. She'll owe him for the rest of her life.*

"Are you taking him up on the offer?" I asked.

"No. Granny suggested I get scholarships like I did for undergraduate school."

I breathed a sigh of relief. Granny might be the smartest woman on earth. "You said you were moving to Atlanta. When did you tell Jacob?"

"This morning. I've thought about it for weeks and have finally made my decision." She lifted her steepled fingers to her mouth. "We've talked a lot about the future. At a company party just a few weeks ago, he got on his knee and asked me to marry him. Made a big production of it as he slipped a tab on my pinkie finger."

Tab? Good grief. What a tool.

Of course, she accepted the proposal, and everyone—especially his mother—was thrilled. Such a special moment, with everyone rushing up to them to offer congratulations.

She sighed happily. "But he hasn't asked Granny's permission. He thinks he should. So, do I. We'll see. But I dread telling Granny about the move."

I listened patiently to her recounting of the Jacob-Ginny love story but couldn't understand her anxiety about telling Granny. Wouldn't her grandmother be happy, delighted her granddaughter had found someone she wanted to spend the rest of your life with?

Why couldn't it be me?

"Jacob is my best friend," she continued. "I tell him everything.

Well, *almost* everything." Ginny rubbed her naked ring finger and glanced at her phone.

Why didn't she tell him everything? Best friends do that. Well, that wasn't completely true. Bryan was clueless about why I avoided relationships, but Aimee surely knew.

Eventually Ginny explained her reluctance for avoiding a conversation with Granny—understandable given her grandmother's values. Granny didn't approve of shacking up or premarital sex and thought both undermined the God-ordained institution of marriage. People should never give in to their fleshly desires, regardless of the reason, Granny believed. To avoid an all-too-certain conflict with Granny, Ginny suggested to Jacob that she rent her own place until they tied the knot. Jacob poo-poohed the idea. Medical school would take up her time. A job was out of the question.

"He's probably right, as usual," she said. "My finances are limited. And Granny doesn't have much to spare. Anyway, he says we'll get married in a few months' time. Can't wait to go ring shopping. Granny will come around . . . eventually."

Within seconds, her contented smile turned into a frown. She gnawed on her lip. "I don't understand Granny. I'm a grown woman, with a good head on my shoulders, thanks to her. Just because I plan to live in his house doesn't mean I'm going to share his bed." A flush crept across her cheeks. "Why can't she see that Jacob is perfect for me and has helped me come out of my shell and feel more confident? Even Granny worries that I'm too quiet." She sucked in her top lip and massaged her temple. "Probably because she doesn't know him well."

She slapped the arms of her chair and gave me a little smile. "Everything is going to be great. Perfect."

What I would have given to know Granny's thoughts.

CHAPTER TWENTY

The Festival, One Year Earlier

I ignored Ginny's optimism where Jacob was concerned. He seemed to rule the roost in that relationship and had succeeded in convincing her to ignore the values Granny had instilled in her. What about the other people in her life? Where were her parents? She seemed to be hiding something.

"I must have missed something, Ginny," I said. "You've shared a lot about Granny and her expectations, but nothing else. You haven't mentioned your parents or anything about your early childhood. How did you come to live with Granny?"

Earlier, before we started talking about Ginny's planned move to Atlanta, I'd shared quite a bit about my childhood. I told her about the gang of boys who gravitated to our backyard, drawn by the dad-built clubhouse, a fifteen-foot rope swing, and a shed full of tools we used to disassemble bikes, lawnmowers, and whatever else we could get our mitts on. As we got older, we ventured farther afield to explore the creeks that ran alongside the heavily traveled roads in our suburban community.

My childhood was, without reservation, idyllic. Simple and worry-free.

Ginny had chuckled at my stories, especially the ones about my grandmother, Mom-Mom. I had every reason to tell them. Ginny appeared to love her grandmother as much as I love mine. That much Ginny and I had in common. Our grandmothers, however, seemed to have very little in common. Mom-Mom is a wild thing and probably influenced my preference for flamboyant people.

"Yep, we had fun with her wig," I said, explaining how Mom-Mom had let her hairdresser conduct chemical warfare on her head. When her hair follicles finally surrendered, she bought a light brown wig that looked like something a clown might wear.

Ginny's eyes glowed. She kept touching my arm.

One Mom-Mom visit came to mind. We'd been sitting on my front porch and watching and commenting on Sloth—the dirtbag who lived across the street. For the first time since I'd moved to the hood—before I'd learned of his dark secrets—he found the energy to pick up his yard, littered with trash, rowboats, and rusted appliances. The city should have condemned the property. Rats that munched on his trash had become a neighborhood problem. That's when Georgie hurdled my makeshift barricade spanning the two porch posts and took off. He didn't stick around, and I had no other choice. I had to find him.

Getting Mom-Mom out of the chair took some effort since she's not steady on her feet anymore. As I searched my pockets for the car keys, she rambled down the sidewalk, checked her wig, and hoisted herself into my car. She'd sold the car to me for pennies given the dents and scratches she'd created after backing up into a power pole.

Our madcap chase across the neighborhood ensued.

"You should have seen her, Ginny. As I drove, she hung her head out and yelled his name. Suddenly, she screamed to stop the car. She said I'd hit a small dog. Now, I'm a little shaken, right. I didn't feel a bump, but that didn't mean anything. I was pretty upset and was imagining Georgie dead on the side of the road."

I slammed on the breaks, glanced in my rearview mirror, and saw a furry brown thing lying in a puddle amid fast-food bags. But before backing up, I glanced at her and hooted.

"You should've seen the look on her face and heard the salvo of choice words when she patted her head and realized the wig was gone. As I started backing up, I told her I'd pluck the wig from the puddle, but she wasn't putting that nasty old thing back on her head." When we got home, we found Georgie, sitting on a porch step, wagging his tail like a lunatic. I draped the wig over a citronella candle and handed Mom-Mom a red bandana.

"She looked like a geriatric biker chick," I said.

Ginny threw her head back and roared. "How old is she? Sounds young at heart."

I did the math in my head. "Eighty."

"She's Granny's age. Wow. Granny's nothing like her. As I've told you, she keeps her cussing to a minimum—to quote you."

From her descriptions, I could see Ginny's spitfire of a

grandmother. "Granny spends a lot of her time either frying chicken for church socials or digging in her garden, and she doesn't give a hoot about fashion or hairstyles." Ginny's eyes shined as she described Granny's ugly gardening hats and baggy house dresses that hung off her short, wiry frame.

"Granny is a believer. A wonderful woman," she continued, shaking her head in wonderment. "She understands that everyone sins, including herself. She puts her faith in God and looks to him for salvation, wisdom, and grace. She refuses to judge or condemn others because she knows how it feels when you're on the receiving end of idle talk."

"Wow. Sounds like Granny's the real deal. She sounds like a Christian who talks the talk and walks the walk," I said.

"That she is." Ginny grinned. "I've benefited from her example. She's well-liked and respected by everyone." Her voice quieted. "Granny also understands another truth. Evil exists. The wise keep their eyes on the Shepherd because only He can protect them from the thief in the night, who comes to steal, kill, and destroy."

I didn't know what to make of this. Granny's views on evil didn't surprise me, given what Ginny had revealed about her grandmother's faith. But who was the thief in the night? A hypothetical? Jacob or someone else? I leaned back in my chair and considered everything Ginny had just said. I knew then that I wouldn't be sharing my take on faith.

Like Ginny, I, too, went to Vacation Bible School, belonged to church youth groups—that type of thing—but along the way, my childhood attitudes toward religion changed. My heart hardened.

To me, Granny sounded like an anomaly in how she walked out her faith. Many of the Christians I know are hypocrites and fakes, masters at criticizing others for their own behaviors. Pedophile priests further reinforce my dim view of church people, as do adulterous television evangelists. I don't hate God. I believe He exists and occasionally read scripture myself from a Bible my aunt gave me. But I have given up on organized religion. Most of my friends have given up on church too.

My thoughts must have played out on my face. Ginny glanced at me, and her smile faded. "What's wrong, TC? Did I offend you?"

"Of course not." I waved her off. "Absolutely, nothing is wrong. Just thinking about something else."

By this point, I'd a pretty good idea of how Granny raised Ginny but knew instinctively Ginny was withholding critical pieces of information that might explain why she wouldn't talk about her parents. Or brothers and sisters. Did she have siblings? Why did she evade questions about them? Something wasn't adding up.

"Honestly, Ginny you're not telling me everything."

She furrowed her brow and pressed her lips together before answering. "I had a sister—once. Laurel. She's gone. I probably wouldn't be sitting here with you right now or making plans for medical school if Granny hadn't come and rescued me. She's never left my side, and I never, ever want her to think I'm abandoning her. I will always be loyal to her." Her voice grew quieter. "That's why I dread telling her about my move to Atlanta. I respect her, want her blessings." She sighed. "I just wish she were more enthusiastic about Jacob."

CHAPTER TWENTY-ONE

The Festival, One Year Earlier

Ginny's blunt revelation about her sister and Granny's lack-luster opinion of Jacob hung in the air.

"You can't lay that down and not explain what happened to you and Laurel," I said.

Ginny sat still, watching a girl riding piggyback on a guy's back. She massaged her forehead, exhaled, and looked toward the overcast sky. Then she shut her eyes and seemed to utter a silent prayer. She turned to me.

"TC, before I tell you about Laurel, do you mind watching out for Jacob? I need to go to the bathroom, and I want to make sure someone is here when he comes for me." She offered a barely noticeable smile.

"No prob." Although I gave her my mega-watt grin, I really wanted to grab her by the shoulders. Shake some sense into her.

Neither one of us should be here when he arrives. Serve him right. She left her bag and cowgirl hat next to her chair, assuring me she'd come back and tell the rest of her story. But did I really want to hear it?

Something traumatic had happened to Ginny. Intellectually, I understand the ramifications. Kids react to events over which they have no control. Their brains get rewired. Some tragically become incapable of leading fulfilling, productive lives, without serious intervention from mental health professionals or someone who cares.

My family isn't perfect. I know that. But the death of a sibling or a threat on my own life has never happened to me or those in my circle of close friends. Maybe my friends keep their tragedies hidden, only telling a few about the catastrophes that have shaken their lives. But I am unaware of them and live in an innocent bliss, wandering through life.

Her phone rang inside her satchel as I mulled these thoughts. Though tempted to answer, I let it go to voicemail. Within seconds, it rang again. And again.

To fill the time, I texted Bryan to see what he was up to. He didn't answer my question about his whereabouts. He wanted the inside skinny on Ginny. His question went ignored, and the phone went to its place in the cupholder. I didn't notice Ginny's return until she sat in the chair.

"Jacob didn't come, did he?"

I shook my head. She frowned and looked at her muddy boots. I found Bryan's towel and handed it to her, thinking she wouldn't relax until she removed every speck of mud from her footwear.

"Sort of pointless, don't you think?" She grinned before taking the towel and giving her boots a cursory wipe.

"Well, you won't find perfection here." I looked at my flamingo shirt and saw the faint stain from the earlier dribbling. "Oh, almost forgot…your phone kept ringing while you were gone. Maybe it was him."

"Oh, boy. First time he's called." She found her phone and listened to the messages. I could hear his voice, louder when she pulled the phone away from her ear. Although his words were muffled, I could tell he was unhappy—livid after his third unanswered call.

Ginny called back, but I guess he didn't answer. "Hi, Jacob. Sorry I missed you. I had to go to the bathroom and left my phone here at the tent. I'm fine. Wondering where you are. I'm wearing out my welcome. Call or text. I'll make sure to keep the phone with me." She hung up and pinched the bridge of her nose. "I don't get it."

"No worries, Ginny. And you are *not* wearing out your welcome. Glad you're here. By the time he shows up, we'll be best friends." I had no idea how prescient my comment would become.

She smiled uncertainly. "We'll see. You might not like me after I tell you my story."

"You might not like me either, once you get to know me better."

"Is that so?" She scowled at me. "You've been honest about who you are. I know about the people in your life, your attitudes, the trouble you caused. You even told me about your arrest and the reason you withdrew from college."

Why did I tell her that story? Her good opinion mattered to me, and stories like that didn't help. Another example of my talent for self-sabotage. I am the leading character in my own Greek tragedy.

On that afternoon, I had slow rolled through a stop sign. Within seconds, the cruiser's siren blared, the blue light flashing. That's when I noticed the bag of amphetamines in my console. The bag got shoved into my shoe.

The jig was up. The cop slapped handcuffs on my wrists and hauled me to jail. My only call was to a lawyer specializing in representing stupid college kids, like me, a serial class skipper and gifted partier who had to pull all-nighters just to get passing grades on final exams. I knew my run-in with the law paled in comparison with the troubles of others, but it embarrassed me then . . . and now. My friends aren't angels, but they don't get busted either.

The entire episode underscores a flaw. I can see the problems in others but refuse to face my own, which only leads to poor decisions. Too many parties. Too much procrastination. I go about as if I have all the time in the world. No one, including my friends and family, can figure me out. How many times has Bryan questioned my motivations? Or told me I wasn't living up to my potential . . . whatever that is.

But deep inside I know. I don't know what I want to do with my life and feel like a failure, a feeling exacerbated by Chelsey's dumping of me. Why can't I remain a kid forever? It would be so much easier.

"I'd never condemn you, TC." She touched my arm but spoke

with force. She admired me, she said, because I didn't involve my parents in my legal troubles, and I eventually finished school. "But I sense you don't appreciate the advantages in your life. Despite yourself, you've been blessed."

Until that moment, this side of Ginny had remained hidden. In our time together, never once did she raise her voice. She was polite to a fault. "Okay, okay." I threw up both hands in surrender. "You win."

"This isn't a matter of winning." She sounded exasperated. "You need to realize how fortunate you are. You have parents, grandparents, a huge extended family, and friends who love you, care for you, and only want the best for you."

I looked at my lap, noticing grass stains and dried mud on my cargo shorts. I flicked a blob and watched the crusty morsel take flight.

"Just tell me about Laurel, okay."

Her fervor dissolved. "You need to hear the whole story, not just the part about Laurel, and why I moved in with Granny. Once you know my story, you might understand why I called you out. I am sorry I raised my voice at you." I dreaded hearing about her childhood now. Whatever happened to her had never happened to me. No wonder she was annoyed.

CHAPTER TWENTY-TWO

The Festival, One Year Earlier

Once Ginny started telling me about her family, she couldn't be stopped. She spat out her story, each word a high-caliber bullet that pierced my naiveté. Other times, her voice got quiet. While speaking, she showed me just how much I *had* taken for granted. Why hadn't I gotten on my knees to thank God, whom I rarely thought about, for my good fortune in matters that really counted?

Pictures formed in my mind. I could see a younger Granny, her hard-working husband, a bricklayer, and their two little girls. I began to know them as if they'd been my kin—my parents, grandparents, and extended family, people who keep me from going completely off the rails. Over the years, my procrastination and mistakes have disappointed them because I am capable of more. But they love me all the same.

Her story also made me consider how inconsequential moments could alter the paths people take in their journeys through life and how those choices affect generations to come. *How would my choices affect the people in my life?*

Ginny stood, clasped her hands above her head, then shoved them in her pockets. She rolled her shoulders and massaged the back of her neck before returning to her chair.

She seemed to be reading my mind.

"Life is full of what-ifs," she said. "Choose this door, this happens, choose another door and something else altogether different happens."

What if her grandfather hadn't gone to work early that day? What if he had spent the early morning hours with Granny, reading the newspaper and enjoying a second cup of coffee, as was his habit? For whatever reason, he didn't. He went in early, mixed a pan of mud, and climbed the scaffolding alone.

She waited a beat. "He tripped over a bucket and fell twenty feet and hit his head on a pile of cast-off bricks. He laid there for an hour or so before the other bricklayers started arriving and saw him lying on the ground."

"Your grandfather didn't make it, did he?"

"No." She rested her head in both hands and said she sometimes wondered about the other outcome, the one where he hadn't deviated from his normal routine and showed up with his coworkers at the usual time. Maybe they would have seen the hazard and warned him before he took the fatal step.

"I think my mother—her name is Audrey—would have turned

out differently had he lived." Ginny looked sideways at me.

"Wait a minute. Is your mom still around? Since you wouldn't talk about her, I got the impression both your mother and father were dead."

"They are to me." Her eyes turned dark. "Please, TC, let me tell this my way. This is hard enough, okay?"

CHAPTER TWENTY-THREE

Ginny, The Festival, One Year Earlier

've heard Granny's stories so often they've become my own. TC said nothing as I recounted my family history, or at least Granny's version of it and the fragments I remembered. I'm not sure why I told him. His openness and honesty? Certainly, that factored, but more than anything, TC made me feel safe as we sat beneath his lemon-flavored canopy in a private world of our own making. No longer ashamed, and knowing he wasn't the type to blame or make snap judgments, I told my deepest secrets . . . to someone I'd just met.

The first part, I knew, would be easy. Or comparatively so. I wasn't so sure about the middle or the end. I needed a drink of water, and started rummaging around in the cooler, coming up empty-handed.

"Girl, move over." One hand dragged through the ice water

and TC found a bottle, the label hanging on, but barely. He handed it to me and shook his head. "What would you do without me?"

He had no clue. I took a sip and then began.

Granny was my age—twenty-six, in the prime of her life—when tragedy struck. She had few job skills and couldn't drive, let alone balance the checkbook. Her life's ambition was to be a wife to her high school sweetheart and the mother to his children. But Grandpa's sudden death forced her to reimagine a different life. She was overwhelmed and terrified, worried she couldn't raise her two girls alone after the neighbors, church friends, and relatives moved on.

"In the end, though, she powered through . . . one of many reasons I admire her so," I told TC.

Even today, decades later, Granny's eyes will well up when she recalls those days. The peace and the blessings. A simple life . . . the one she always wanted living in a modest, two-bedroom home where she eventually raised me.

Back then, my six-year-old mother would sit on the front porch steps every night waiting for Grandpa to pull into the driveway. As he climbed out of his truck, my mom would run to him and call, "Daddy, Daddy, Daddy!" and launch into his arms. For him, and him alone, she sang and danced. While Granny and Adele cleaned up the kitchen after supper, Mom would invent reasons to curl up beside him in his recliner. She always found a scratch for him to kiss or a book for him to read out loud, a nightly ritual until the evening he didn't come home.

"Granny knew she had to be strong. She needed to assure her

girls that while life might change, they would survive. They would emerge stronger. God would provide and equip them for the challenges ahead."

Nothing went as expected. The thief in the night had come to steal and destroy.

About the time my grandfather normally got home from work, my mother slipped out the front door and sat on porch steps. The house was packed with Granny's neighbors and friends who brought food. A few women sat with Granny in the living room. No one paid attention to where my mother was or what she was doing. When my grandfather's arrival time came and went, my mom came inside and asked when he would be home.

"Granny pulled Mom onto her lap and told her that Grandpa wasn't coming home, that he'd gone to be with Jesus in heaven, and was dancing with the angels. Mom wasn't buying it." I looked at TC, who was studying his lap. "She wiggled out of Granny's arms and started pummeling Granny's chest with her fists. She said she hated Jesus and his lies. She needed her daddy, and Jesus didn't. She would never pray to him again."

I can imagine how still the room went. I've heard that stillness myself . . . when something horrible happens. And I can imagine how Granny felt, with everyone staring at her, shocked by my mother's outburst.

TC looked up. "I feel sorry for your mother. I don't know what I'd do without my dad."

But I didn't want to hear TC's sorries. "Granny smacked her so hard across the face that it left a red mark. She ordered Mom to her room." I looked directly into TC eyes as if to challenge him.

"Granny overacted," TC said. "Six-year-old kids say whatever pops into their heads, especially when they're angry and confused."

I shrugged. TC was probably right, but I wasn't about to give my mother one inch.

"Granny shouldn't have smacked my mother, but in this instance, I'll give her a pass," I said. "Granny always had trouble relating to her. My mother has a real skill for drawing attention to herself and causing havoc." I stopped for a minute to get my breathing under control. "Granny was embarrassed too. To her ear, Mom's hate-filled words . . . her hitting needed correcting."

Within a second, Granny realized her mistake, but she had to save face. She wanted those women to know she *could* control her child. She waited until everyone had left before going to Mom, to apologize and explain why she shouldn't hate Jesus or anyone else, why hitting never accomplished anything. She found her asleep underneath her bed, cuddling a stuffed toy that my grandpa had won at a carnival game. That conversation never happened.

As the days turned into weeks and months into years, Granny came to peace with Grandpa's death. She grew stronger, more capable and evolved into a one-woman tour de force. She got her driver's license, worked as a waitress during the day while Adele and my mother went to school, and completed a secretarial correspondence course at night.

Despite her skimpy employment history, Granny convinced the school board to hire her as a secretary, a job she wanted because the work schedule accommodated her family needs better than most jobs. She moved up the ranks to become the executive secretary for the school superintendent.

"My mother didn't fare as well." I stared at my hands, feeling utter sorrow for Granny, Adele and *even* my mom. "Granny blamed herself and pointed back to that moment when she'd let her anger and pride get the better of her." Granny paid for that mistake. It only got worse as my mother got older.

Withdrawn and sullen—at least around Granny and Adele— my mom began acting up in school. Teachers would call at night to discuss Mom's behavioral problems. "She had a mouth and a temper, and she'd pitch a fit every Sunday morning, refusing to go to church until Granny yanked her from her bed and told her to get dressed."

Granny won those skirmishes, I told TC, but the war had only begun.

"Granny knew things were going south, but Grandpa's death happened before people went to counselors and talked openly about their problems. We're Southerners. We soft-pedal everything," I said.

TC massaged his forehead. "What was going on with her sister? Did she cause as much trouble as your mother did?"

"Adele toed the line," I said. "She went to school and studied hard. Kept her nose to the grindstone."

"She sounds a little like you."

"Yes, I suppose that's true. I can only hope I'll be as successful. She's a vice president with one of the Wall Street investment companies." She, like Granny, look for silver linings in hard times and believe they can learn from them. They persist and stay focused.

I took a big breath and exhaled. I could feel my eyes narrowing. "My mom lets setbacks cripple her. She makes lots of mistakes and then refuses to accept responsibility for any of them. She is the quintessential victim."

"Don't you think you're being a bit harsh? TC asked. "Like I said, I couldn't imagine growing up without my father. He and Mom have done everything to help me get on with my life and settle down."

"You haven't heard the rest of it, TC. Hear me out before judging." I slammed an open palm on the chair arm, surprising even myself. Clearly, my memories hadn't been dealt with. The barn door had been opened, and I couldn't turn back now. I wanted to exorcise every bit of it from my spirit and soul. It had taken up far too much space.

Tired of the constant turmoil, my aunt often took Granny's side. She advised my mother to use her head. Cooperate. Do household chores. Be polite. Stop running after boys. Sass and laziness wouldn't move Granny's needle, and neither would my mother's dramatic door-slamming and name-calling when she didn't get her way.

"The big-sister lecture had the usual effect."

"How?"

"Mom usually flipped Adele the bird."

TC sort of smirked.

"But I also think other issues affected their relationship."

TC raised his eyebrows. "Like what?"

"I've never asked her, but I think Aunt Adele resented my mother. My grandpa loved both girls, but even Granny admitted he showed favorites. He called Mom his little pixie. He loved her spirit and how she'd made him laugh. Aunt Adele is . . . what's the word, TC?" I thought for a moment. "Handsome. Yes, that's it. Handsome."

TC sat still and nodded slowly.

By the time Mom turned fifteen, she was smoking dope, popping pills, shoplifting, and sneaking out to meet boys. She told lies. Granny grounded her, complained about the clothes she wore, and warned her of damaging her reputation. The gossip had become rampant. Granny told me her fears about my mom had become her worst nightmare.

"In public, Granny squared her shoulders and held her head up—but in private, she worried," I said. "She begged God to open my mother's eyes because nothing she did worked. She only rebelled more, accusing Granny and Aunt Adele of conspiring to ruin her life."

In these moments, even Granny herself doubted the existence of God.

CHAPTER TWENTY-FOUR

Ginny, The Festival, One Year Earlier

Night began to fall, and I wasn't close to finishing my story or telling TC what had happened to Laurel. But I stopped. My growing affection for him couldn't be ignored. The way he listened and urged to me to unload and tell more. I started comparing. The clothes, the jewelry. Surface appearances that were so important to Jacob. He thought I needed improvement and coaching. But TC seemed to accept me unconditionally, dressed in my filthy clothes, my hair and make-up a wreck due to perspiration and the rain. All this confused me. It made me wonder if God was trying to tell me something by putting TC in my path.

"I don't know. I don't know." I started pacing, wearing a path into the vinyl tarp. I wasn't sure about what I was unsure of . . . telling TC the rest of the story about my dysfunctional family or admitting Jacob might not be right for me. TC seemed oblivious to my warring thoughts.

"Take your time, Ginny." His voice softened. "If you don't feel comfortable telling me what happened, then don't. I won't push."

"I just hate thinking about my mother." I sat down and pushed aside my confused thoughts about TC and Jacob. "She's horrible." I glanced at the neighboring tents and then at him. His eyes looked sad as if he felt true compassion for me. I wanted to hug him but thought better. TC seemed to keep boundaries.

I breathed in and exhaled, closed my eyes, and sent up another silent prayer. My confusion over TC and Jacob hadn't evaporated, but I knew TC could be trusted with the rest of my secrets.

"Sorry about that little meltdown. How about I start with one of the last fights my mother would have with Granny before she left Georgia."

A quick nod from him, and I continued with a renewed sense of purpose.

That night, my mother had run from the house. She slammed the door and plopped down on the porch step. Granny didn't think much of her behavior—another chapter in the Smith family saga. But then she heard voices outside. Before she could investigate, she heard a car door slam and tires squealing.

"How old was she?" TC asked.

"Ten days shy of her eighteenth birthday." My mother had quit high school and worked as a waitress at a truck stop. Unlike Adele, who attended the University of Georgia under a full scholarship, she didn't have any other plans.

"Granny made some big mistakes," I continued. "She didn't

appreciate the depths of Mom's loss. People say children are resilient, but death is hard. I'm not blaming Granny. She loved her. Cared for her. But Granny didn't understand or appreciate my mom's special relationship with Grandpa. And as I mentioned earlier, no one in our world went to counselors. People saw therapy as a weakness. But Granny could've used the support. She didn't know how to handle her."

I can only imagine the endless cycle of strife between Mom and Granny, thankful Granny had realized her mistake when it came time to deal with me.

"You know that term *crossing the Rubicon*?" I asked.

"Yeah. It's when you reach a point where you can't change a decision or course of action."

"Right. Well, they crossed the Rubicon the night Mom took off in the car without telling Granny where she was going."

My voice sounded far away as I recalled Granny's turmoil . . . her guilt. After this confrontation, Granny had prayed hard to come to terms with her mistakes, realizing she'd failed my mother and had driven her away with her nagging. She, too, had shown favorites raising her daughters, preferring the company of the reserved, hard-working Adele over my frivolous, uncontrollable mom. Had she gotten therapy for my mom and herself, Granny thought that their relationship could have been healthier. The knowledge made Granny weep.

But the night my mother took off, Granny hadn't come to terms with that yet. She waited in the living room in the dark, fuming, until my mom stumbled through the front door.

When Granny asked where my mom had gone and with whom, Mom ignored her. Granny had had enough. She started yelling, told her she smelled of booze. Mom laughed. She said she was the town drunk, the neighborhood slut, but not to worry. She'd come home to pack her stuff, and to quote her, "get the hell out of here."

My mother knew which buttons to push. She wanted to provoke a reaction from Granny, who'd no more utter an off-color word than take a sip of sherry. Granny didn't take the bait. She leaned back in her chair, crossed her arms, and waited, watching as Mom staggered to the front door and started shouting to a guy named Jimmy.

"That got Granny's attention," I told TC. "She shot out of her chair, shoved my mother aside, nearly knocking her over to get a better look at this man whom she'd never met. But then, Granny didn't know most of my mother's friends."

As she stepped out onto the porch, Granny saw the man getting out of his mud-splattered car. He looked as disheveled as his car, but Granny said there was no mistaking his roguish good looks, despite the greasy, jet-black hair that hung in his eyes. She watched as he took deep draws from a flask and then wiped his mouth with the back of his hand. His well-developed biceps were covered in tattoos.

"Granny said he looked ominous, and that the hair on the back of her neck stood up, especially when he started hollering and cursing at my mom, telling her he'd give her only five minutes to pack her bags. He was hitting the road, with or without her."

The bellowing triggered barking from the neighbors' dogs,

spoiling the late-night peace. He got back into the car, leaned his head against the seat and closed his eyes. Granny wouldn't lay eyes on him again for several more years.

"You cleaned up Jimmy's language, didn't you?" TC asked.

"I did. I don't know what he really said. Granny said she'd never repeat his words. She said she'd never heard anything so common in her life."

TC nodded. "What did your mom do?"

"She complied. She went to her bedroom to pack her stuff, with Granny hot on her heels."

Granny asked where my mother had met Jimmy, why she hadn't seen him before, why he didn't have the common courtesy to come inside and introduce himself. When my mother ignored her, Granny grabbed her arm and told her she'd leave only over Granny's dead body.

I pressed my lips together. "Granny was mad. She accused my mother of acting like trash and how Grandpa was turning over in his grave. He'd expect so much more from my mother."

The comment was incendiary, like a match on gasoline. The mere mention of my grandpa stopped my mom dead in her tracks. She whipped around and snatched her arm from Granny's grasp, her face contorted in rage. She warned Granny to never mention her father again. She said her daddy loved her and thought her special. Granny did not.

"Knowing my mother, I know her words were meant to wound, and they did. She dredged up every criticism Granny ever leveled, including those she'd overheard during Granny's calls with friends—people my mother dismissed as old, nosey hags."

Though TC appeared spellbound by the story, I had to put the narrative on pause. My phone buzzed. "Jacob," I said, apologizing for the interruption before reading the message. "*Humph*, he claims he's on his way over here." I hit the thumbs-up emoticon before I put the phone down. I was tired of typing, annoyed with his behavior. *Was I having second thoughts?*

"Where was I?"

"You were telling me about their last blowup." TC prompted. "How Granny didn't care for your mother and thought she wasn't good enough. What did Granny say about her? Whatever she said, your mom never forgot it."

I leaned back in my chair and tapped my knuckles on the arms of the chair. "Who knows. Granny never told me."

But I can imagine.

Straightlaced Granny has always believed women should act like ladies. No cursing, drinking, smoking, carrying on. Her friends think the same. My mom had done that and more.

"Had she just toed the line a little," I said, "life would have been so much easier for her. I know that from personal experience."

"Personal experience?" TC eased to the edge of his chair.

"Yes, I'm getting to it, TC." I continued with the story.

My mother said she was getting married and moving to South Carolina, the Spartanburg area, where some of Jimmy's family lived. Jimmy loved and appreciated her. She loved him. He'd make a good living as a mechanic for his uncle. Mom wanted a life far from Georgia, Granny, Adele, and the small-town gossips, and nothing would change her mind. She said she'd call, but she would never come back.

"What could Granny do?" I asked. "She knew she couldn't stop my mother. By then, she wanted to wash her hands of Mom and live in peace . . . for once. She figured my mom would learn a hard lesson and eventually return with her tail between her legs."

When Mom realized she had won the war, she turned wordlessly for the bedroom she shared with Adele. She tossed a few belongings into a suitcase as Granny watched silently from the doorway. What my mother couldn't cram into the baggage, she shoved into brown paper grocery bags. She made several trips to pack everything inside the back of Jimmy's car. He never lifted a hand to help, Granny told me. Before Mom could even pull the passenger-side door shut, Jimmy hit the gas pedal and peeled out of the driveway, flinging gravel on the grass. The neighborhood dogs resumed their wild barking. Granny slammed the front door.

"A precursor of things to come," I said. "Mom kept her word too. She'd call occasionally, always collect, but she'd never come home again. At least to stay."

I glanced at my phone and tossed it back into my bag.

"Didn't you say Jacob was coming soon?" TC asked.

"I thought he was."

TC checked the time on his phone.

"What do you want me to do, TC? I could walk over to the food pavilions to see if I can find Jacob there. Isn't there a nice bar or something over in the higher-end camping area? In my texts, I've asked him where he is, but he hasn't told me. I feel horrible for holding you up. This is unfair to you. Your friends are waiting."

"Ginny don't say that again. I've told you that you're welcome to stay," he said. "Go look for him if you like. I won't stop you." He then shrugged and suggested that I call Jacob and get his location. He would personally escort me. He put his phone back into the pocket of that crazy flamingo shirt. "But if you run off, I may never find out what happened next."

"Okay. We have a deal. And really, TC, I can't thank you enough for all you've done for me." I rifled through my bag. *He didn't know the half of it.* "Would you like to see a photo of her?"

"A photo of whom?"

"My mother."

"Sure." TC leaned back in his camp chair and rubbed his neck. My story must have made him tense.

I scrolled through my photos until I found the one I wanted, and then handed the phone to him. The photo showed my mom and Laurel sitting at the picnic table in front of an old mobile home where we lived.

"That's Laurel, my big sister." I pointed to my then six-year-old big sister who was dressed in flowered shorts and a matching top. "And that's me." I pointed to my mother's extended abdomen.

"Big hair." TC commented. "Has anyone ever mentioned that you're a clone. I can't believe how much you look like your mom."

"Yes, Granny tells me that all the time. As for the hair, I suppose Mom liked the look . . . The bigger the hair, the closer to God."

"Never heard that one before." He laughed. "Need to jot that one down."

"A southernism. Her hairdo certainly didn't put her closer to God." I could have made light of my mom's style but couldn't. I did understand that Mom had needed help when she was little, but sometimes I struggle coming to terms with the damage she inflicted on me. "This photo has been sitting on Granny's mantel for as long as I can remember. Granny doesn't have any others of the two of them. I look at it every day. Still do, but now I have it on my phone. I should have photoshopped Mom out of it though."

TC raised his eyebrows.

I shrugged.

"No one should make assumptions, but I guess your mom got married." TC squinted at the slightly out-of-focus photo. "Where did your mom meet Jimmy anyway?"

I'd never asked if they'd gotten married and didn't know for certain. "Jimmy's the sperm donor. That's all I can tell you."

The photo had been taken in South Carolina a few weeks before I was born. "I vaguely remember this dump." Leaning in close to TC, I pointed to the mobile home in the background. Weeds grew knee-high along the foundation, partially hiding cast-off furniture, car parts, and other garbage. The front door hung open.

TC studied the photo and shook his head. "I still can't believe your likeness to your mother. She's beautiful. Just like you."

People do comment on my looks, but I don't think that much about it. But TC's admiration gave me goose bumps all over. *Wasn't I engaged to Jacob?* I moved on quickly. "As for how they met, Granny heard the rumors and eventually put the whole story together."

Jimmy, as I prefer to refer to him, had served in the U.S. Army before he met my mom, and indeed Uncle Sam trained him as a mechanic—an aptitude that shined brighter than Sirius when the Army tested him after his enlistment before the Vietnam War ended. What my mother didn't tell Granny, or perhaps didn't know, was Jimmy's dishonorable discharge. He went AWOL to spend time with his civilian buddies smoking dope, snorting cocaine, and getting into brawls at the local dives.

Unemployed, Jimmy decided to visit his kin who lived on the outskirts of Granny's town. As fate would have it, my mother's best friend—one of Jimmy's relatives and a girl with a reputation as scurrilous as Mom's—introduced them at a field party.

"News of her late-night skedaddle traveled fast and caused a scandal. My mom had known him for only a month before she ran off."

TC's jaw dropped. "One month? Dear God. The women in my life take months planning weddings. Running off would be my preference, of course, but eloping with a near stranger seems over-the-top even to me."

I put my head between my legs, not wanting TC to see my face. Tears had started to well up. TC had zeroed in on one of my mother's most fundamental flaws, and I wondered if therapy would have ever corrected it. She *was* reckless, and Laurel and I certainly paid the price. After a few moments, I reached over to take the phone from TC's hand and threw it back inside my bag.

"What is your first true memory, TC?" The question seemed random even to me. "Not the things someone tells you about, but the events you remember vividly, memories that are distinctly yours?"

He thought about the question, a quizzical look on his face. "Where'd that come from? Are you trying to remind me of my good fortune and how our lives couldn't be more different? If that's your motive, you've succeeded."

How different could his first memory be from mine?

CHAPTER TWENTY-FIVE

The Festival, One Year Earlier

The memory that popped instantly to mind happened decades ago. And it did underscore just how different our young lives had been.

My middle brother, Cameron, hadn't arrived yet. He was still swimming in a sea of amnionic fluid. I was in preschool then, skinny, and short for my age. But what I lacked in physical size was offset by my command of the English language—a skill learned early, speaking in full sentences long before my second birthday—and the decibel at which I spoke. My soul may have occupied a pint-sized body, but it made sure it was heard.

Complete strangers called me *precocious*.

So did my great aunt. One night, when the whole family had gathered to watch one of the national political conventions, I planted myself on the floor in front of the TV and gobbled my

Mike & Ike candies. I watched the speakers take the podium and listened to the newscasters opine, fascinated by the balloons and patriotic-themed hats and shirts. "They sure talk a lot but say nothing," I said. "Is that all they do?"

"I think you're right, TC," my aunt said, laughing as I provided a running commentary on the goings-on. "You're more insightful than they are."

Later that night, when I should've been asleep, I crept out to the hallway to listen to the adults chatting in the kitchen. "How many little kids sit and watch a political convention?" my aunt asked. "He's special, very bright, and what a vocabulary. I think he's going places."

I carry her words in my heart, hauling them out when I feel low and unaccomplished. That has more to do with my insecurities and inability to figure out what I want to do with my life. Careers that afford money, prestige, and position don't inspire, even though I'd pretended with Chelsey. But then again, neither does mooching off the government, my parents, or anyone else. I work hard, yes, but I go through the motions, always thinking something better might be hidden around the corner.

"What about you, Ginny? What's your memory?"

"I can tell you it doesn't compare to yours."

I knew Ginny's sister, Laurel, was gone, and assumed her dead. That's all I knew, and I wondered how bad her first memory would be. The details would knock the rose-colored glasses off my face. Ginny hadn't exaggerated. Her first memory was nothing like mine. Hers was a nightmare.

We couldn't have known it then, but Jacob wouldn't find his way to the yellow tent for several more hours. A godsend.

By the time she finished telling her story, I appreciated Ginny even more. She'd peeled back her layers. I'd never met a woman who faced so much adversity but remained on her feet, refusing to succumb to self-pity.

My attraction had turned into something more, and I could hear Aimee's warning inside my head.

CHAPTER TWENTY-SIX

Ginny, The Festival, One Year Earlier

Telling this memory is something I always avoid. Just the thought of Jimmy and my time living inside that ramshackle trailer triggers me, sometimes causing my heart to race and my hands to shake. Like what happened earlier when TC's friend, Bear, stopped by to visit. That came out of nowhere.

"Are you sure you want to hear this story?" I asked, hoping he'd say no. I was afraid of dissolving into a blubbering mess or losing heart. At home, when I feel anxious, I'll go to my room and declutter a closet or to the living room to dust furniture that needs no dusting . . . my way to assert control over my surroundings. It's not obsessive or compulsive. Just a technique I've found helpful when needing to de-stress. I've come to appreciate tidiness. It's restorative. But here, I had no room to clean. I'd already cleaned up the campsite.

"Only if you want to," TC said, resting his head in one hand, watching me chewing my lip and flapping my hands. They seemed to have taken on a life of their own. I trapped them under my thighs, exhaled, and pulled my body into a straight position. I needed to get this off my chest, and here, sitting inches from me, was someone who wouldn't judge or blame me. I started my narrative, something no one, aside from Granny and a few trusted therapists, had heard.

"Within a year of my mom leaving Georgia, she gave birth to Laurel and then me . . . six years later. Why they hadn't had other kids, I don't know. I never asked."

"Why didn't you ask?" TC asked.

"Mom never gave me the chance." I left it at that.

Demons had bedeviled Jimmy, and he assuaged his torment with pills, alcohol, and cocaine. Quick to anger, he fought constantly, especially with those smaller and weaker than he was. When that happened, which seemed to happen all the time, I'd crawl into bed with Laurel at night, afraid of the loud voices, the thumps, the broken glass, and Mom's cries coming from beyond the paper-thin walls.

"Jimmy scared me. In my child's eyes, I saw a shaggy-haired giant." He wore steel-toed boots and mechanic's shirts, and his name, which I could read, was embroidered over the breast pocket. He towered over us and the men who dropped by at night to drink get high at the outdoor picnic table. Peeking out the window, I'd watch them pass around a glass cylinder pipe.

He must have worried Laurel too. When she'd hear Jimmy's

car pulling into our gravel driveway, Laurel would grab my hand and drag me outside to play on our rusted swing set, well out of Jimmy's reach. Laurel's intuitions were spot on. He always came home itching for a fight.

"I remember one night. Mom must not have fried the chicken to his satisfaction. He hurled the dish at Mom's head, then turned the table over, upending our plates and glasses of milk onto our laps. Laurel grabbed my hand, and we ran. Outside, I think. I remember spending a lot of time at that swing set."

The table had been overturned so often, two of the legs snapped off that night. The next morning, I watched Mom haul it outside with the rest of junk piled up around the trailer. After that, we ate meals in silence on TV trays set up in the cramped living room.

"I've never understood why women stay in abusive relationships," TC said. I didn't infer his comment as a judgment, but rather a desire to understand a dynamic he'd never witnessed growing up. "Did she use too?"

"I don't remember her doing drugs, but she did drink wine. She smoked a lot of cigarettes too. They both did. Now that I'm older, after years of counseling, I suppose she believed she was stuck. She didn't work and I assumed that Jimmy wouldn't let her." I paused and freed my right hand and cupped my chin. "But I think more than anything else, her pride got in the way. She didn't want Granny to be proven right."

TC nodded. "Yep, pride goeth before the fall. My youth pastor used to talk about that. He was trying to warn us kids about a haughty spirit, which he said led to mistakes, setbacks, and failures.

A haughty spirit isn't my problem. I am."

Why does he think that way?

I didn't comment on his remark then. I filed it away and resumed my story.

Some mornings, I would see my mom sitting on the sofa, staring off into space and crying. She held a bag of ice on her lip and bruised eye. On those mornings, Laurel made my breakfast, fixed my lunch, and told me to stay in our room until she got home from school. "I guess Mom cared for me. I have only vague memories. It seemed Laurel had done all the heavy lifting where I was concerned. Sometimes I wonder if those memories are even real."

Tears began to pool in my eyes and my skin felt clammy. Uh-oh. Was a panic attack coming on? I took a few deep breaths.

"You don't have to tell me the rest if you don't want to." TC cupped my face and then reached down to find a leftover napkin. He started dabbing my eyes.

"No, that's okay." I took the napkin and balled it into my fist. "I want to tell you."

The horror began on a hot, humid day in late July. Rain came sporadically. I remember the month because I was only a few weeks shy of entering the first grade and was excited. I could already read the hand-me-down children's books stored in our bedroom and couldn't wait to get around other kids. Living in the boondocks, we didn't have playmates. Laurel and I had ourselves.

Due to the weather, Laurel and I stayed inside most of the day. I played with my Barbie on the living room floor while Mom and Laurel watched TV. Around supper time, my mom turned off the television. She told me to pick up my toys and asked Laurel to help with supper. She fidgeted with her clothes and hair and glanced around the room. Not surprising. Laurel and I heard the loud shouting the night before.

I didn't want to tear down the house I'd made from cardboard boxes and decorated with old-fashioned dollhouse furniture. My dawdling proved ill-timed.

Jimmy came home earlier than usual. He reeked of cigarettes, booze, and that burnt-rubber aroma I frequently detected on his clothes and hair. He pushed the front door open and tripped over my makeshift Barbie house. He sprawled flat on his face a couple of feet from where I stood.

All hell broke loose.

He got up on his hands and knees and started cursing. Then he lunged for me. His intoxication hadn't impaired his aim. As I stood immobilized and crying, he slapped the side of my face, and I flew across the room before landing hard against the wall. My head spun and my cheek throbbed.

Mom had been washing the day's dishes and came running. She sailed into him, her soapy fists thrashing his chest. A cigarette dangled from her mouth.

"I'd never seen her confront Jimmy, let alone physically attack him," I said. "But whatever nascent mama-bear instincts she possessed emerged in a fury."

Jimmy roared and swatted Mom. She soared in the same trajectory as I did, and we both sat slumped against the wall. Her cigarette smoldered on the carpet. She looked dazed. So, I crawled over to retrieve it, doused it in an overflowing ashtray, and scrambled back to her. I kept my head low, not wanting to draw Jimmy's attention.

From the corner of her eye, I saw Laurel, armed with the kitchen knife. She came in at full sprint. Tall for her age, she looked like Jimmy's female mini-me—a blessing that negated his occasional claim he wasn't her father.

Laurel screamed in rage, as she sliced Jimmy's tattooed forearm . . . a flesh wound that marred the grim reaper inked into his skin. "He looked momentarily stunned. I guess he never expected any of us to stand up and defend ourselves." He shook his head, reached out, and Laurel's weapon—her only means of protection—was in his hand.

"For as long as I lived with that man, he bullied us, called us names, and smacked my mother around, but he never touched us kids before. Only threatened." I glanced at my lap and then at the small gatherings of people who partied and danced beyond where we sat. A surreal scene given the intensity of our conversation beneath the yellow canopy.

"I couldn't move. I sat next to my mother, bawling, sucking on my finger. I remember seeing the blood dripping down his arm. I remember the fear in Laurel's eyes. I kept thinking, *Why won't she run? Why won't she run?* TC, she just stood there."

We sat without speaking. TC squeezed my shoulder while I tapped my mouth with my fingers.

Jimmy tossed the knife to the floor and then kicked Laurel in the stomach. She curled herself into a tight ball.

His expression morphed from crazy to demonic. He then picked Laurel up by the scruff of the neck and slammed her head against the television stand. Her mouth bled and her nose bent sideways. Laurel whimpered and tried to ward off the kicks that rained down on her back, legs, and buttocks.

Jimmy hurled more invective before he delivered one final kick to Laurel's head.

My mother shook her head and muffled a moan. She whispered in my ear. Told me to go to her bedroom and call the police—a number Laurel had drilled into my head daily. "She called me *sweet pea*," I said. "I was struck by that. I don't think Mom ever called me that before."

As I crawled away, I saw Mom leap onto Jimmy's back, her arms around his neck and fingernails digging into his flesh. He didn't seem to notice. He stared at Laurel who remained still, her blood soaking into the carpet. I scuttled to my mother's room on all fours, not fully understanding what I'd just witnessed.

I clasped and unclasped my hands, took a sip of my now lukewarm bottle of water. The details I'd pushed away had come back to me and now I was back at the trailer, with its smells of stale cigarette smoke and mildew. Word for word, I recounted my conversation with the dispatcher. Even to me I sounded like a six-year-old girl.

"'And what is your emergency?'"

"'My daddy beat up my sister. She's on the floor. I don't know where Mommy is . . .'"

"'Where are you, honey?'"

"'I'm in their bedroom, hiding. Mommy told me to call. I'm scared.'"

As I whispered into the receiver, I heard more shouts, my mother's cries, and then a thud. The room went silent. The screen door slammed, and Jimmy's car revved to life. Tires squealed as they spun in the gravel before fading. A calm fell over the trailer.

"Do you believe in miracles?" I asked. The question seemed to throw TC off balance. His brow furrowed.

"I've never given it much thought. I assume you do, or you wouldn't have asked."

I nodded and sat still, looking intently into his eyes. My gawking must've unnerved him because he looked away. "A miracle happened." I said this with an authority I never knew existed. "Nothing will convince me otherwise."

"I'm confused," TC said. "This isn't a miracle. This is evil."

"Let me finish."

I didn't move from my hiding space between the bed and nightstand. Not until I heard the sirens. Then heavy footsteps pounded up the wooden steps that led to the front door. As they stormed into the trailer, shouting, I heard another vehicle screech to a halt, followed by a woman's voice that I didn't recognize.

That's when I met Granny face-to-face for the first time. Dressed in a simple blouse and skirt, she pushed past a female deputy who'd already stepped inside the bedroom.

"'Lady, this is a police matter.'"

"'And I'm this girl's grandmother. She needs me.'"

Now crouching next to me, the uniformed woman asked in a reassuring voice, "'Do you know this lady, honey?'"

And for reasons I've never understood, I told the policewoman that, yes, the older woman was my Granny Smith, how she'd send Laurel and me cookies and Valentine's cards. How we'd never share with Daddy.

Before the female deputy carried me away from the mobile home, Granny told me to keep my eyes closed. She stayed glued to my side until the deputy placed me alone inside her cruiser. I didn't open my eyes until I heard more shouts and saw the medics coming down the steps carrying my mother on a gurney. Her face was a smeared and broken mess.

"Granny was walking alongside, touching my mother's hair and arms. She was crying and refused to step aside until Mom was loaded into the ambulance and the doors were shut. I don't know what I was thinking. The cruiser door was open, so I crept out and ran to where Granny stood. I wrapped my arms around her thighs, buried my head, and cried. I stayed like that until the social worker came to take me to the home of a foster family. Boy, did she struggle trying to pry my hands loose."

The family, especially the mom, showed kindness and kept reassuring me that everything would be okay. But I was scared and couldn't understand why I couldn't stay with Granny.

"They had to protect you," TC said. "They didn't know if Granny was related."

"I know, but it was cruel. Once they straightened things out, Granny visited me before and after she checked in on Mom at the hospital. I bawled. I wanted to stay with her in her hotel room."

Later, the police found Jimmy squatting in an abandoned trailer in rural Cherokee County close to the North Carolina border. Once the hospital released Mom, Granny took us back to Georgia. That's where Granny buried Laurel . . . next to the grandfather she'd never met.

"How did Granny know?" TC's voice sounded incredulous. "She lived so far away, and yet arrived within seconds of the cops. This is unbelievable."

"I told you. It was a miracle. Granny said she couldn't shake the feeling that she had to make that drive. She said she dismissed it at first, thinking her coffee was playing tricks on her mind. She went to work, but the voice inside her head became more insistent. You know what I'm talking about, right?"

TC cleared his throat and continued the vigorous nose rubbing. "I do, but I don't usually listen to mine." He looked at his lap.

It was a throw-away question, one I didn't expect him to answer. But his admission revealed so much about him. *Whose voice did he listen to?* As I tossed that around in my head, he looked up.

"What?" He must have wondered why I was staring at him.

"Well, Granny calls her voice *the Spirit*," I said this quickly. "She said she'd never experienced it so intensely. Consider this, TC. Granny made that drive before GPS. She was at the wheel, but someone else did the driving. Can you imagine what could've happened to me had she not obeyed? Like I said—it was miracle."

We sat quietly for a few minutes. I was humbled by how God had arranged my encounter with TC. Because of him, I had mustered the courage to tell my story.

"Tell me about Granny's experience . . . the miracle." TC leaned over. Our faces were inches apart.

"Granny told me about her premonition and the power of the Holy Spirit long after Jimmy's trial and murder conviction—long after my mother left. Granny told me to always seek His counsel and wisdom."

TC frowned. At what I didn't know.

"Please, don't ask me about Jimmy," I said, thinking the mention of Jimmy had prompted TC's puzzled expression. "He's in prison, or at least he better be. Don't ask me about that uncle of his either, or any of those fools who came around. Everyone knew what was happening to us. Especially to my mother. And no one lifted a hand to help. Evil people, all of them."

"Hold on a minute." TC was again taken aback by my ferocity. I couldn't imagine the look on my face. "I don't care about Jimmy or anyone else. I'm not even questioning Granny's premonition. I sort of get that. What did you mean about your mother leaving?"

CHAPTER TWENTY-SEVEN

Ginny, The Festival, One Year Earlier

Rage filled me. *Audrey did leave me.* That is a truth in my life, and I wanted to lash out. Break something. But I gathered my wits, took a few more deep breathes as recommended by my counselors over the years, and started talking.

Again, my mind raced to places I'd kept submerged. Without so much as a snap, I was six, living with my mother and Granny, sleeping in my mother's old room, my mom on the couch. Nothing had changed between the two. Granny criticized Mom for the hours she kept. Blasted her for smoking and drinking. Mom attacked Granny for not minding her own business. I hid as often as I could, burying my head beneath my pillow to muffle the angry voices.

After a few half-hearted attempts to get an office job, Mom returned to the truck stop. She worked hard, showed up on time, and covered extra shifts when someone called in sick. Her work ethic wasn't the problem. *Men* were. Particularly one.

He was older and married, a regular at the truck stop. Granny told me he wooed Mom with compliments and little gifts, and eventually she agreed to meet him at an economy-style chain motel along the highway. The relationship continued, giving Mom plenty of time away from Alma Smith and me—a reminder of what had happened in South Carolina and the mistakes she'd made.

"How'd you know this?" TC piped up. I'd nearly forgotten he was sitting at my side, so engrossed in my memories.

"I heard Granny talking on the phone. She thought I was out of earshot. Even if I hadn't overheard, everyone knew my mother." People talked, including the mothers of kids my age. I'd heard their whispers. Noticed their looks. "Thank God, Granny's reputation canceled Mom's. It didn't matter. Everyone knew who was raising me."

The night before Mom left about a year after we moved in, I was lying in my twin bed. Perhaps before midnight, I heard the front door open, squeaking on its hinges. I got up and snuck to the hallway. Granny sat in her armchair next to the fireplace.

"I guess Granny had reached the end of her rope. I think she finally realized she *had* no power or influence in my mother's life, but she couldn't live with the constant instability and watch its effect on me. Something had to give."

TC propped his head on his hand and gave me a sideways glance. He gave me a quick nod and I restarted.

Granny had acknowledged Mom's God-given right to make her own decisions. If she chose to carry on with a married man in motel rooms, that was her choice. But Granny believed Mom had been negligent. I did need her. I needed counseling. Strategies to cope with the trauma and classmates' bullying, their sidelong glances, and whispers. Nightmares started soon after I went to bed at night. During the day I needed constant reassurance from Granny. Regardless of what she was doing, I'd ask that she hold me, let me sit on her lap. And always, Granny drew me close. "I could cry just thinking about what she whispered in my ear: 'I love you big. Nothing will ever change that. And when those blue meanies start attackin', remember this . . . You are beautifully and powerfully made. God doesn't make junk.'"

I was too afraid to ask how my mother felt. Did she feel the same way as Granny did?

Granny knew the director of a private, all-girls Christian school in the more populated neighboring town. Scholarships were available, and Granny thought I would do better there. Local kids knew too much about what happened in South Carolina, listening to, and then repeating, the adult gossip further fueled by Mom's affair with the married man. Granny was adamant. I needed a clean start, and she had no authority to make those decisions. She wasn't my mother.

I slipped back to bed, not wanting to hear the rest.

"When I woke up the next day, the sun was just coming up. I don't know why I'd gotten up so early. Maybe I needed the bathroom. But something felt wrong. The house was completely silent. No rustling of bedsheets. No creaking of sofa springs. I got out of bed and walked the few feet to the living room. Mom was gone. Her sheets and blanket were folded and placed on the couch, next to a note written in large block letters."

"What did the letter say?"

"Mom said I was better off without her."

"Did you show it to Granny?"

"Of course. She read it a couple of times, folded it, and stuffed it in her pocket. I didn't hear from Mom again until a few years ago. She mailed a postcard, postmarked in a little town in Nevada. She said she thought about me and hoped I was well. I guess she's still there. I don't reach out."

TC scratched a spot above his right eyebrow and shook his head. "And no one else has heard from her either?"

Granny stayed in touch—she had to. She became my legal guardian and, of course, Mom needed to sign the papers. But no one talked about her, including Aunt Adele who washed her hands of Mom, disgusted by her treatment of Granny and abandonment of me. Granny had made her peace and advised that Adele and I do likewise. She had forgiven Mom . . . and herself.

"Anyway, so much for that." I dismissed my mother's departure with a wave of my hand. "I told you. Granny saved me. She did."

CHAPTER TWENTY-EIGHT

The Festival, One Year Earlier

No wonder Ginny wished to erase Audrey from her photo. No wonder she avoided Bear. Big and scruffy looking, he probably reminded her of Jimmy. Had years of counseling succeeded in healing Ginny's soul? Something else seemed to be eating at her then, but I couldn't put my finger on it.

Ginny looked exhausted. She leaned her head against the camp chair and closed her eyes. I looked away and noticed Bryan and Mo headed toward us. The always-joyful Mo smiled broadly and waved, her bangle bracelets bouncing, but my expression must have communicated bad timing on their part. She whispered to Bryan, and he nodded. He gave me the peace sign, and then they turned away, weaving through the drunks gathered a few yards in front of our tent. The stadium lights in the distance were now turned on.

"I've never told any of my friends or coworkers the whole story." Ginny's voice was small. "I haven't told Jacob any of it."

"Why? Are you afraid to tell him?"

Wrinkles appeared between her eyebrows. Hadn't she thought about this? Why would she hide this information from Jacob? *Her one true love?*

"I don't know. Would you want someone knowing your father murdered your sister or that your mother had abandoned you? It's bad enough the townspeople know my backstory. Maybe I'm afraid Jacob won't want anything to do with me."

Jacob's family, she then explained, was well established in the upper echelons of Atlanta society. The big-ticket donor class. The type of people who give hundreds of thousands each year to charitable causes, especially to those catering to people who live on the fringes. People exactly like her parents. *Would they see Ginny's mom and dad as deserving of their help?*

"No . . . Audrey and Jimmy don't need a hand-up," Ginny said. "They're trash."

"So, let me get this straight. Your parents' sins are your sins? Is that what you're saying? Are you saying Jacob's family is better than yours—and by this, I do mean Granny? Geez." An indignation grew within me, and I couldn't tamp it down. "You know what bugs me? Classism. No one is better than someone else. Everyone has issues. And money doesn't cure all ills. If Jacob can't handle what happened to you as a child, so what? You shouldn't want anything to do with him."

I kept rambling, never more adamant about expressing my

opinions. Ginny wasn't the only one needing to exorcise demons and hurts. My voice got louder, maybe motivated by my disgust for people like Chelsey who lusted after the almighty buck, which would give her passage into the upper stratum…as well as the fakes and phonies. By then I'd started thinking Jacob and Chelsey might be perfect for each other and that I'd managed to dodge a bullet. *If only Ginny could see that.*

"Why would you allow yourself to be judged?" I asked. "You have no reason to be ashamed. You aren't to blame. Screw Jacob if he thinks that." I told Ginny this and more, surprised by the words that flowed from my mouth. For the first time, my impressions of Jacob, his money, his material stuff had slipped out. My live-and-let-live attitude along with it.

Ginny rubbed her temples.

"Why did you tell me your story?" Seeing her widened eyes, I toned it down and brushed a stray hair off her face.

"I don't know. I don't even know why I agreed to wait out the rain in your tent. Not my nature, but I sensed I'd be okay. You give off a positive vibe." She smiled a little and touched my arm but wouldn't look me in the eye. She went on, her words tumbling over one another. "Furthermore, every person I met today sang your praises, called you a reliable, trustworthy friend. I guess I figured it wouldn't hurt to unload on you." She moved her hand to pat my leg. "Plus, we might not see each other again. I hope that's not the case, but you never know . . . What's the harm, anyway? You spilled your guts and I've spilled mine."

Shame and sadness filled me. I had wished Ginny would tell

me about her family and contemplated using whatever she revealed in a joke or two for my performances. Her story wasn't funny. It was raw. And my stomach roiled, thinking about the lie Ginny was living and her misplaced hope that Jacob could rescue her from her past—or at least that's how I saw it.

But she was right about one thing. Growing up, I had enjoyed a privileged life. A life that wasn't defined by money and prestige, but good old-fashioned stability and love. I may not have thanked God for this blessing, but she was wrong on this count: I sure thanked my parents. They did know the depths of my gratitude for their unconditional love of me.

I studied my memory bracelet, thought about my childhood friend, his mother, and the words in the Bible verse. I pulled the band off my wrist and handed it to her. "Here, I want you to have it."

She hesitated.

At that moment, I had never felt so good about giving a gift in my life. Who better to have the bracelet than Ginny? My soul seemed to merge with Ginny's at that moment, and it felt cosmic. We evolved from being strangers to intimates, a relationship that transcended even my physical attraction to her.

I hoped she'd always think of me . . . tomorrow . . . and the next day. And I hoped she'd thank her God whenever she did.

CHAPTER TWENTY-NINE

The Festival, One Year Earlier

Ginny's face radiated as she slipped the band on her wrist. Maybe she thought, as did I, that we'd entered a new phase in our relationship. In each other's presence at the tent, we could just *be*. At ease. Comfortable. And at that moment, I was okay with it. I loved and admired this woman, regardless of what she saw in me.

"I've been thinking, TC. You're right. I've nothing to hide. By not telling Jacob, I diminish Granny. She's done everything in her power to bring normalcy to my life. What is wrong with me?"

What could I say? I've asked that question often about my motives and actions in life.

"Oh, I don't know. Insecurity. Sometimes we slap on a veneer to make ourselves look better." I shrugged. "Sometimes we don't want to confront a problem because we're too lazy to fix it or want to avoid the truth. That's me," I told her. "I don't lie to others. I lie to myself. I slap on the big personality instead of dealing with my own feelings of inadequacy. I honestly don't know what to do with my life, and I know I've let people down, including myself." I probably should've mentioned Chelsey, but I didn't.

"Has the avoidance worked?" Ginny nodded and touched her lip, like a notion had been confirmed inside her head.

"Sweetheart, what do you think?" I narrowed my eyes. "What *have* you told Jacob?"

"I told him my father had a heart attack and died at work, and that my sister had leukemia and died when I was too young to remember her. Mom struggled and couldn't afford to care for me."

"You told him that?" I covered my face with both hands and tossed my head back and forth. "If I were you, I'd I come clean with him. If he loves you, he'll understand why you didn't want to tell him about Jimmy and all the rest. No point in marrying a guy embarrassed by who you are and where you come from. It's best you find out now."

Ginny nodded but cast her gaze everywhere but at me. She slapped her thighs and then stood. She lifted her arms over her head, swaying side-to-side to work out the stiffness. "I think I've grown roots in this chair. Not used to sitting for so long." She leaned over to pick up her hat. She arranged the hat sideways on her head and then winked at me coyly—a distinct improvement over Aimee's cringe-worthy, full-face contortion.

She reminded me of so many exercise gurus. I decided to join her in the calisthenics, but with my own special twist. I ran my hands through my hair so that it stood up on end. I pulled dance music up on my playlist and cranked the volume.

Ginny stopped stretching. She squinted her eyes and cocked her head, probably trying to figure out what had come over me. I knew. I'd been hunkered inside a foxhole, bombs exploding around me. I needed to forget this ugliness. I wanted to laugh. Dance. Be in the moment with Ginny.

"Come on, you slacker. Move those feet. Don't you feel the music?" I sang and did a toe-tap number in beat to a Motown tune. It was a bouncy little dance I'd learned from my wig-wearing grandmother, Mom-Mom. She likes nothing better than dance parties on the porch of her beach house.

Ginny confessed she had two left feet, but then she must have gotten into the spirit. Because before I knew it, we were dancing. She caught on quickly and proved to be a twinkle toes. We stepped to our right, crossed our left feet behind our right, and did it again. We reversed direction. We couldn't have wanted better dance music for the grapevine, another dance my Mom-Mom had taught me.

The song ended. Ginny tapped her toe in anticipation, and again my playlist didn't disappoint. I grabbed Ginny's hands and launched into a jitterbug, complete with turns and spins. We made a scene. We toppled the camp chairs, nearly fell over the cooler, and twisted the tarp in a bunched knot and had to hang onto each other just to remain standing. At some point, her hat flew off her head and landed on the ground.

"You're dangerous," Ginny bent over to catch her breath.

"If you can't run with the big boys, then go home." Sweat collected on my forehead, ran down my cheeks and into my beard.

"I can't. I don't know where my ride is."

The absurdity of her situation hit us at the same time. We howled.

"I can't remember the last time I danced . . . or laughed so hard," Ginny said, still bent over, her hands on her knees. "Jacob doesn't like to dance. He doesn't laugh either. He titters."

"Titters?"

"Yes, titters."

"You need to hang out with me more."

She grinned. "You're right. You're certainly more entertaining than he is." She retrieved her hat and brushed off invisible specks of dirt on the rim before surveying the toppled chairs and bunched-up tarp. "Better fix this."

"It can wait," I said, trying to calm my heavy breathing.

"I'm a neatnik. I like order," she said. "If you ever see me living in squalor, not taking care of myself, that's when you worry."

As Ginny straightened up the campsite, her off-hand comment about Jacob ran through my head. *Titters? Spending more time with me?* I opened the cooler and grabbed Aimee's Mountain Dew. As I started twisting the top, Ginny launched herself into my arms. My spirits took off at warp speed. *Maybe this wasn't a lost cause after all.* "You're the best." She wrapped her arms around my neck. "I adore you."

I returned the hug, not knowing what do with the soda. I dropped it and started swaying back and forth with her pulled close to my chest. She threw her head back, grinned, and then planted a tiny kiss on my cheek.

My skin tingled. I remembered the last time the same burning sensation ripped through my body . . . when Chelsey kissed me. Until that moment, I believed I'd never experience the thrill again. *Was the tide turning? Did I have a chance with Ginny?* I shoved those thoughts aside. Ginny was head-over-heels in love with Jacob. Or was she?

"I mean it. You're good medicine. I'm so glad we met." I didn't want her to leave my arms because it felt good, but she pulled away and looked me in the eye. Could she see the longing in my eyes because I'm sure I saw something in hers. She kissed me again— this time on the lips. Not a peck. Her lips lingered too long for that. I'd been a gentleman all day, taking my lead from her. So, I reciprocated and pulled her in, deepening the kiss. The mood ended as quickly as it began. She pulled away.

"Oh, I shouldn't have done that." A flush spread across her face and down her neck. She covered her mouth with her hand and used the other to guide her movements as she backed up and slipped into her chair. Her cowgirl boots had her full attention.

What would Bryan say if he saw what had just happened? He'd probably give me a hard time for not taking advantage of the situation. But he didn't have the full picture. She was engaged and felt embarrassed and guilty. We both had acted in a moment of weakness having spent hours in an emotionally charged conversation. Not smart to read too much into it. So, I turned my back on her and started searching for my dropped soda.

An awkwardness fell over the camp. Ginny sat quietly for a few minutes, avoiding eye contact, and then started hunting for her satchel. "Did you see my bag when you went for the bug spray?" She scratched her head.

"Yep, next to my backpack." I rose to retrieve it and handed it to her, thankful for something to do.

"I know I packed that stuff." She removed a few items and placed them on the tarp.

"What are looking for?"

"Body spray and wipes. I'm sweaty." She pulled off her cowgirl boots and wiggled her toes.

"You don't stink. You smell like lavender." The comment made her blush. "Give that thing to me." I took the bag and upended it. "Why would you need all this stuff? No wonder you need a satchel."

She shrugged and lifted her hands. "I was a Girl Scout. We know how to prepare for all emergencies."

"True, but better ways come to mind. My wallet, for example." I patted the big pockets on my cargo shorts. "It goes there. The phone here, and sometimes there." I pointed to my shirt pocket and back pocket. "Bam. All I need. Less stress on the back. I bet you have a twisted spine from humping that thing around."

She showed her dimples. "I go to a chiropractor." She found the body spray amid the jumble on the tarp and spritzed her legs, arms, neck, and face. She used a package of wet wipes to clean her feet.

"Ahh. I feel so much better. I bet you would too," she said.

I unlaced my hiking boots and peeled off my socks. My wrinkled feet were a sickly white, and the smell of dirty boy, mixed with rotten eggs, wafted over our heads. I nearly gagged. What had possessed me to take off the boots? Good grief. Another bonehead move that would have annoyed and embarrassed Chelsey.

"Yikes." Ginny fanned her face but seemed unbothered. She knelt in front of me and started spraying my feet with her lavender-scented spray and used the wipes to clean my feet and toes. It reminded me of Jesus washing his disciples' feet. An intimate, selfless act. The heart of a servant. Ginny was in a class alone. "That should take care of it. Your flip-flops, by the way, are in the bin."

Now refreshed, and smelling like a drawer sachet, we reloaded the satchel. Our hands brushed and the tingling began anew, as did a simple truth:

I wanted to spend the rest of my life with Ginny. But I wasn't sure the feelings were mutual.

CHAPTER THIRTY

The Festival, One Year Earlier

After tossing the boots behind the tent, throwing the socks in the trash, and retrieving my flip-flops from the bin—as Ginny suggested—I sat next to her beneath the canopy. She appeared to be in a debate with herself. She closed her eyes and bowed her head, her hands clasped on the back of her neck and her elbows anchored to her knees. I didn't intrude, only wondered what was going on inside her head. After several minutes of silence, I couldn't help myself.

"Have you heard from Jacob?"

She looked up. Her eyes flinty and hard. "He has some explaining to do. He's been rude to me and has taken advantage of you. This is beyond ridiculous. I'm almost ready to take you up on your offer of taking me home to Granny's."

I liked where this was headed and nodded. I reached into my

pocket and grabbed the keys. "I've already told you." I jingled them. "Say the word and we're out of here." *I'd take her to the ends of the Earth if that's what she wanted.*

"What's it been? Eight or nine hours since we met?" she asked and eased herself out of the camp chair. She walked to the edge of the tarp and crossed her arms. Was she looking for him or wrestling with more inner talk? She sighed heavily, turned, and then sat down next to me.

"I believe God wanted us to meet today," she said after a long pause. She touched her mouth with her hand. She started nodding. "I know He did. He made sure our paths crossed, and then made sure Jacob stayed away long enough for us to talk. God used you to open my eyes. Maybe I shouldn't give Jacob a hard time when he gets here. I should thank him."

Worry lines then appeared on her forehead, like the internal debate had started up again. She looked sideways at me, not smiling. "I want to tell you something. I've been thinking a lot about what we've talked about." She sat upright and took a deep breath. *Was she going to give Jacob the heave-ho.* "Number one, you're absolutely right about Jacob."

Eureka!

"I shouldn't be ashamed of what happened to me," she continued. "I should embrace it. I'm going to tell Jacob everything. Deception is a recipe for disaster." *Is she going to tell him about our kiss?*

"Okay, good start. What else?"

"Before I get to that, let me explain why I haven't told Jacob everything, why I shy away from people. I'm afraid they'll abandon me, like my mom did, if they know the truth." She looked at me. "I can see you don't understand this."

Who knows which expression played across my face. I didn't understand her fears of abandonment, but then again, I hadn't lived her childhood as her story so vividly brought to light. She'd already shown me the disparities in our childhoods. But the look on her face made me uneasy. She appeared determined to open my eyes to something else.

"That leads me to my second point," she said. "I had to trust in something larger than myself, and you figured you were okay on your own."

My mouth opened, but she cut me off.

"Didn't you say you couldn't make sense of why you're here, what you're supposed to be doing with your life?" she asked. She didn't wait for my response before she said, "Have you ever asked God? He put you here for a reason. Don't you understand that?" She inclined her head to look at me, putting me on the spot.

She was sailing into a riptide, and this was the last topic I wanted to address.

Faith doesn't factor into my worldview. I believe in an omniscient creator, but I would rather debate the pros and cons of religion than ruminate over God's master plan. I hadn't revealed these attitudes to Ginny or anything about my heartbreak over Chelsey.

"I'm just here, doing my thing." I glanced at Ginny. Her eyes were boring into my cranium. She frowned.

What did she want from me? Why can't we talk about body

spray or even Jacob? Anything but this. This conversation wasn't going in the direction I wanted. I blustered a little and tried to change the topic.

I know I'm not living up to others' expectations, including my own, and don't want to even imagine what God thinks or wants for me. So, I keep the bar low. Does this bother me? It does. But I rationalize. Don't I have a slew of friends, a quick and creative mind, and an enviable command of language? Don't they serve me well in my role as the conversationalist, the crowd pleaser, and the party-boy jokester? Don't I get jazzed in my side job as an amateur comedian?

My rationalizations don't work. I brood. Major setbacks reinforce my fears and erode my confidence bit by bit. While my friends settle down and get on with their lives, I remain stagnated. My career as a real-estate agent came about because nothing else seemed better. I never get off the teeter-totter either. Confident one minute and then down in the dumps the next.

Now and then, my often-ignored inner voice—my *better angel,* as I like to think of him—will urge me to consider the questions Ginny had asked. Maybe I am missing something. Maybe the world and its offerings do consume too much of my time. Maybe the man upstairs has a bigger, wiser, and more meaningful plan, one that doesn't consist of me running away from myself and from my own fears of rejection.

But those thoughts are pushed to the dusty corners of my mind. I yank my better angel off the stage and listen to a podcast or watch a random video instead. Comfortable. Momentarily content.

Ginny appeared oblivious to my inner thoughts.

"Tell me." She moved her chair closer to mine and tapped my forearm.

"I don't know," I answered somewhat truthfully and scratched my nose.

"Oh, my sweet, confused friend. You can see through other people's issues. You've certainly seen through mine, but you can't see your own." She leaned over and got into my space. I could smell the lavender, the body spray. She gently touched my leg and spoke in a light, non-confrontational tone, perhaps sensing my inner turmoil.

"I think you need to hear what I have to say."

"Haven't stopped you yet, have I?" I sounded like a bratty kid.

"You don't have all the answers where *you're* concerned," she said. "We've spent a lot of time together and this is what I think. Deep down inside is an insecure man who doesn't realize his true value or purpose. He hides behind his big personality to avoid the truth. He wanders through life, hoping for the best, expecting the worst. God has given you"—she tapped my chest with her finger— "a purpose. You don't have to go through life confused by the vagaries of life."

"Vagaries. Good word, Ginny. I'll add it to my everyday vocabulary."

She squinted her eyes and shook her head.

I watched the drunks and other merrymakers who congregated in groups around us. Never did I expect this conversation at an outdoor festival. This was a new experience. I examined my bottle of Dew. Said nothing. I knew she was right. I didn't think about purpose or life's meaning. This beautiful woman saw through me and examined my heart.

We sat in silence for a long time, listening to the music blasting from my portable speakers. She hummed to a Phish tune, one I didn't particularly like, but one my mother had always asked that I play when we sat on the porch appreciating the mountain views. "Waiting All Night" was the song. The lyrics seemed oddly appropriate. A man's lament over his lost love, wanting to know where she'd gone. He cried out. He was so alone. Was that me? Or was that the man upstairs crying over me?

"What about you?" I asked in a monotone. "What *is* your purpose in life, Ginny?"

"You've played a big role in helping me understand it. That's another thing I've been thinking about. Like I said, God orchestrated our meeting." She smiled and leaned back, clasping her hands behind her neck. "God did me a favor. My past *prepared* me for the future, helping kids like me. Our conversation helped me to make up my mind. I'm going to specialize in child psychiatry. I want to do my part to end cycles of dysfunction that pass from one generation to the next, ruining lives." She looked victorious. "I must carry on where Granny left off."

Though I'd no clue about my life's path, it made me happy she'd discovered hers. She probably had known the whole time but needed a sounding board—me. I'd take that.

"Without Granny's encouragement and support, I may have ended up a drug addict like Jimmy or a flake like my mother, jumping from one bad situation to the next. The things Granny taught me can only strengthen what I'll learn in school."

Why then had she ignored Granny's opinion of Jacob?

"What did I do to bring about your epiphany?" I asked instead, sensing our time might be ending. I wanted to know specifically how I'd helped. I needed to feel better about myself.

"You listened to me. Encouraged me. Gave me honest advice. You showed me it's okay to take risks and to share my life with others. It was cathartic." Ginny grinned. "You've accomplished more than the army of counselors that Granny hired. Like I told you, you're the only person, other than Granny, who knows *everything*."

"Make sure you follow through on everything you said you're going to do." I lifted my head and waited until we made eye contact. "I don't necessarily share your worldview about God having a purpose for our lives, but you've given me some food for thought. I admire your convictions. Go for it, Ginny. Become a doctor. Make a difference, a lasting difference."

I grinned, trying to ignore my other feelings. Jacob wasn't the guy for her, and I feared he'd turn her from her faith and resolve. A sense of failure consumed me. I had ignored my intuitions and listened to the voice who'd advised giving Jacob the benefit of the doubt. That voice insisted that jealousy underpinned my attitudes toward Jacob.

"Promise me you'll go home and make things right. Okay?"

She nodded and twisted the memory bracelet around her wrist. She went into the tent and came back with my hat of many colors.

"My favorite hat." I gave a sad smile, knowing I had missed my chance. "Forgot I brought it. Where you'd find it?"

"When I cleaned up that mess in there."

She placed my cap backwards on my head and arranged her cowgirl hat. She leaned over my shoulder and snapped the selfie.

That was when we heard Jacob. He didn't take a shine to me or seem to appreciate Ginny's displeasure with him. Did I really see his eyes turn pitch black?

CHAPTER THIRTY-ONE

The Festival, One Year Earlier

"Well, isn't this cozy." Jacob spoke loudly as he picked his way through clusters of people. He stood out, dressed in his boat shoes, dressy tan shorts, and pale-blue Oxford shirt. The visible trappings of his wealth. I didn't know where he had spent the past eight-plus hours, but it didn't look like he had filled the time in the heat and humidity. He was relatively spotless, except for his mud-caked Docksiders.

Although it hadn't rained since we moved our party to the canopy, the ground was still slick, and Jacob struggled to navigate the terrain. He was no mountain goat. He slipped but didn't do a face plant. I had to give him that, but nothing more. Moments ago, one of my inner voices—the one listened to more often—told me not to judge Jacob prematurely. But now, seeing Jacob face-to-face as he shoved people aside, I knew he was a jack wagon. The other voice, the one I often ignored, was dead on.

Please, please let Ginny see the light. Was that a prayer?

As he stumbled closer, the contrasts between us became clearer. Where I was short, he was tall. Where I looked like I'd spent the night in a ditch, he looked like he had stepped out of *GQ* magazine, aside from the specks of mud on his otherwise clean shorts. My wrinkled flamingo-themed shirt looked tacky, as did my favorite cap, and I'm sure my beard still harbored drops of Asian barbecue sauce. He looked at me, turned his nose up, and sniffed.

"I leave you for a few minutes and you find yourself a new man?" He stood a couple feet from where I sat. He spoke in a cultivated Southern accent, revealing a private-school education and position in Southern high society. "You move quick, Ginny."

I couldn't tell if he was kidding or deranged. *A few minutes?* I snorted and he glared at me. But I couldn't help it. I guess we weren't supposed to believe our lying eyes.

Ginny straightened, squared her shoulders, and smiled. She tucked her phone into her back pocket and touched my shoulder, a gesture interpreted to mean she would handle Jacob.

"Don't look at him that way," she commanded, unflappable and cool. She no longer seemed to be interested in thanking him for his unexplained disappearance. "Where have you been?" She walked toward him. He grinned at her and held his arms out as if he expected her to jump into his embrace or something. She crossed her arms and shook her head in disapproval.

Jacob looked confused. The sweet, accommodating Ginny— who hours earlier had gushed at the mention of his name and fretted about his safety—appeared to have grown a spine.

A good sign.

Neither one of us was buying his rubbish or weird gaslighting. He leaned down to kiss her cheek, but she turned away.

"My goodness, Jacob, you've been gone for hours. I didn't know if you were ever coming back. You owe me an apology. You owe *him* an apology." She angled her head in my direction. "You shouldn't have put us in this situation."

Jacob frowned. His face contorted in anger for a second before he regained control. "Ginny, what's the matter with you?" His voice sounded concerned. Maybe he sensed the shifting ground and wanted to reassert himself, assure her of his reasonableness. "You know I ran into a friend. You're the one who told me it was okay to hang out with her for a while." He held out his hands like a peace offering. "I wasn't gone that *long*. You know I wouldn't do something like that. You're overreacting."

I stood next to Ginny for moral support. I didn't know which lie she was reacting to, but her eyes widened in disbelief. She ignored his outstretched hands, pulled her phone from her back pocket, and looked at the time.

"You're full of it." Her voice rose in pitch. "Eight—no, nearly *nine hours* seem like a long time to me. And I never told you to take off with some woman I don't know. You didn't introduce me. Remember? You took off in a flash. You stranded me in the rain. Where was I supposed to go, Jacob? Thank goodness for him"—she glanced at me—"and his incredibly generous nature. You could learn something from him."

Jacob's blue eyes turned icy. "You're telling me I'm full of it? Did I hear you correctly?" He tilted his head to the side, no longer smiling. "Answer me."

Ginny chewed on her lips. I could tell she wasn't sure what to make of this Jacob, but I did. This type of behavior is known to me. My neighbor behaves similarly, and for my own mental health, I no longer socialize with him.

"We'll talk about this later." Her spunk seemed to wane.

She stepped back and I moved in.

"I'm TC. Nice to meet you." I sounded phony even to my ears. I extended my right hand and caught a whiff of something, a sweaty, musky smell that was easy to identify. While Ginny and I shared our lives through conversation, he smelled like he had shared his more intimately. Probably in a nicely equipped RV or motel, given how long he was gone.

He didn't take my hand. Instead, he clasped his hands behind his back and stood on his toes. It was a ploy, typical of guys like him. He wanted me to feel inferior. I shoved my hand into my pocket, glad of the slight.

I hadn't packed hand sanitizer.

"Get your stuff." His eyes turned black. Despite my involvement with a guy like Jacob, this was new. He looked like a demon, and a chill crept up my spine.

Ginny was over her head in dangerous waters. This guy made my former friend look like a rookie. My better angel had urged me to say something earlier. Now that opportunity had passed. I shuddered.

He looked at his expensive-looking watch and barked at Ginny to hurry up, to get her stuff. His eyes returned to normal, but he looked like he wanted to snatch and devour her soul. *Did Ginny see what I saw? Or was I only imagining it?*

"You can wait one second." Ginny held her own. Was she channeling Granny? Had Aimee's in-your-face persona rubbed off on her? She sat on her camp chair and pulled on her boots, taking her time. I held my breath, hoping she might escape a bad situation.

Jacob then threw a curveball. Should've seen it coming having seen the tactic before. But it caught me by surprise. That quick, he flipped the switch. Turned on the charm. His voice lost its intensity. He sounded accommodating . . . gracious. Mr. Nice Guy.

"You are right, baby. I do you owe you an apology," he said. "But I'm sick of this place and want to go home." He gave Ginny a warm smile, his eyes crinkled at the corners. His bleached teeth looked like Chiclets. He glanced at me. "And yes, ahem . . ." He seemed to be searching for my name. "Thank you for keeping my girl company. I owe you." He then stepped toward her, and gently took her elbow. "You are the best thing that's ever happened to me. I know I don't deserve you." He gently caressed the side of her face. His eyes looked dreamy. Lovesick.

That was when an elusive thought blasted through to my conscious mind. Ginny was just like her mother. Her pride, like her mom's, couldn't abide by Granny being right. She was going to choose badly, and I knew, beyond all doubt, that nothing good would come from this union if I didn't say something now. *Dump him. Stay with Granny. Come with me. Do anything but go with him. He has a problem.*

"Ginny, wait," I said.

She turned to face me and drew me into an embrace. "What did you think? That I'd leave without first saying goodbye to you, especially after all you've done for me helping me find my true calling? Oh, my goodness, TC."

"Don't go." I whispered in ear. "It's a mistake."

She leaned back and a look of sadness fell over her face. "I pray you find someone who deserves you, TC," she whispered back. "You're going to make some girl very happy someday. Can't you see Jacob loves me?" She bit her lip. "Loyalty is important to me, TC . . ."

Love. Loyalty?

"I'm not sure what happened today," she continued. "Why he stayed away for so long. Like I told you, Jacob's never done anything like that before." She glanced away . . . and then nodded. "But I do think he's sorry."

No, he isn't.

Jacob touched her arm again. "Darlin', let's get going."

She rotated her head away from me. "Jacob, one more minute. Please."

He nodded. "Absolutely." He took a few steps back and gave us space.

She turned back to face me—her arms still wrapped around my shoulders. Tears gathered in the corners of those gorgeous blue eyes of hers. "Think about what we talked about."

"What are you referring to?" I whispered, wanting to cry myself. "We talked about a lot of things."

"Consider what God wants for your life," she said. "You might find peace in the answer. Think about it, okay?"

And with that—before I could ask for her phone number or last name—she draped her oversized bag around her torso and walked away. He slung his across her shoulder and nuzzled her ear.

She never looked back.

CHAPTER THIRTY-TWO

Ginny, The Festival, One Year Earlier

I wanted to look back at TC standing alone at his campsite, but I didn't trust myself. I was afraid I'd start bawling. As we walked back to Jacob's car, he apologized again for staying away so long, and then asked my advice on what he *should have* done with the family friend.

"If I know you, you would have done exactly what I did." He smiled and touched my upper arm. "She needed my help, and you never turn anyone away. Just taking a page from your book, darlin."

I let him talk and started thinking that I would have probably done the same thing. Granny would drop everything to hear me out and offer comfort. I glanced down and stepped aside to avoid a mud puddle. "You're probably right."

He grinned and winked at me. "Hey, I've been thinking." He paused and inclined his head to the side, wrapping his arm around my waist. "When's the last time I came to visit you and Granny?"

"It's been a long time, Jacob."

He nodded. "Don't make plans for Atlanta next weekend. How about I drive down next Saturday?" He pulled me in closer. "I need to ask my future Granny-in-law for your hand in marriage." His eyes crinkled and he tickled my sides. "We need to make our engagement official with the woman who matters most." He then took my left hand and raised it to his lips. "Maybe I'll bring a special gift."

By the time he pulled out onto the highway, I was laughing, my earlier irritation and confusion nearly forgotten, washed away by his attention and interest in me. He seemed overjoyed by my decision to concentrate on child psychiatry.

"I know you've struggled with that," he said. "You're going to be perfect."

At his encouragement, I told him about TC and Aimee's banter, Sugahbear's provisions, the things I saw sitting beneath the yellow canopy. I examined my mud-splattered shorts and pulled down the visor. The light switched on as soon as I opened the mirror. What did my Granny—the gardener extraordinaire— always say? *A peck of dirt will never hurt you. Sometimes it just means you're having fun.* My mascara had run, and mud speckled my legs. I giggled. I did have fun.

"I hope you enjoyed your day as much as I did." I closed the visor and glanced back at Jacob. "It's good meeting new people."

He stared at the road ahead. His jaw twitched. He made no comment until I asked what I thought was an innocent question . . .

"What did you do today, Jacob? I wish I could have met your friend."

My question had flipped the switch. His body looked taut, ready to snap. He was tapping his fingers on the steering wheel, his eyes laser focused on the highway, when he said, "By the way, Ginny, grunge is not a good look on you."

But it was too late to run back to TC. I touched the memory bracelet. And that's when I remembered I didn't know his last name.

CHAPTER THIRTY-THREE

The Festival, One Year Earlier

Watching Ginny walk away depressed me more than any setback in my life. It was even worse than when Chelsey left me. But Ginny had made her choice, and I knew exactly what lay in store for her. I felt powerless.

I went inside the tent, grabbed my backpack, and headed for Sugahbear's campsite. It was time to anesthetize myself with a few more beers.

After just one sip, I could tell I wouldn't find solace there. The beer tasted bitter. I didn't say much. Had nothing to say. Retreating to our yellow tent and thinking about Ginny appealed to me more, but nothing good could come from sitting alone. Bryan gave me a few side-long glances but kept quiet. Mo didn't ask questions either, but she seemed to instinctively know exactly what to do. God bless her big ol' heart.

"Looks like you got the short end of the stick." She wrapped her immense arm around my shoulder and drew me close. "There's nothing a hug won't fix." She smiled and pinched my cheek, her skin glowing, her eyes twinkling. "You are something, Little Big Man. Smile, honey. Makes you look prettier."

Maybe everything would be okay after all.

The next day I plastered on my festival face, anticipating the Phish performance later that night. In my years of being a devout fanboy, I rarely miss a performance, provided my finances allow it. I wasn't disappointed this time either. I was glad I'd made the trip. Jamming to my favorite band made me forget Ginny and Jacob.

This was my happy place—at least for a little while.

But by noon the next day, the dark mood returned. Bryan talked incessantly as we packed our camping gear. I didn't feel like small talk and didn't want to answer his probing questions about the "beautiful babe" I'd spent time with on Friday. He meant well and only wanted to encourage me. But he made it hard. So, I told him to shut his pie hole. He took no offense.

Let it go. Move on. I'm not telling anyone about my feelings for Ginny.

As he drove the back roads and highways to my place, I rested my head against the headrest. Scenery rolled past the window. I couldn't help but worry about Ginny and wonder if she'd tell Jacob the truth and how long it'd take before he took a wrecking ball to the foundation she'd laid. I thought about my own experience with a guy like Jacob and shut my eyes.

"What's eating you?" Bryan glanced at me. "What's up? Why

do you look like you've lost your best friend? You haven't. I'm still here, bro."

"Did you ever meet Adrian?"

"Yeah, met him once, but you haven't talked about him lately." Bryan kept his eyes on the road. Traffic was bad. "Why are you bringing him up now?"

"I met someone just like him."

Bryan turned down the radio. "Talk."

My friendship with Adrian had started out great. He liked the same music and listened to the same podcasts. We always had a good time, cutting up and discussing the ways of the world. He seemed to latch onto my every word and made my opinions his own. I was flattered, all too happy to share my take on the world.

As time passed, though, I noticed obvious unsettling behaviors. He couldn't tell the truth if he wanted. A lie here, a lie there, especially where it concerned his skills and talents. I let it go, figuring embellishment didn't do any harm.

One night, Georgie and I had gone to their place for dinner. Dusty, his wife, had knocked herself out preparing our meal. Sitting at the dining room table that she'd set, Adrian started bragging about how he was the family chef. He was the one who spent the day cooking. I nearly choked on a clump of noodles. He hadn't lifted a finger to help at all.

That was the beginning. Over time, his lies became more grandiose. He acted like the world revolved around him. He either dominated the conversation or told me I didn't know what I was talking about. He'd launch into diatribes about his struggles, friends who betrayed him, and bosses who underestimated his value. He expected favors from me and tried to shame me when I wouldn't comply.

He was never wrong. About anything.

I couldn't imagine how Dusty felt. She slept with the dude. She didn't say much during his rants and would look at her lap, her fingernails, or leave the room, claiming she needed to use the bathroom or grab a drink. Given the circumstances, it seemed strange that Dusty became a close friend.

On walks with their flea-infested mutt, when Adrian wasn't around, she'd stop by if she saw me sitting on the porch. We'd talk about her work and mine, gossip about the Sloth or the beer-mooching Bud and our weekend plans. She had a great sense of humor. But that humor was kept in check when she was around Adrian because he didn't like being upstaged. She'd offer improvements to my comedy routines and suggested possible topics. I enjoyed her company, and she mine. She seemed starved for a normal conversation with someone who appreciated her and didn't need to be the center of attention.

One night, she'd stopped by. She looked worried, jittery. Adrian had quit his job that day, claiming he lined up something that paid better. She was worried about how she'd cover the rent, groceries, utility bills, and car payments on her waitress income. "You know, TC, Adrian is a liar. He doesn't have *anything* lined up." She then questioned her sanity for getting involved with him in the first place. Neither one of us had ever talked about his lies before.

"Hours after I went to bed," I said, glancing at Bryan, "I heard pounding on the front door. He shouted for me to open. He had a bone to pick."

I turned the doorknob to open the door, but before I could open it all the way, Adrian pushed through like a maniac. He grabbed my undershirt and slammed me against the wall. Enraged, his spittle flew all over my face. He accused me of sleeping with Dusty.

"Were you?"

I rolled my eyes. Bryan knew me better than that. Like my other female friends—a sorority that I supposed now included Ginny—Dusty offered easy companionship. She was someone to hang out with.

"You're jealous of me," Adrian yelled, his face inches from mine, before calling me a loser and a slob. "Stay away from my woman." I shoved him out and locked the front and back doors.

My heart pounded like a jackhammer. Since going back to sleep was impossible, I turned on my computer. Adrian's off-the-wall behavior, fierce accusations and lies, weren't normal. Something was wrong with him.

I typed "personality disorders" into the search engine and started reading. I read enough to suspect a severe problem . . . narcissism, a condition that was difficult to treat. Did he feel entitled? Did he show envy? Did he possess an overstated sense of importance and need constant attention?

I checked every box.

The sun was already over the horizon by the time I powered off my computer and went to bed, tired to the bone.

The discovery rattled me. I did feel empathy for him, but he didn't feel any for me or his wife of seven years. Did I really want to hang around with him? Life was hard enough without being reminded of my flaws or being accused of things I'd never do. His friendship *wasn't* good for me.

The next day, as I drove past Adrian's house, he saw me and waved me down. He wanted to apologize and buy me a beer. He blamed everything on Dusty, said she had gotten on his nerves with her constant haranguing about money. I begged off. I'd already decided to steer clear of him.

"Sounds a little like someone I know at work. Difficult to be around." Bryan nodded as he pulled into a gas station. "We need gas. Want something?"

"Orange Fanta."

I gassed up the car and returned to my seat on the passenger side, watching Bryan scurry around inside the store as he gathered food supplies.

Bryan returned and handed my drink to me. He opened a bag of pork rinds. Human garbage disposal. "You said you met someone like Adrian." He munched a few before putting the car in reverse. "Who'd you meet?"

"Ginny's fiancé. We talked only briefly, but I got the sense he *feasts* on hurting people . . . he's in league of his own. His eyes . . . they creeped me out. And the thing is, I can't help her."

"Why not? You spent the whole day with her. Just call or text and tell her you need to talk."

"I didn't get her phone number, and I don't know her last name. Wanted to get it, but he dragged her away before I could."

Bryan sighed and shook his head.

Not wanting to hear his criticisms, I leaned my head against the window and closed my eyes. Bryan gobbled another bag of snacks before I finally fell asleep.

I didn't wake up until he pulled into my driveway.

CHAPTER THIRTY-FOUR

Today, May 30

I hear Laurel whimpering from her crib. Ginny doesn't seem to hear, so I check. The baby's kicked off her blanket. I caress her head until she quiets and return to Ginny. She doesn't look up. She talks in a flat, lifeless tone, telling me what's happened in her life since we saw each other last.

After I returned home from the festival, I halfheartedly tried to find Ginny on social media. But that was impossible without her last name. And even if I had, then what would I have done? She'd made her choice. Like Chelsey, she appreciated my friendship and nothing more. I even searched for Alma Smith in Georgia and found many results, but I couldn't muster the courage to call anyone. Floating through life—not delving too deeply into how I might change my trajectory—seemed a better course. Easier. Less painful.

So, I'd let it go and cleaved to my well-worn habits. I hung out at the bar or with Aimee, who stopped by at least once a week to fill me in on her latest exploits, guiding the guileless into the wilds of the East Tennessee mountains and filling their heads with stories. Thank God, comments about Ginny went unsaid. I also went on a handful of fishing trips with her grandfather, visited my parents on Sundays, and entertained Bryan when he made the drive from Baltimore. And, of course, I continued my practice of listening to podcasts and falling into online rabbit holes seeking fodder for my comedy routines, my little black book at the ready.

Ginny tells me about her ride home to Georgia after she and Jacob left the festival. As he drove, he ranted about his hurt feelings, Ginny's insinuations when she asked what he'd done during his hours-long absence, and her failures to understand and remember events correctly.

She couldn't reconcile the Jacob who brought her to the festival with the one who took her home. Who was that guy? Was she mistaken? Did she *really* say what he claimed she'd said? She was pretty sure she hadn't. She also knew spending less time with him was a good idea while she figured things out. Moving to Atlanta wasn't going to happen. When they finally got back to his house, Jacob asked her to stay. She refused even though it was late, collected her suitcase, and then drove home to Granny's.

"He called you every day, didn't he?" I ask. "He apologized, said he couldn't live without you, and pleaded for you to return." His behavior was so predictable. "He gave you gifts, sent you notes. Told you how special you were. Promised things would be different, right?"

Ginny's mouth falls open. "How did you know?"

"Firsthand experience. One of my good friends married a guy like Jacob. Not sure where he is these days. I ended the friendship with him and advised her later to leave him. I'm glad she listened. He nearly ruined her life."

Ginny stares at me, her forehead creasing. "Why didn't you tell me?"

"When was I supposed to tell you, Ginny?" The memory of the past opportunity at the festival taunts me. "You probably wouldn't have believed me anyway."

She looks off into space, her mind far away. She seems lost in what I suppose are memories and possibly regrets. "My life hasn't turned out the way I envisioned. I've tried so hard to make our relationship work. He never admits he's wrong about anything. Everything is my fault. Why won't he love me the way he used to?"

I could spend the rest of my time here telling her why. I touch her shoulder, and she looks at me. "Ginny, what happened to Granny?"

She shakes her head and runs her hands down her thighs. Her black sweatpants are pilled. "I told you. She died."

"How? What happened? Ginny, look at me. I came here to talk with you." I put my arm around her and draw her close. She rests her head on my shoulder and then pushes away. Tears run down her cheeks, and she covers her face with her hands. She starts, stops, then starts again.

As Ginny tells me the whole sorry tale, filling in the details leading up to Granny's death, I marvel at Jacob's persistence. He'd wormed himself back into Ginny's life within weeks. Despite Granny's protests, Ginny moved into Jacob's posh house in the posh neighborhood having convinced herself that his festival behavior had been an anomaly, a one off.

"With the hoopla surrounding Jacob and me, and Granny begging me not to move to Atlanta, I'd initially ignored what my body was telling me." Ginny looks at her wrist as she twirls the memory bracelet. "I did the calculations in my head and realized I might be pregnant. After Jacob left for work one morning, I did the test. I was thrilled. A new baby . . . our baby. A family. I got so excited and was convinced Jacob would be ecstatic too. We had turned a corner in our relationship, and he was adamant about getting married sooner than later."

I understand why she might have thought that. According to her, Jacob talked endlessly about their life together and the family they would have. His work colleagues—the only people Ginny socialized with regularly—heard his talk too. Her spirits soared . . . until the night she told him about the pregnancy, along with her decision to defer medical school.

"I told you he didn't take the news well," she says. "He stormed out of the house, and I went to bed. He didn't talk to me for days."

As the pregnancy progressed, Jacob stopped talking about marriage and Ginny stopped visiting Granny as often as she once did. Calls and texts from her small circle of friends went unreturned until it no longer mattered. They had stopped reaching out to her. Having Ginny to himself improved Jacob's mood for a while, but he'd always revert to his complaining self.

"I threatened to leave once before the baby arrived. Had my bags packed and everything," Ginny says.

Predictably, he poured on the charm, convincing her anew of his reformed mindset, blaming his moods on work pressures, and begging her to be patient. She stayed with him as her abdomen swelled.

"Other than for refusing the abortion, I go along with Jacob on everything," Ginny admits. "It's easier that way. But it's taking a toll. One minute I'm brilliant, the next I'm a dunce." Her eyes fill, but she rubs the tears away. "He stole my Bible once. The one Granny gave me on my twelfth birthday. He says only fools believe the stuff in that book. I found it in the trash and put it inside a box." She points to a closed door across from where we sit on the bed. "I guess it's still there."

I raise my eyebrows in surprise.

"Well, Granny gave it to me," she says in defense. "Don't you think I should keep it?"

"You didn't tell Jacob about your parents, did you?"

"TC, I had no reason to tell him. At first, things were going so well. When he's charming, he's wonderful. When he's in a bad mood . . . To this day, he calls me selfish, thoughtless, disloyal, sneaky, and a liar." She taps her fingers while rattling off the insults. "It doesn't matter what I do. Nothing changes. Right now, he's not talking to me."

"Do you care?"

"Of course, I care. We have a child. His parents think we ran off to get married because my family couldn't afford a big wedding.

Everyone we know thinks we're the perfect couple, a match made in heaven."

"Do you confront him with his lies? And why would you care what others think?" I ask.

This conversation seems like a re-run. Hadn't I already pontificated to her on why she shouldn't hide her background from anyone? I feel like a district attorney, lobbing questions at a defendant.

"I did at first. I begged him to stop telling people we're married. But he claims he wants to protect my honor and insists he knows better. He doesn't want his mother, her friends, or the neighbors thinking ill of me, especially now that the baby is here."

I'm annoyed. Really annoyed. Her entire life is a lie. Why hadn't she come clean with Jacob as she promised a year ago? He'd have dumped her—fast. No doubt in my mind. And the truth would have spared Granny, Ginny, and her daughter from the smoldering wreckage that is her life.

I run my hands through my hair. She still hasn't answered the one question that completes the picture.

"How did Granny die?"

Ginny chews the inside of her mouth. "It's all my fault. I shouldn't have called Granny."

The day Ginny went into labor, she called Jacob at work, but no one knew where he was. She almost drove herself to the hospital but thought better of it and called an Uber instead. The contractions had started, and she couldn't wait.

The delivery was hard. The baby went into fetal distress. Just as her doctors started preparing for an emergency Caesarean, Jacob rushed into the delivery room garbed in scrubs. He was out of breath and begging her forgiveness in front of her doctor and the nurses.

"You would have thought I was the Virgin Mother, and that Laurel was the baby Jesus, the way he clucked and preened," she says. "He held my hand and told me how proud he was and to hang tough. With all I'd gone through, the private hospital room would be a treat. He made sure to mention that."

How many times had I listened to Adrian's boasts and self-congratulations?

When Ginny returned to her private room, she called Granny to tell her about the C-section. She told her that she and the baby were fine and would probably go home in a few days if everything went well.

"The baby was in her bassinet," she says. "Jacob sat in a chair, looking at his iPhone. I told him that Granny wanted to know what we were naming the baby. He looked up and shrugged, said he had to go to an important afternoon meeting and didn't have time to talk about it. And I said, 'Oh, come on, Jacob, this is important.' I told him that he used the same excuse every time I brought up the subject. He then got up, walked over to my bed, and leaned down as if he wanted to kiss me. But then he whispered in my ear, 'Name her whatever. I don't care. She might not even be mine.' And then he left."

"Are you kidding?" I can't believe my ears. Or can I?

Jacob didn't come back later that night. He didn't come the next day either. Ginny called his cell. His office. He didn't answer. She left voicemail messages and asked his administrative assistant to have him call her. He didn't. When it was time to leave the hospital, she had no choice. She called Granny, not feeling comfortable contacting his parents.

"I'll never forget what Granny said." Ginny massages the back of her neck. "'I'm on my way, sweet pea. I'll be there in an hour. But I'm tellin' you, you're not going back to that man. You're comin' home with me where I can keep you safe. He's no good.' She couldn't even say his name, it was that distasteful to her."

But Granny never made it.

Driving north on Interstate 75, someone cut into her lane, and she swerved to avoid a collision. She lost control and slammed into a concrete barrier. Ginny tells the story in bits and pieces, interrupted by uncontrollable weeping. I try to touch her. She pushes my hand away, punches the mattress, and looks for something to throw. She finds a pillow and heaves it toward the dresser.

Firefighters struggled for at least an hour extracting Granny from her crumpled car. She was still breathing. Ginny's friend, Melinda, was an emergency room nurse like Ginny, and she was on duty when medics rushed her in.

Granny died a few minutes later of massive internal bleeding. Melinda recognized Granny's name and went upstairs to the maternity ward to give Ginny the devastating news.

"I couldn't understand a word she was telling me. I started shaking, couldn't stand, felt completely detached from my body. Nothing made sense. I kept thinking, *This is a bad dream and soon I'll wake up.*" Ginny wipes her face with the back of her hand.

When she saw the look on Melinda's face, Ginny knew it wasn't a dream. Melinda helped Ginny pack her few belongings and took her home with the baby. Jacob was still incommunicado.

"Obviously, he came back, right?" I ask.

Jacob was home when they arrived. Melinda tore into him, accused him of shirking his responsibilities. And it was because of his carelessness that Granny was gone.

That got his attention. He acted concerned and told Melinda that he would've rearranged his busy schedule had he known he was supposed to bring Ginny home.

"Well, that's what fathers do," I say.

"He didn't ask Laurel's name either. Wouldn't look at her. Melinda was furious."

Ginny had never seen Melinda behave so aggressively. "Say her name!" she shrieked. But he refused. His indifference sparked another verbal assault. Melinda accused him of being self-centered and cruel. Ginny didn't have the energy to intercede. She was too busy beating herself up for calling Granny instead of an Uber.

Ginny handed Laurel to Melinda as she left the living room and asked her to bring the baby upstairs.

She climbed the stairs slowly, clutching her abdomen with one hand and the banister with the other. She overheard Jacob say he worried about Ginny's lies. The whoppers that made him look bad. He blamed her erratic behavior on hormones. He promised Melinda that he'd call Aunt Adele and help with funeral arrangements since Ginny was emotionally incapable of it.

"Did Melinda believe him?" I ask.

"She's always called him the pretty boy. After that confrontation, her opinion seemed to sour. She'll ask about Jacob when we talk on the phone, but I get the sense she's being polite. I don't think she cares much for him."

"*Did* he help with the arrangements?"

Ginny didn't think so. Her mind had been in a haze, overcome with grief, guilt, and the responsibilities of being a new mom. The stress made healing difficult. The physical pain immobilized her, and the doctor-prescribed painkillers barely made a dent. She cried herself to sleep at night and felt guilty because she didn't have a personal connection with Laurel. And it scared her.

"I felt incompetent and completely alone after Granny died," she says. "I *was* alone. Jacob ignored me for the most part." Her voice is void of emotion. "He'd check to make sure I'd taken my pain meds. That's about all. I guess it was better than listening to his tirades."

Why did he worry about her pills? The off-hand comment registers. The alarm goes off inside my head. I need more information, a better understanding of the people closest to Ginny this past year.

"Didn't Melinda come around? I ask instead. "And how about his parents?"

Ginny nods and sniffles. "Melinda's been great, but she has a family too. I don't know his parents well. We're cordial when I see them at special events and the occasional dinner party at their house. They're nice, but that's the extent of things."

Ginny notices the puzzled look on my face. "What?"

"Don't his parents want to see Laurel? Seems odd to me. New babies are always a cause for celebration in my family."

Ginny pauses and scratches her head. "His mother stopped by a day or two after I got home with Laurel. She brought a baby gift and expressed her condolences over Granny's death."

Ginny shrugs. "She doesn't visit, and the lack of contact suits me just fine. His mother makes me uncomfortable. I feel inadequate, not good enough, an unwanted house guest, especially when Jacob and his father are around." Ginny closes her eyes and exhales. "But she did ask where my wedding ring was."

Ginny wrings her hands. "Oh my gosh, the lies. The deception."

Her grief was swallowing her whole. She felt like a zombie but knew she had to rally, pull it together for Granny's funeral—an event that Jacob used to play the doting father, the loving spouse.

"He blew so much smoke up Aunt Adele's rear-end that it poured out of every orifice north of her neck." Ginny says, again without emotion.

After the funeral, Aunt Adele commended Ginny for the life she'd created. Beautiful baby, gorgeous and caring husband. Jacob told her that lie too.

I shake my head. The picture is clearer. The lies had piled up, closing all exit ramps.

"I didn't have the energy to set the story straight." Ginny gets up to check on her child who hasn't uttered a sound since whimpering many minutes ago. "I didn't want her to think badly of me, to compare me with my mother. I'm nothing like her."

She trudges to the window and peers through the slats. "I don't know why I let my mother bother me, but she does. I thought I'd moved past her stuff, especially after we talked about her last year, and I try not to think about her. When Aunt Adele called to tell her about Granny, do you know what she said?"

"Tell me."

She turns to face me. "She didn't have the money to fly east for the funeral. She lives in a commune or something. Or at least that's what she told Aunt Adele. She could work in a brothel for all I know. She also said her family didn't live in Georgia or New York. Her family was in Nevada."

Why can't people keep their ugly thoughts to themselves? And why did Aunt Adele pass along that intel to her grieving niece?

"Can you believe that?" Ginny shakes in anger. Deep lines form between her eyebrows. "This is how much she cares for her mother, daughter, and granddaughter. *Zippo.*" She says this in a snarl and squeezes her finger against her thumb. The veins in her hand pop.

"I feel like I'm going crazy." She rubs her face with both hands and moans. "I don't know where to turn." She pulls her hands away and looks at me. "You said you were here to help. How can you help me? If I leave Jacob, as you suggested earlier, where am I to go? I have nowhere to go."

As Ginny explains, she and Aunt Adele inherited Granny's house, but her aunt wants to sell it once it's out of probate. One less worry since no one needs the house. Ginny is supposedly married to a rich guy and lives in a big, expensive house in Tuxedo Park, and Adele has a nice condo in Manhattan.

"Aunt Adele thinks Jacob is a dream come true." Tears roll down Ginny's cheeks. "Why didn't I correct Jacob's big lie? Why did Granny have to die? I miss her so much. I can't stand it."

She walks back and sits next to me, oblivious to the irony. Her mother used the same language when her father died.

"For years, I listened to Granny talk about the Lord and how he had our backs. Look where that got us. Look where that's gotten me. Jacob *is* right. I did put my faith in an imaginary God."

My heart breaks for this woman. Before Jacob entered her world, faith and Granny anchored Ginny. Made her world understandable. Without them, her foundation crumbled and made her especially prone to Jacob's machinations. I draw her close to me, but her sorrow has no bottom. She spirals deeper into a black pit where all options are viable, even reasonable, if they will end the pain.

"Life is too hard," Ginny mutters hiding her face in her hands. She begins rocking. "I just want to end it all."

I sit up straighter and glance toward the hidden pills. "Stop it. Do you understand what you're saying?"

She doesn't seem to hear me. Her mind can't let loose of Jacob. "I know he doesn't love me. Maybe he never did. I'm such a fool . . . You're here to help, right?"

I nod, and that quick she jumps off the bed with the energy of a dervish. She darts to the closet and drags a large suitcase into the middle of the room. She then opens dresser drawers and haphazardly pulls out piles of shirts, jeans, and socks. Most of them are shoved into the suitcase. She then hurries to the crib, grabs the bag of disposable diapers and the hanging hamper, and tosses them in the general direction of the suitcase. The pile is high and disordered.

"What are you doing?" I take hold of her arms. Leaning down,

I force her to look into my eyes. She tries to look away, but I grab her face with both hands. She stops. I ask her again, "What. Are. You. Doing?"

"What does it look like? I'm packing."

"Okay, good, but where are you going?"

"With you. You'll take me back to Tennessee. You'll let me and Laurel stay with you for a while, won't you?" She bites the inside of her cheek, looking everywhere but at me.

Had I known about her plight two weeks ago, two days ago or earlier today, I would have swooped down to rescue her. I *would* have changed my plans.

"I can't."

Those two words wound her deeper than anything I could have done to her physically. It makes me sad, concerned that she's too fragile to bear the news I've come to tell her. She pulls away from my arms, trips over a pair of shoes and falls to the floor. Her body is convulsing. She can't catch her breathe.

"Ginny, look at me." I crouch next to her on the floor.

She lifts her head, her face blotchy and wet. She swipes her nose with her forearm.

"If I could, I would take you home with me in a heartbeat. But that's not why I'm here. That's not how I can help you. I've come to tell you what has happened to me, to tell you my story. I think it will help."

All doubts are gone. The sugar has completely dissolved. I believe the words I've said. And I know what to say to Ginny.

CHAPTER THIRTY-FIVE

Uriah, Today, May 30

I round the corner, headed for the sidewalk, when I see Jacob. He talks on the phone as he leans against a red BMW convertible parked in the driveway. I backtrack and look for cover. A large flowering bush ten feet from Jacob's car offers a decent vantage point. I conceal myself within the branches and pray a dog doesn't wander by, sense my presence, and start barking. It's happened before.

"Dad. Got a problem. It's Ginny. She's worse. I think she's addicted to pain pills, and she drinks all day. She's turned our bedroom into a pigsty. That's how bad it's gotten. I've tried talking with her, but she won't listen." He kicks a piece of gravel and switches the phone to his other ear, listening. Frown lines form when he notices a scuff mark on his loafer. He leans over to rub it with his finger.

"Of course, I'm sure. I live with the woman. Apparently, it runs in her family." He pauses. "I haven't had time to tell you. Hired a private investigator. She's as bad as her father, maybe her mother. Still trying to find her." Several moments pass as Jacob listens. "Look, I can fill you in later. I'm headed out and don't have time to talk." He looks at his watch. "Really, gotta go."

I can't hear the other side of the conversation, of course, but it appears Jacob is pleased by what he hears. "Good. We're in agreement then. As a family, we'll get the help my wife needs. And I agree. At this point, she's unfit to care for my child and your granddaughter. I'm grateful for your support. The kid deserves better." He laughs. "No, I don't think she'll do anything drastic. I'm about to run an errand. A friend of Ginny's promised to come over in a few minutes. Maybe she can talk some sense in her. Do me a favor, though, prepare Mom for what we need to do. Okay, then. Later."

Jacob pockets his phone and smiles broadly. "Yep, getting Mom onboard will be easy."

Just as the streetlights turn on, I look to my left and see an older man, maybe a neighbor, walking toward Jacob's driveway. "Jacob. So glad I caught you." He throws up his hand in greeting. "Could I have a word?"

"I'm in a hurry," Jacob says. He opens the trunk with his key fob, loads his overnight bag, and slams the hood. He checks his watch before walking to the driver's side and opening the door. "Could this wait? I have a plane to catch and I'm running late."

"Oh, I won't keep you," the man says, as Jacob climbs into his car. "Just wanted to ask about Ginny. You know, my wife broke her foot over the winter and can't get out as much as she'd like . . ."

"What does that have to do with Ginny?" Jacob cuts him short and starts the engine.

From the flowering bush, I see the man's jaw go slack. His eyes open wide. He stammers. "Well, my wife enjoys your wife's company and loves seeing the baby. The visits lift her spirits, and Ginny hasn't dropped by in more than a week. That's why I'm asking. Are Ginny and little Laurel okay?"

"I'd no idea Ginny spent time with your wife." Jacob doesn't break eye contact with the older man now standing close to his car. "I will ask her about this."

The man frowns and shakes his head slightly. "I don't want to cause trouble . . ."

Jacob's eyes narrow and his voice sounds harsh. "As I said, I'm in a hurry, but since you've asked, my family is okay. I'll be sure to call the moment we need your help. Until then, assume all is well. I must be going." Jacob waves dismissively and puts the car in gear.

The neighbor shakes his head, perhaps in disgust or disbelief, as he watches Jacob back into the street and drive away. He walks slowly back to his house, mumbling under his breath.

Could anyone be more arrogant?

CHAPTER THIRTY-SIX

Today, May 30

Ginny lies in a heap, refusing to get up after her slapdash effort packing a suitcase. I wrap both arms around her waist and drag her to the bed to prop her up. Though she can't weigh more than one hundred pounds, she feels like dead weight.

"Ginny, look at me." She's sweating. Her pulse seems normal, but what would I know? "Are you okay?" She slumps down, and she doesn't respond for a minute or two, making me worried she's in shock. Or reacting to the alcohol. Did she swallow a pill without me noticing? Or have I made the situation worse? I'm not telling her anything until I'm convinced she's physically okay and can mentally handle what I'm here to say.

Eventually, she nods and looks at me. Her face has a grayish cast, but her eyes are focused. She's gotten her breathing under control. But if looks could kill . . .

"I'm here to help, not to hurt. Maybe I should just go." I stand and head for the door. It's a ploy, a gamble. Will it work?

"Say what you came to say and then go." Ginny says. "I want to be alone."

"Okay, but if you want me to leave, tell me. I'll honor whatever *you* want."

I've made a big deal about my story, but where to start? Should I tell her everything that happened today? Or confine it to the important parts? I tell her everything.

I had to get up early. I would've preferred spending the morning in bed, but a deadline loomed. My next listing needed repairs before a photographer could take pictures. Dad, a former home remodeler, accepted the job and hired me as his gofer. He wanted to get in, get out, finish the job in a day. He told me to expect him early and to be ready.

I was in bad mood. I woke up that way. Money was tight. Making matters worse, Georgie had thrown up on my rug, forcing me to waste valuable minutes scraping up chunks and scrubbing the slimy residue. My backyard wasn't fenced so his usual twenty-minute walk couldn't be avoided. He spent the time sniffing every bush in the neighborhood, and I didn't have time for his nonsense. I yanked his leash—a homemade contraption looped across my shoulder to afford hands-free walking—and told him to move on. He looked pitiful, so, I gave him another five minutes to do his thing.

By the time we got home, Dad was in my driveway. Georgie jumped on the sofa, and I watched him burrow beneath his favorite down comforter. "Is there a dog under there?" I asked. The blanket moved as his tail wagged. I laughed. "Thatta boy." The blanket moved again, and I walked out the front door.

After days of torrential rain, the sunshine nearly blinded me. The heat was oppressive, and the air was thick and smelled of rotting vegetation. How I wanted to be back in bed, with the ceiling fan zipping around keeping me cool. The heat and humidity only worsened as the day progressed. We were working in a small bathroom without air conditioning. Between the tile dust and ninety-degree temperatures, my mood and attitude got worse. My throat felt like it had been dragged through sawdust.

We knocked off for the day and stopped at the quickie mart to buy a six-pack. Sitting on my porch, Dad and I drank our beers and made plans to watch the hockey championship after dinner with Mom. I mentioned I wanted to cool off at the river before coming over. Would he take Georgie with him? By that time, Bud, the mooching neighbor, limped over, no doubt looking for a free beer. And Dad left with Georgie in tow.

"I never did that," I say to Ginny.

"What?"

I never let anyone take Georgie anywhere. He only travels shotgun with me. If I go somewhere and need my parents to dog sit, he gets dropped off first. I didn't do that this time. Even now, telling Ginny, I'm amazed by my out-of-character behavior. Did I know something even then?

Ginny looks at me and deep lines form between her eyebrows. She still looks a little green around the gills, but at least she's tracking. Maybe I'll get through this and be on my way, assured of

Ginny's well-being, confident she'll overcome.

With Georgie gone, I changed into my swim trunks, locked my house, and took off in my damaged Chrysler Pacifica, Mom-Mom's former ride. Even if I had the Benjamins to fix it, I wouldn't have. My mother loaned her fancy crossover whenever I needed to squire a client. Furthermore, Georgie and I didn't mind being seen in the wrecked hand-me-down. A car is a car, and where I was headed, looks didn't matter.

I couldn't wait to get there . . . a former grist mill, a fav among the locals. Although I'm probably only one of few who knows, the site—along with the mill's crumbling foundation and low-head dam spanning the Little River—is listed on the National Register of Historic Places. Aimee and I have spent a lot of time there and call it our hillbilly resort.

We coined the term, not to make fun of the regulars who go there, but because it's accurate. I can't imagine the country club or monied class, people like Jacob or Chelsey, stepping foot on the place. Bathrooms don't exist. Neither do picnic tables. One lonely trashcan serves the entire area, which is rough and ungroomed, especially below the dam where heavy rains have washed out the ground and created deep ruts.

The weekend warriors, many covered from head to toe in tatts or attired in bathing suits several sizes too small, aren't looking for fancy. They're looking for a free place to cool off and hang out, hassle-free and unmolested by what they consider onerous rules. So, they pack their cars with coolers, lawn chairs, towels, and blankets, and spread them out on a narrow swath of green above the dam, or along the rutted, pebbled area below beneath the trees.

I get it. Aimee and I go there for the same reason. We aren't looking for fancy, and we certainly don't rock the bathing suits.

When I got there, I saw an older man leaning against the only truck in the gravel parking lot. I thought it was odd, but I shrugged it off. A pre-adolescent boy walked along the bank, heaving rocks into the river. I said "hey" to the kid and headed toward the rope swing.

"Ginny, no one was in the water. That was so strange. Regardless of the day, hot weather draws people like flies. I knew it had rained, but the water looked calm."

Why wasn't anyone in the water? I scratched my head and wondered if Aimee would advise against jumping in. She could read the river better than anyone I knew. I again dismissed my second thoughts, thinking only about how good it would feel to wash off the day's grime and get into a better frame of mind. *Cooling waters. A baptism of sorts. Yes, that's what I needed.* I walked back to my car and threw my phone and wallet on Georgie's seat before heading back to the bank and rope swing.

The boy was only a few feet way. He stared at me but said nothing, despite my friendly thumbs-up. I kicked off my flip-flops.

Ginny bites her lip.

"Do you know anything about low-head dams?" I ask her.

"Not really."

I nod. "The experts call them drowning machines. Within seconds, Ginny, I knew I was in trouble. Big trouble."

The current was strong beneath the surface. My heart

hammered as I flailed around, trying to reach the bank. In a blink, the current propelled me over the dam and dumped me amid the more powerful recirculating currents—the vortex—below. It was the very place Aimee and I always avoided. I felt like I was inside the drum of a commercial clothes dryer, tumbling relentlessly. I couldn't free myself and was losing my breath.

Ginny's eyes widen as she bites her knuckle. She wants this to end well. Who wouldn't?

Stress takes your mind to weird places. For a second, my thoughts went to our family dog. She fell into our neighbor's pool and got trapped beneath the solar blanket, but I don't divulge that. I want to give Ginny hope and know the next part of my story will help.

"Ginny, I never explained why I didn't talk to God. You did, and your high opinion of me mattered. But this time I did. I asked God to save me, and that's when I saw a hand reach through the water. I grabbed it."

CHAPTER THIRTY-SEVEN

Today, May 30

At that moment, my joy was indescribable. Another chance at the brass ring. When death seemed certain, someone had saved me. Who was it? The old man? A rescuer? Either was possible, and I marveled at how fast God worked. Maybe Granny had been right. Maybe an all-powerful God had our backs. Maybe He orchestrated my rescue, as well as another two weeks earlier. The local newspaper published the story, along with color photos of a swimmer clinging to a rope as rescue workers pulled him to safety.

Ginny moves closer to me on the floor, our legs outstretched. She touches my arm. The tingle doesn't come this time. How much my life has changed.

"I didn't dwell on who saved me—not at first," I say, debating whether to tell her about Uriah, who confirmed his identity at the river earlier. I *had* invited Uriah into my life when I was a little kid, scared senseless when a stranger asked me if I needed a ride. I knew then that I needed a protector. And unbeknownst to me, Uriah had come. He urged me to run like a jack rabbit, and I did, my legs and arms pumping, as I fled from someone who meant me harm. From that point forward, Uriah never left my side.

"No. One of my first thoughts was Aimee and a special gala she's invited me to," I say. "She's receiving an entrepreneur-of-the-year award and wants me to be her date."

Ginny's face softens, maybe happy that the conversation has veered to a different, cheerier topic.

"Of course, I accepted. Free food and a chance to see Aimee dressed up in fancy clothing. . . . Well, I couldn't miss that." I shake my head. "Then she invites me to go shopping with her to buy an outfit . . . *at a thrift store*. Ginny, I wish you could see the get-up she bought. One hot mess, and I told her that if she wore that outfit, I'd relinquish my man card and wear my Richard Simmons Halloween costume. Red-and-white striped bootie shorts, wig, and all."

Ginny tosses her head back and laughs. Her eyes look a little brighter. Though momentarily pleased my Aimee moment has amused her, I'm procrastinating, a lingering trait. I look at the dresser and results of Ginny's haphazard effort to pack a suitcase. I study the towel she used after she'd gotten sick earlier and the dirty diaper lying a few inches from her feet. So much is at stake, but I hold fast to Uriah's words about this being a mountaintop moment, how Ginny would listen to me. I get on with it.

I didn't think only about Aimee, I tell Ginny. I thought about my life in general. My mind raced from one memory to next, but one stood out, relived in vivid detail—the time my parents had taken me and my brothers to southern Maryland. I may have been six or seven at the time and hadn't thought about the trip in years. Ultimately, it would foreshadow what happened to me, and I suppose that's why it popped into my head.

"Why did you go there?" Ginny moves to get more comfortable. She seems to have forgotten Jacob and seems to be listening intently.

For a spell, as I explain, my parents would spend weekends hunting for property along the river. This was one such trip. We had stayed at a large hotel chain and marina on one of the many creeks that feed the Patuxent River, which flows into the Chesapeake Bay. We'd arrived late in the afternoon, and after settling in, we went outside to investigate the hotel's pool and marina. With all those boats bobbing in their slips, it looked like a floating city to me. Condominiums ringed the property.

Dad had been wearing flip-flops, the cheap kind without any tread. My baby brother, Scott, was perched on his shoulders. My brother, Cameron, the kid in the middle, held one of my mom's hands and she made me hold the other. We walked slowly behind Dad and Scott. The docks had been slippery due to an earlier rain.

"What happened?" Ginny asks.

"He slipped."

"Who slipped? I'm not following."

"My dad slipped, and Scott fell into the river. I saw Scott's hair floating above his head before he sank from view. I never saw Dad move so fast. My mother was shrieking as he dove into the water."

He snatched my brother around his torso, and in one fluid

motion, plunked him, wet and screaming, onto the wood planking at our feet. Dad hoisted himself back onto the walkway and bear-hugged him. Unlike me, Scott never said much as a little kid. He and Cameron always let me do the talking. What Scott lacked in language skills, he certainly made up for in temper. He pounded the top of Dad's head with his fists.

"Dad was a hero. But I guess Scott thought Dad had let him down. He hadn't protected him, and boy was he mad."

I then re-experienced the long walk back to the hotel . . . Dad's flip-flops flapping his feet and the creek water coursing off their hair and clothing, leaving puddles on the corridor floor with each step that Dad took. As the elevator doors opened, the desk manager ordered a housekeeper to mop the floor.

We spent the rest of the night inside our room. I don't know what we ate for dinner or how it got there. My mind never captured that detail. What it *did* capture was the sound of the too-loud television and Mom changing my brothers' diapers, washing their faces, and getting them into their pajamas. She told me to do likewise, and I balked. Too weary to enforce her order, she pulled the covers down on one of the two king-sized beds, plumped the pillows, and laid down. Dad eventually joined her. Side-by-side, they stared in numbed silence at the television set for what seemed hours. I soon lost interest in their doings.

My brothers and I took advantage of the situation. Because we weren't allowed to do so at home, we jumped on the other bed until our muscles ached. Scott flopped around in the middle of the mattress, laughing. He had already forgotten his plunge into the river.

My parents never forgot. My mother told me later that, until Scott's fall into the drink, she never thought about the death of one of her children.

But his fall forced her to consider the capriciousness of life, and the thought made her physically sick.

CHAPTER THIRTY-EIGHT

Today, May 30

I sit next to Ginny on the bedroom floor, crack my knuckles, and rock my head from side-to-side. My neck and shoulders ache from the tension.

Ginny hasn't made a sound. She absently plucks tiny lint balls from her well-worn sweatpants. "No one is ever prepared for the unthinkable, are they?"

"Never. The thief in the night."

She rubs her forehead. "Sounds like you had a near-death experience. I've read where people recall or relive important moments in their lives. You said you grabbed someone's hand after you were drawn into that vortex, or whatever you called it. Isn't that what you said? Whose hand did you grab?"

I don't want to reveal whose hand I took but confirm her observation. "It *was* a near-death experience." I felt like a drone,

---

Lori Keesey

hovering high over the river, the dam, the parking lot, my vision never clearer. I watched everything happening on the ground below. Never had I experienced anything quite so surreal or frightening. I had absolutely no control over my body and instinctively knew my fate rested in the hands of another.

Ginny's mouth falls open. "This is amazing," she says. "What happened next?" She moves a little closer to me on the floor.

The young boy ran toward the older man who was leaning against his truck. I couldn't make out the boy's words, but he was yelling, pointing frantically at the river. The poor kid looked upset and scared. The man glanced up from his phone, his eyes narrowed. He seemed annoyed by the boy's interruption but started walking fast toward the riverbank, following in the boy's wake to the exact spot where I'd jumped, close to the rope swing. The man moved his head slowly, cupping his eyes with his hands to block the glare. He pulled his phone from his back pocket, tapped three numbers, and started shouting into his phone.

That's when I saw myself. Floating face-down in the water.

Within minutes, a large pick-up truck roared into the parking lot. The driver, a barrel-chested man with well-defined biceps, sprinted to the bank. As he waded into the thigh-high, rushing waters on the other side of the dam, he struggled against the current and slipped on the river stones, but kept his footing as he pulled my body to the pebbled shore.

He pushed my T-shirt up around my neck and started to administer CPR. His biceps bulged each time he compressed my chest. Sweat formed along his hairline, and the veins in his neck

262

popped. He wiped his face and began anew. My head bobbed each time he pressed down, and angry red spots began to form on my chest. I couldn't feel pressure in my chest, I couldn't feel anything but an overwhelming feeling of gratitude.

This man put his life on the line to save mine.

An ambulance and several sheriff's deputies arrived next. As they got out of their vehicles, they shouted into their radios and at one another. They worked like a well-oiled machine as one strung up yellow police tape and another walked toward the old man who now stood next to his truck, smacking his phone against his thigh as the young boy burrowed his head into his belly.

I wanted to tell the boy it would be okay. I would be fine, but the words wouldn't come. How would I tell him anyway?

My attention was then drawn to the other man—the well-built guy who'd pulled me from the river. As he tried to blow life into my lifeless body, the EMT maneuvered the ambulance closer. Both he and his partner jumped out and shouted something as they pulled the gurney from the back. They loaded me onto the stretcher and slammed the doors. The siren screamed and the tires spun as they sped onto the highway, leaving my rescuer at the scene, kicking rocks.

"Seeing your body disconnected from your soul, your personality, and everything that defines you is strange. My body was gone, but I stayed on the scene. Weird. I wondered how I could be in two places at once."

Ginny absently plays with the wristband. She doesn't look at me.

That's when I saw my mother and father at the side of the road. Why were they there? That's right, we had a dinner planned, a hockey game to watch. They lived only a few minutes away. No doubt, they'd left a million texts and voicemails before they jumped into their car to see what had become of me.

Dad was barefoot and Mom wore a pair of old shorts and an oversized T-shirt—an outfit she'd never wear in public. She stood on her toes and saw the yellow crime tape and police cruisers, their lights flashing. Her eyes darted back and forth until she spotted my car parked at the other end of the lot. She pointed, grasped my father's arm, and rushed toward the taped-off area. Dad followed, picking his way through the rocks and debris in his bare feet.

"Mom has never been able to hide her emotions very well. She wanted answers, and the police were ignoring both her and Dad, along with others who showed up just to gawk at the scene."

Mom crossed her arms and then let them drop to her sides. Her eyes widened. A deputy glanced up from his notebook and saw them standing next to the strung tape. He walked over and asked a question. She nodded. He glanced down at his notebook and said something. My father's shoulders fell, and his chest seemed to cave in. He looked like he would collapse.

Mom stepped away and covered her mouth with her palm. She glanced once more at my car, said something to my father, and then they rushed to their car, speeding off in the same direction as the ambulance.

CHAPTER THIRTY-NINE

Today, May 30

Ginny pulls her legs to her chest and buries her head in her knees, her back against the side of the bed. She must sense I'm watching her because she turns her head to look at me.

"Ginny, are you okay? Do you want me to continue?"

She shakes her head. "What's going on, TC? I don't understand any of this. Are you real or am I hallucinating?"

How do I tell the rest of my story?

"I used to think near-death experiences were bunk, the imaginings of devout people who interpret a brush with death as evidence of God's existence. I'll never doubt again." Ginny's worry lines disappear, and she lets out a heavy sigh. "What people say is true," I say. "I saw that blindingly bright light people talk about. I found myself speeding down a long tunnel. I remembered things that had happened in the past, like the episode with my brother, Scott."

But I also saw video clips. I don't know how else to describe them. It was like re-watching a movie and seeing details that you hadn't noticed the first time.

I tell Ginny about the first one involving my friend, Dusty. She was the one who had been married to the man who reminded me of Jacob. The scene showed us sitting on my front porch, eating my specialty chili. I could smell the peppers, the cumin, the Sriracha sauce. I could smell her perfume and shampoo. My senses heightened. I don't know where Adrian was. I didn't ask. I'd started avoiding him weeks earlier but kept in touch with her. We only talked when he wasn't home.

At the time, I had noticed her nervousness. But in this video, I saw her anguish through a clearer optic. She looked pale and the dark circles under her eyes made me think she hadn't slept in days. She dragged her hands through her hair. She wouldn't look at me.

Adrian had been her one and only. She felt bad that her marriage wasn't working, and she wondered if she should try to salvage it—but life with him had become intolerable. He was unemployed. They were broke. And now he was physically threatening her. He nearly killed her when he purposely crashed his car into a concrete jersey wall during a fit of rage. She called it a death by a million cuts, and she couldn't find another way out. She was considering leaving him and wanted my advice.

By re-experiencing the event and seeing the interaction in a new light, I realized I'd done the right thing. Dusty simply needed confirmation. She couldn't fix him. Nobody could fix him unless he admitted his problems and sought professional help. And that wasn't likely. How could he be wrong when he was always right? I'd encouraged her to leave, to see a therapist. If he agreed to get counseling, give it another go. But until that happened, I'd never tell Adrian where she was, regardless of how much he threatened me.

"What did she say?" Ginny wets her lips and nods slightly. *Does she recognize herself in Dusty's story?* "What did she do?"

"She hugged and thanked me. She left town a few days later, early in the morning, a bittersweet moment for me. She didn't tell me her plans, and I didn't know she'd made up her mind until I found her note shoved into a tiny crack between the front door and jamb. It would've been nice to see her again, but I never did."

"What did the note say?"

"She said I saved her from a life of unending pain." I look at my lap and describe the crumbled, tear-stained note now folded and placed inside the Bible that my aunt had given me, along with other papers important to me. I take a big breath. "She said she'd miss my hugs."

"I understand her affection for you," Ginny says. "I can relate."

I nod. The compliment would have launched me into the stratosphere a year ago.

As one scene ended, another queued up. They were incredible in their lucidness.

The visual then shifted to the night that one of my parents' tenants had called me. She was a recently divorced newcomer to the area. Lonely and depressed, she needed to talk with someone. I had a lot going on the next day and planned to go to bed early, but I couldn't put her off. I suggested we go out for a beer.

We ended up staying until closing time. She needed a night out, a chance to connect with someone face-to-face. I tell Ginny that she's since moved to another apartment, but I see her now and then at Brady's, hanging out with her coworkers and having a good time. She always speaks to me and reminds me of how I showed up when she most needed a friend.

"These near-death stories fascinate me," Ginny says, sitting up straighter. "In a weird way, they're hopeful. They give you a whole new perspective. Don't you think? What else did you see?"

They do give you a different perspective, I agree, and in my case, one that was long overdue. I then watched one of the many times I'd counseled Mitchell, a guy I met through Aimee. I felt bad for this guy. His father had a drinking problem. His mother jumped from one guy to another. All his siblings had different fathers. She couldn't handle Mitchell, so she shuttled him off to one relative after another until he landed at his father's. He made Mitchell's life worse than it already was.

"I don't think Mitchell ever heard an encouraging word from his dad," I say. "And the thing is, he is bright, talented, and funny. If you hear nothing but criticism, though, you start doubting yourself."

I'm striking a nerve now. Ginny resumes the cheek chewing and lip biting. Maybe she's not so sure about hearing more about my near-death experience.

"You question your worth, right?" I ask.

She doesn't comment, but her narrowed eyes and far-off gaze tell me she hears everything.

"Mitchell looked up to me. He trusted me. I told him to never settle, to go back to school, to believe in himself. Sometimes being his personal self-help guru grew old—but, you know, my advice helped. He's back in trade school, training to become an electrician. He'll be okay."

This is where the videos changed direction, I tell Ginny. They gave me even greater insights into the people who'd entered my life long before I met her. In this one, I saw the after-school kids camp where I worked as a teenager. There, I met one of my favorite kids, a runt with an attitude larger than my own.

He lived with his single mom in a neighborhood dominated by gangs. His father was in jail. Within minutes of meeting this kid, he mouthed off, telling me that he did what he wanted, and nobody bossed him. He was mad at the world. Eventually, I got through to him. Did he want to spend his life in and out of jail? I didn't pull any punches. He could be great—he *was* great—but he had to dump the bad attitude and stop blaming others. He had to start thinking of what he *could* do with his life, not what he couldn't.

Why hadn't I heeded my own advice?

"The coolest thing about that video is that I also saw him, as he is today. He's a counselor, helping kids who grew up like he did. He's doing what you planned to do."

Ginny shakes her head and holds up her hand. She doesn't want to discuss her plans. I don't either—not at this point anyway.

"But the scene that impressed me the most was the time a friend came for a week-long visit, the last time we spent any time together under the same roof. We hung out in my living room and listened to music, talking about movies, books, and stuff we cared about."

Ginny exhales, perhaps relieved that the story's moved on, past the kid who grew up and became a counselor. "Don't you see this friend anymore?" Her question sounds like a diversionary tactic. Ginny doesn't want me talking about her. I'll play along . . . for now. But time is short. I can feel it in my bones.

"We're still close, but she lives in South America," I tell Ginny. "Emailing and texting aren't the same. I miss our face-to-face conversations. They were epic."

She, too, is ambivalent about God—not because she doesn't believe in a higher power. She just doesn't think about it. Like me once, she puts her faith in the tangible, the things she can touch and see. We thought we knew everything. We had the world figured out.

I choke up. "Now I want to tell her we couldn't have been more wrong. We didn't know anything. I believe I re-experienced that conversation for a reason."

"I don't understand."

"The worldly truth we both revered isn't truth. I needed to see how misguided I had been."

Ginny buries her head in her knees.

CHAPTER FORTY

Uriah, Today, May 30

Other than for the senior who asked about Ginny's well-being, I don't see anyone. No one is out and about. I shouldn't be surprised. People today hide inside their air-conditioned cocoons, protecting themselves from unwanted conversations. I look at the streetlights that now cast shadows across the neighborhood. I better go back inside. I've seen and heard enough anyway.

I retrace my steps to the back of the house, looking around to make sure I'm still alone. What if the French doors are locked? What if I can't get back inside? Why am I so worried? No one can see me anyway. I can just slip in quietly, check on TC, and go home. Time is getting short.

CHAPTER FORTY-ONE

Today, May 30

'm conflicted. I want to go with Uriah, but I also want to stay with Ginny.

I want to take her back to Tennessee, to Georgie, to my crazy oddball neighborhood. I want to belly up to the bar at Brady's and talk politics with Bryan. I want to stay up late at night, watching videos, listening to podcasts, and writing jokes in my little black book. The one I left on my kitchen table before I headed out for my swim. I want to hike. Sell houses. Make money. I want to hang out with my grandmother, Mom-Mom, and yuk it up with my brothers, aunts, uncles, and cousins. See Aimee and go to her gala.

I want to live my life.

But I have a job to do, and it's one I've been doing my entire life.

Before I went to the river and re-experienced those special moments while traveling toward the light, though, I'd never fully appreciated the impact I had made in the lives of others. I'd convinced myself that I wasn't destined for distinction. Wouldn't find the cure for cancer. Wouldn't become a gazillionaire or change the world, for better or worse. I'd ignored the voice of my better angel and listened to the other the guy, the one who called me random, a fluke, a clump of cells that evolved into a sack of flesh and bones. I would live, like millions of others, "a life of quiet desperation" as once described by Henry David Thoreau.

Standing takes effort. My legs feel wobbly, but I manage to lean down and pick up one of the empty bottles of wine. Ginny watches but doesn't say a word. She narrows her eyes as if daring me to mention her drinking.

I take the challenge.

No more procrastination.

It's showtime.

"What's going on here, Ginny?" I wave the bottle in the air. "You told me you didn't drink, that you had no interest given your experience with Jimmy and your mother." I set the bottle on her nightstand. She opens her mouth, ready to say something, but my upheld hand stops her. "I'm not judging. That would be a touch hypocritical, don't you think?" I shrug. "Just curious. Seems out of character for you."

Several seconds pass. Is she going to tell me?

"Well, if you must know, Jacob has a wine cellar." She lifts her chin higher.

"Lots of people have wine cellars, especially in tony neighborhoods like this one. You still haven't answered my question."

She doesn't say anything for what seems minutes. She frowns, and I can tell she's confused by the sudden change in conversation and my insistent tone. Eventually, she tells me about the night Jacob had offered a glass of wine. She'd been crying all day thinking about Granny. The baby had colic and screamed for hours. Laurel's abdomen was tight as a drum. Jacob placed his arm around Ginny's waist and told her that a small glass might help. And it did. She relaxed and had a nice evening with him. They cuddled, something they hadn't done in a long time. He seemed so understanding, Ginny says, assuring her that time would heal. The baby would outgrow the colic. He would take care of her and Laurel.

I glance at the other bottle and marvel at Jacob's manipulation. He would no more take care of them than admit he was wrong about anything.

"What do you think I'm doing?" Ginny interrupts my thoughts. Her voice sounds defensive. "Do you think I'm drinking in this bedroom all alone?"

"Kind of looks like it." I gesture to the piles of clothing and trash. "It doesn't look like you leave this room either."

She scoffs and shakes her head. "At night I'll have a glass or two." She glances at the empty bottles. "And don't be silly. Of course, I leave this room."

Does she think she can snow me? We're friends. Why can't she see I'm not judging, just wondering? I've come to help.

"Not buying it, Ginny. Tell me the truth."

She confesses she doesn't go out much. Too much effort getting ready. Taking care of Laurel every day consumes her, drains her of what little energy she has. "Sometimes, I slip out to visit the lady next door. She took a tumble and can't get out to golf or lunch with her lady friends." Ginny chews her lip. "She and her husband are empty-nesters without grandchildren, and I get lonely. They love the baby."

I scratch my nose and ponder my next move. I take a couple steps toward the bed, lean over, and retrieve the bag of pills from beneath the pillow.

"What about these?"

Her head swivels to see what I'm talking about. She gasps.

"How did you find those?" She gets up faster than I thought possible and tries to snatch them from my hand.

I sidestep her and lift them over my head and am reminded of the time Aimee tried to steal my phone at the festival, one of many wild episodes, a turning point in my then-budding friendship with Ginny. A lifetime ago.

I shake the bag. "Where did you get them?"

"Give them back."

I shake my head. "Not a chance."

I sit on the edge of the bed. Ginny stands in front of me, radiating fury.

"You have a nice mix here." I open the bag and dump some of the pills onto the bed. "What's this? Looks like Tylenol. This looks like Ibuprofen. Not sure about these." I examine a fistful of white pills, each of them etched with a number. "Could these be painkillers of some sort?"

"What are you now? A pharmacist?"

"I don't need to be a pharmacist to know what they are. Is your doctor still prescribing painkillers? What's it been—*three months* since Laurel was born? You shouldn't need these by now. Not unless you have a problem."

She shakes her head. "They're old. I didn't take them all."

She reminds me of a trapped animal. Her head pivots as she backs up. "You know what? I don't have to explain anything to you." She turns her back to me and walks toward the dresser.

"So, they're just a stash for a rainy day?" My voice sounds sarcastic and in-your-face. One that's used only rarely around friends. I can't even believe the change coming over me. I look more closely at a couple of blue pills still in the bag. They are imprinted with "M" on one side and "30" on the other.

One advantage to keeping current on national affairs shines bright now. Does she think they're pharmaceutical-quality Oxycodone Hydrochloride? That would be bad enough. But that's highly doubtful. Their color and etching are off. More likely they're fentanyl or fentanyl-laced, cooked up in some foreign country. Doesn't she read the news? Hear the nurses talk about the fentanyl overdoses? She is an emergency-room nurse, after all. Living in a big city like Atlanta, she must have had firsthand experience with the fentanyl crisis sweeping the country, causing thousands and thousands of deaths.

"What about the blue ones? Where did you get those?" I cross my arms and wait.

She faces me and stares at the pills, rubbing her jaw. Her body seems to tremble.

"I'm on maternity leave," she finally says, turning her back to pick up one of the decorative boxes on the dresser. "I'm supposed to go back in a few weeks."

"If you take this stockpile, you won't have to worry about going back to work." She looks over her shoulder. "Actually, all you need is one of those." I point to one of the blue pills. If my suspicions are correct, even a smidgeon can cause an overdose.

My frustration grows. "Why don't you just crush one and use a rolled dollar bill to snort it. Works faster that way."

Ginny spins to face me, shaking her head.

"Is that what you want, Ginny?" I ask. "What about her?" I tilt my head in the direction of her sleeping child. "I guess you figured Melinda would take care of her." I don't let up. "That's why you called her, isn't it? You hoped she'd find you stiff in your bed and then take Laurel home with her. Why would you traumatize Melinda? And do you really believe that Jacob would give up custody? You're deluding yourself, Ginny."

I place each pill back into the bag and rub my hand on my trunks. "Were you planning an overdose? Was that your answer to your problems?"

Ginny is completely still. She opens her mouth to speak, but her words seem to dry up before she can say them. She stands away from me but takes another step back and bumps into the dresser. She shakes her finger at me.

"How do you know this? Why are you here? How did you get here?" Her eyes dart.

"I know a lot of stuff, Ginny. I know your last name.

Carmichael, right? Didn't learn that until, I don't know, a few hours ago. But it doesn't matter anymore."

She tries to say something, but I don't let her speak.

"I saw everything, Ginny. I watched you. Heard your phone conversation with Melinda. Saw you trip over your shoes. Witnessed Jacob's cruelty. By the way, his manhandling has left two red bruises on your face. Bet that wasn't the first time he decided to get rough."

She touches the bruises and blinks slowly.

"We have free will. You know that better than anyone. Do what you want with these, but an overdose was never a part of your future. The world will be a far uglier place without you in it."

I toss the bag at her.

She catches it and shoves it into her front pocket. I see the hideous bulge. The empty bottles of wine and broken wineglass. Laurel's bottle and dirty diaper. I can see everything except the thoughts inside her head.

CHAPTER FORTY-TWO

Uriah, Today, May 30

I slip through the French doors. The house is quiet, except for the hum of Jacob's Sub-Zero refrigerator. As I start toward the staircase, curiosity gets the better of me. I turn the doorknob on the formerly locked foyer door, and to my surprise, it flies open. Interesting. Jacob must have been in a hurry and got sloppy. I step in.

The desk at the center of the bookshelf-lined study is piled high with folders. A map of Georgia rests on top of one, and a brochure advertising a romantic getaway in Savannah on another. The laptop is open. I touch the trackpad, and a website pops up. Why isn't this thing passcode protected?

Not my problem.

I sit down on the leather desk chair and start reading.

Ginny might be in more trouble than I thought. Substance abuse. Georgia custody laws. I glance at the desk and see a list of family law attorneys. I check the browser's history and am convinced he's scheming a custody battle over Laurel. Jacob's cruelty has no bottom. He has no interest in that child. I saw his interaction with the baby. Didn't he wipe his hands after placing the baby on the bed? He acted as if he'd touched something unpleasant, much like whatever is decaying in this room. I sniff. What is causing that putrid smell?

I'm not hanging around to find out. As I head for the door, my eyes fall on another framed photo of Jacob. I look closer. He's pictured at a costume party, dressed appropriately enough as a long-fanged wolf. The mask shows only his eyes—the window into the soul. They appear dead, flat, and I turn away. Jacob is a predator. Why is he allowed to prey on Ginny? I make a mental note to ask the Big Man. He knows. He knows everything, including how this mission will turn out.

I've been cheering for TC for as long as I can remember and sense now that he needs me. I turn from the photo and head for the staircase.

CHAPTER FORTY-THREE

Today, May 30

I may not see the thoughts in Ginny's head, but the lucidity in my own staggers me. Before Jacob had snatched Ginny from my life, she asked me to consider God's purpose for my life. I did think about it, but I never came up with an answer that satisfied. But the foolhardy leap into the river and my trip here have changed that.

My eyes are wide open now. *Why hadn't I grasped it sooner?*

I'm not supposed to be a doctor like Ginny. My purpose is simpler, maybe even more important. At some level, dancing around at the edges of my consciousness, I knew I had the ability to connect with people. I practiced it and took advantage of it. But my gift never struck me as anything special.

I thrashed around, hyper-focused on my failings. I tried to figure out why I wasn't like everyone else, especially my friends who pursued careers and made tons of money—the world's definition of success. I felt like an oddity, an extraordinarily unaccomplished one, bobbing alone in a big sea.

The trip to the river and this mission to Ginny's have made my destiny crystal clear. We're all called to greatness, even in the smallest ways, and failure to carry out the plan for our lives could prevent others from accomplishing theirs. *Hadn't Granny said that once?* She did. And she was right. We're inextricably meshed, like the finest tapestry.

Hard to believe, but the roles have been reversed where Ginny and I are concerned. Who could've known a year ago? My job is to remind Ginny of her purpose and to stop her from doing the unthinkable, an action that would reverberate down through the generations—starting with little Laurel.

The biggest obstacle to success is glaring at me from across the room, waiting to hear what I'll say next. Ginny wraps her arms around her middle. Her narrowed eyes tell me she wants nothing to do with me. One year ago, that would've been impossible. Who, after all, had thrown her arms around my neck and thanked me for helping her see her destiny? The anticipated stop along a smooth highway paved in gold.

I understand her doubts. What do I expect? I show up unannounced and tell her things no one else could possibly know. And then confront her with evidence of her suicidal intentions, all while dodging questions about how I landed here in the first place.

She'll find out soon enough. Time hasn't stopped. I need to finish the job I was asked to do. Uriah is waiting.

"What happened to that girl who believed in miracles and knew exactly how she planned to live her life? What happened to that girl who believed she was destined to carry on Granny's legacy?"

"Don't you think it's kind of obvious?"

I figured she'd respond that way. Within a few hours' time, Ginny gave birth to a child and lost her Granny, the heroine who taught a traumatized little girl about faith and intrinsic value and provided a safe harbor where her granddaughter could heal from the violence and abandonment experienced so early in life. Ginny was alone now, or she thought she was, and she allowed herself to become dependent on a deceiver whose true motivations still eluded her.

More tough talk is needed, and I'm amazed at how God has used me to do His will. The voice inside my head, the one who had always led me astray before, is gone. Forever.

"Granny's looking down, wondering where she went wrong. You weren't created to become someone's plaything. And that's what you've become—Jacob's toy. He's a master at deception, Ginny, and you've let him swat you around for far too long. Don't let him knock the life out of you."

I look around the room and see the clothing heaped on the floor next to the suitcase. Ginny seems to have lost all interest in herself.

"I'd say he's nearly finished the job."

She walks over to the crib, her stringy hair falling into her eyes. She finger-combs it into place and stares at her baby. She exhales and sits in the chair next to the crib. I sit on the edge of the bed. I'll give her space if that's what she wants.

She might think she has nowhere to turn, but that's not true.

She will survive. No, she'll *thrive*. She isn't alone and she never was. I offer the same advice given to Dusty and tell her *again* to pack her clothes, bundle up the baby, and leave. Fast. She must flush the pills, along with her misguided thinking. She should never look back because the world's a big place and is filled with opportunities for women as smart as Ginny.

"Whatever you do," I say, "don't believe his lies."

She touches the bulge, almost protectively, and gives me a fierce look. I shouldn't be surprised by her bitter-sounding voice that I hear next, but it does knock me back a few paces.

"Boy, you're good at telling others what to do, aren't you?" She points her finger at me. She nearly shouts but lowers her voice to avoid waking Laurel. "What happened to that live-and-let-live guy I met? What did you say your motto was? Oh, I remember. 'Hey, bro, not my business.'" Her voice drips with sarcasm. "Guess what? This isn't your business either. Especially since you're only offering advice. No one can help me, including you. And *I will do what I want.*" She touches her chin. "Hmm. Where did I hear that phrase before?" Her grin is ugly. Cynical. "Oh, I know. *You.*"

Why did I think my lecturing would work? A ludicrous strategy. Never worked on me. I look at the ceiling. No answers there. I get why she's disappointed with me. I refused to take her to Tennessee, which was something she suggested. She'd been casting about for solutions, temporary or *permanent*. And as soon as I showed up, a new plan had entered her head. She figured she could escape her situation by going home with me. My refusal had removed that option, boxed her in further. Why hadn't I grasped that before?

I give it another go.

"You're right." I nod. "Talk is cheap."

She crosses her arms and legs, scowling from her safe space across the room. Neither one of us speaks. I wait her out. Eventually she relaxes. She leans her head on the back cushion. I see her swallow as she glances at the crib.

"You're different," she says after a few moments. Her voice is barely audible. "And I'm not talking about appearance either." She glances at her lap, then she looks at me. "You're the same guy, but you're not. I can't put my finger on it. Maybe more somber? Less irreverent? I think that experience in the tunnel has affected you."

Me too. Things are sharper because the gauze has fallen from my eyes. Going to the river and coming here have granted me *perfect* eyesight. "You're right. I've changed because of the truths I've learned. Ginny, do you remember telling me to think about my purpose? It took me a while, but I get it now."

She furrows her brow, looking at me as if I'm talking in riddles.

"I *can* help you understand why you're here, trapped by this." I gesture at the artwork, expensive furniture, piles of clothing, and the bottles. I point to her pocket. "But you must open your mind and listen."

She rubs her temples and squeezes her eyes shut. "You shouldn't have come," she whispers.

Whether she wants me here is immaterial. I'm here and single-minded in my focus. I *will* get through to her and I will start with Jacob. She must see him for who he really is. Otherwise, the cycle will continue.

She was easy pickings for a guy like him, I tell her. I don't give her a chance to interrupt even though she tries. She's beautiful. Intelligent. She makes him look good, and he needs that. But that's only part of it.

"He has a beast to feed, and you're the perfect food source."

"What do you mean . . . a food source?" She pinches her lips together in a straight line and touches the bag that is still in her pocket. *What is she doing? Taunting me?* "You're not making sense. He doesn't need me. I need him, and I've ruined our relationship. I'm not the woman he fell in love with. He might be right. I have deceived him. My life has no meaning or worth. I am everything I *never* wanted to be."

I take a deep breath. Why is she so blind to Jacob and his behaviors? Shouldn't *she* know the signs?

I shut my eyes. *I need help.*

I open my eyes and see Uriah. He stands beyond the threshold. He gives an encouraging nod, and my confidence is restored. Of course. She's a co-dependent. She gives. He takes. She lives her life through him and has lost all sense of herself.

"Do you even know what he is? Love plays no part in his attitude toward you, Ginny. Jacob could be a narcissist or something else. I don't know. I'm not a shrink. But it's obvious he cares only for himself . . . satisfying an insatiable need to control and manipulate others. That's his life force. He beats you down. Love-bombs you. Calls you worthless—an endless cycle of his creation. You must get off that carnival ride."

Ginny covers her face and rocks back and forth.

"If you're embarrassed, don't be," I say. "I have firsthand experience with people like him. Remember, I got involved with that guy, Adrian. I know how easy it is to fall under their influence, swept up by their attention. But your experience is different from mine. Your childhood trauma, Laurel's birth, Granny's death, and your own basic personality . . . the desire to help others . . . made it easier for Jacob to entangle you in his web."

She looks at me. Tears run down her cheeks, but she still looks defiant. She won't break eye contact.

"You don't know everything," she says. "You don't know what it feels like to lose the most important person in your life and then be scorned by another when you've tried *everything* to make the relationship work. What are you trying to do? Make my life worse? Why should I believe you?"

She hasn't a clue about my own feelings of rejection, but I don't let her derail my thoughts.

I speak quickly, reminding her of a conversation we had a year ago. By her own admission, she'd kept most people at arm's length, trusting few. She had to work hard, very hard, to shed her discomfort around people. With Granny gone, she only had Melinda to help her when life threw curveballs.

I glance at the doorway. Uriah nods.

"Jacob knows this. Maybe you didn't tell him everything about your past, but he innately sensed your reticence and took advantage of it."

First, he chipped away at her outer shell, which she erected to shield her from potential hurt and rejection. Once he had a tiny opening, he pushed through, overwhelming her with affection and attention, making her think she needed him alone. The perfect food source for a guy like Jacob.

My mouth dries. Too much talking. No forward motion.

And because her network was already small, his attempt to further isolate Ginny was easy. "He discouraged you from seeing Granny or getting closer to Melinda, right? He ridiculed your friends from home and convinced you they couldn't be trusted. With that done, he had you where he wanted you. Alone. Unsure. Off balance. Completely dependent on him."

Ginny doesn't respond. She bends down and places her hands on her knees. She starts gasping for air. But under her breath, I hear a mantra . . . *"This will pass. This will pass. This will pass."* I hate this part of my mission, but Uriah's nodding confirmation reminds me that Ginny can handle the tough talk. She's lost. But she's picking her way through the obstacles in this torturous diversion from her true path. She simply needs a guide—me—to help her over the finish line. I pick up my narrative.

"Granny's death made it easier. Where else would you go? I get why you might feel trapped. He's good. But guess what? At some point, he'll get bored and discard you. Or worse—he could become more ruthless."

I can't read her face. She stares at her lap and takes big breaths.

"Call Aunt Adele. Come clean. Work out financial arrangements until you get on your feet. And I'll say it again: *avoid him.* Based on everything you've described, he enjoys hurting you, and only makes amends when he feels he's losing control over you. He will destroy you." I pause. "Do you know what's sad? If you follow my advice and leave, he'll find another woman—perhaps someone as loyal as you who will supply his needs. Guys like Jacob don't often see themselves as problems. When they're rejected, they look for other prey. Am I making sense?"

Ginny rests her head on her knees and says something in a small, muffled voice.

"Sorry, didn't catch that."

She lifts her head. "I said, I let you in too."

"The happiest day of my life, Ginny. But you mustn't conflate our relationship with the one you have with Jacob. Controlling people or exploiting their trust isn't me." My mind spins and I can't focus. *What will convince her? Why is she fiddling with those pills?*

I try another tactic, one that—if I'm not careful—could backfire on me.

CHAPTER FORTY-FOUR

Today, May 30

"Jacob isn't your only problem, Ginny." I cup my head in my hands, my arms resting on my thighs. My time here is ending soon, and I know in my core she *must* hear what I'm about to say. Otherwise, she might find herself trapped in the same situation, maybe not here, but wherever she goes next. With another man like Jacob.

"He's just a symptom of a far greater problem."

Ginny sits in the armchair next to the crib and rolls her eyes. "How long do you plan to stay, TC? You've made your point, and frankly, I want to sleep." She covers the bulge with her hand.

"Do you want me to leave? I told you I would."

"I don't know what I want. I'm tired, TC, so unbelievably tired."

"You're not going to like it."

"I haven't liked anything you've said." Again, those challenging eyes. I let her stew for a minute.

"You and your mother are a lot alike." The comment lingers in the air. I'd picked up on some of the similarities when we met last year. But much has happened since then and the comparisons can't be denied . . . or ignored.

"What do you mean?" She spits out the words.

I share the parallels: Both Ginny and her mother experienced broken hearts when the people they loved died. Both got involved with damaged, troubled men who were probably abused themselves as kids. Feeling helpless and trapped, both refused to admit their mistakes, and then they blamed God for their heartbreak.

Ginny doesn't seem to know how to respond. She goes completely still.

"Ginny, you suspected Jacob's issues, didn't you? Certainly, Melinda was on to him."

She closes her eyes and nods imperceptibly, a gesture I would've missed had my eyes not been glued on her sitting across the room.

"But the worst characteristic you share is one your own Granny warned you about. You both refuse to forgive."

Ginny's face turns bright red as she pushes herself partway out of the chair, looking ready to rip out my jugular. Did I give her the same look last year when she talked about God's plans for my life and for hers?

"Why should I forgive her? I'd rather not think about her."

"Because it's a problem. Your unforgiveness is directly related to your entanglement with Jacob. You wanted to prove to yourself and everyone else that you weren't like your mother. You wouldn't be spending your life inside a beat-up trailer, living with an ignorant, violent man. You would rise above that, and Jacob offered the ticket out. I let that register.

"Your mother didn't have the benefit of counseling, as you told me. Is it possible she experienced another shock equally as traumatic as the death of her father?" I raise my eyebrows.

Ginny opens her eyes wide and chews her lip but doesn't speak.

"You don't know, do you? Maybe she deserves your compassion. Not your unforgiveness, which keeps you in the past, blinded to the future. For all these reasons, and I'm sure others exist, you need to forgive her. And, oh by the way, before you ask, I *do* know the toxicity of unforgiveness. It happened to my family."

When my mountain-living grandfather left Mom-Mom, the trap door opened, I tell Ginny, hurling my mother, aunts, uncles and us kids into chaos and uncertainty. My sense of family turned on its head. I hated him for what he did. So did they. But Mom-Mom had set us straight. My grandfather had broken our hearts, she agreed, but if we allowed our anger to fester, it would only grow and metastasize, potentially infecting generations to come. We'd be defined by bitterness and debilitated by bad decisions. We deserved more in life, my Mom-Mom said.

I so miss her and her wisdom.

"I'm not saying you must be your mother's best friend." I continue. "I'm saying you need to let go of the hurts. Don't empower your pain. It's a cancer and it's already done enough damage to you, your mother, and even Granny."

She stands next to the crib, grabbing the rails as she faces me. What is she doing? Does she want to protect her baby from my words?

My mind recalls the moment Uriah brought me to Ginny's. My confusion. Worry. Now I'm grateful for this mission. At last, I know and appreciate my special gifts. What if I hadn't shown up tonight? What if she had swallowed those pills or took just one of the blue ones? She needed someone who loved and appreciated her. And I showed up.

Everything hangs in the balance, including little Laurel's fate. The little one is my trump card, and I need to play the hand well. I point to little Laurel sleeping innocently in her crib.

"Your mother abandoned you. What do you think you'd be doing to Laurel? Same thing. But at least your mother made sure you had Granny. Poor Laurel would have Jacob. With you gone, he'd fill her head with lies about you. He'd play the role of a grieving single parent, the doting father. But behind closed doors, he'd play the very game he has played with you. Come on, Ginny. Your love for Laurel is obvious to anyone with eyes to see. Jacob is incapable of loving anyone but himself, and that includes your child."

Ginny's body sways. She grips the rails tighter.

My voice becomes softer as I remind her of Granny's precious contribution. She got the ball rolling. Now it was up to Ginny to keep it going and to forgive both her mother and father. Forget the past. Embrace the future. Think of her own purpose as Laurel's mother, as a doctor. So many will benefit. It was that simple. She couldn't give up because she'd fallen under the spell of someone like Jacob. Many people do, including me—the guy who prided himself in picking amazing friends.

"You understand what I'm saying, right?"

She draws in a big breath and exhales. Her face softens, the anger recedes.

"I'm sorry for my harsh words. I know they're not my style, and I worried they might traumatize you further. But I had it under very good authority that they would help you pull the blinders off." Out of the corner of my eye, I see Uriah. He mouths words at me and makes gestures.

"Ginny, one more thing—if you're willing to hear it."

"Haven't stopped you yet, have I?" She gives me a tiny smile.

"You have everything you need to live your life. You don't need to rely on others or their money, prestige, whatever, to prove your worth." She listens intently and nods. "But you need to promise that you won't turn from the faith you once embraced. Just as it did for Granny, it will gird you for the challenges ahead . . . it will give you hope, even when you think you'll fail. Unfortunately, I gave faith short shrift," I say. "I was too engrossed in the world and what it offered. Big mistake."

She pushes herself off the crib and walks over to the suitcase. She picks up some of the clothes, folds them, and places them neatly back into the dresser. She looks over her shoulder.

"Well?" I ask.

"TC, you still haven't told me how you got here. And where in God's name are your shoes?"

CHAPTER FORTY-FIVE

Today, May 30

Before I can explain the whereabouts of my footwear, Ginny picks up the pillow she'd thrown earlier and tosses it on the bed. The clothing she'd ripped from the dresser during her frantic packing is put away and the empty suitcase is returned to the closet. When she returns, she looks around the room like she's seeing it for the first time. She touches her lips with her fingers, carries the baby paraphernalia back to the crib, and picks up the dirty diaper. I hear it *plunk* as it hits the bottom of the bathroom trashcan. Wordlessly, she walks back over to the dresser, makes sure the drawers are shut, and then catches her reflection in the mirror.

She squares her shoulders, perhaps a learned gesture from Granny who faced her own obstacles but kept the faith. I'm not sure what she plans to do, but the spick-and-span woman who once ordered my tent and toweled mud off her boots seems to be reemerging.

I take it as a positive. I've given this visit my best shot—and now I need to go.

"Look, I need a shower," she says. "Promise me you'll stay until I get back?"

"Take a shower. You'll feel better."

"You won't go, right?"

"I'll be right here."

She draws in a deep breath and closes her eyes. She nods, then she grabs a pair of white jean shorts and clean white shirt. She heads for the bathroom.

I start another tour of the bedroom and peek at the baby who has inched herself to the headboard, leaving the blanket behind. After covering her, I wander over to the window and peer through the slats. Moths dance in the haloed light coming off the landscape lighting and a woman walks her dog down the sidewalk, the leash in one hand, a phone in the other—a sign of the times, something I used to do too. I couldn't disconnect myself from the world for even a few minutes.

What a waste.

I'm still watching the woman walk her dog when Ginny returns. She's scrubbed the black smudges from beneath her eyes and her hair hangs around her shoulders, damp but combed. Her complexion looks creamy. The grayish tone is gone, and her blue eyes shine. The dirty black garb is gone, replaced by clothing that reminds me of what she wore when we met a year ago.

My angel in white is back and she is beautiful.

"Ginny," I say, "you asked how I got here."

She sits on the edge of her rumpled bed. I lean against the window trim and see she's holding the bag of pills. I'm deflated. Why hadn't she flushed them? She doesn't say anything as she places the bag on top of her pillow and looks at the clothing, the books and bottles that still litter the floor.

We'll see if she does the right thing. We'll see if anything I've said has made a difference.

"Remember my near-death experience? The vivid memories, the video clips, the hovering?" I ask. "Remember how I watched my body being loaded into the ambulance, and saw my parents talking with a deputy before they jumped into their car and sped off?"

"Of course, but it doesn't make sense since you're here with me." She pauses for a moment. "But maybe it does make sense. Here's my theory. You had a brush with death, but heaven turned you away. How am I doing?"

I smile, but don't comment.

She purses her lips and walks toward me. I catch a whiff of her lavender shampoo, the scent that made me think of Ginny every time I detected it on other women.

"I don't want to know how you got here," she says. "Please hug me. Assure me you're here in the flesh and not a figment of my imagination or the result of drinking too much. I'll admit I did do that. I should have taken you up on your offer to drive me home to Granny's last year. Open one door, this happens. Open another, something totally different. Remember when I said that?"

She hangs her head. "I chose the wrong door."

The lump in my throat makes it hard to swallow. I close the tiny distance between us and envelop her in a tight hug.

Our encompassing, full-body press of flesh evolves into a slow dance between lovers, but without the heat I experienced a year ago. Now, my love for her is more profound, deeper, merciful, and forgiving. Human words—my calling cards just hours earlier—can't describe it.

"You're the best friend I've ever had. You helped me see the light last year and here you are doing it again." Her voice shakes as she leans back to touch my face. "I have a confession." She burrows her face into my chest and then glances up. Her mouth quivers. "I was falling for you. But I suppressed those feelings . . . misread the cues . . . for reasons you pointed out. Jacob embodied a lifestyle that I thought would prove I was nothing like my mother, my father. How misguided could I have been? And here I am now, begging you to help me escape . . . assuming you have the same feelings for me."

"I had fallen for you too."

She sags against me and hugs me tighter, but sadness overwhelms me. The lump in my throat hasn't dislodged. We'll never share this moment again. We'll never get a chance to try a relationship, as she seems to be suggesting, and she doesn't know it yet. She's gotten part of the story right, but not all. I tear myself from our embrace and she sees my set jaw. Tears leak from her eyes.

"Before I came here, after my near-death experience, I saw my parents walking into the hospital emergency room." I touch her shoulder in a feeble attempt to reassure her. "They looked shell-shocked as they opened the glass doors and walked toward the receptionist. Few people sat in the waiting area. As soon as my mother mentioned my name, the woman's facial features softened. She nodded, looked at paperwork and pointed to a door on the other side of the waiting room. They didn't know I was with them, but I was."

Ginny seems to suspect where this is going. Her face pales. She backs up, and my arm drops to my side. She turns her head, spots the bed, and stumbles backward to sit on the mattress, the bedsheets still in a tangle.

I continue my story.

Inside that windowless room, recessed lighting and table lamps illuminated the space, and sofas and chairs ringed the periphery. The details registered with supernatural clarity. A giant fish tank occupied one wall, and soft, soothing music played through hidden speakers. My parents didn't talk.

Dad was barefoot, rocking back and forth and staring at the carpeted floor. My mother sat across from him, quiet and blank, waiting for someone to walk through the door to give her the news. She looked up anxiously when a doctor and the deputy knocked on the door and stepped in. The doctor sat next to my father. The deputy stood by the door.

I couldn't read my parents' minds. I could only assume their thoughts as the doctor and deputy told them their worst nightmare had come true.

Unlike my brother, Scott, I wouldn't be going home again.

They followed the doctor, shuffling like sleepwalkers down a long, brightly lit hallway to a room where my body lay, still partially connected to resuscitation equipment. The doctor apologized for not removing all the medical devices. He offered his condolences, assuring them that the team did everything it could to save my life.

I felt my mother's pain. She backed away, refused to go into the room, and said repeatedly, "I can't do this, I can't do this. This is not happening." That meant it was my dad's job to confirm my identity. He walked partway into the room, took one glance, and collapsed onto the floor.

I was also with them on their drive home and watched as Georgie greeted them at the door, his tail twirling as he rubbed his nose against Dad's calves. Mom took one look at my sweet, faithful dog and started sobbing. Dad, with Georgie hot on his heels, stumbled out to the porch, staring numbly at the mountains across the valley from their house. My mother asked Dad to call his siblings. She'd make the other calls.

She sounded like a robot while she relayed the news to family members while standing on the back deck. From my mother's side of the conversation, I could tell Mom-Mom ended the call abruptly. I heard Cameron, the brother I'd fought with during our childhoods, yowling like a wounded animal, a sound so guttural and raw it shocked me. Her conversation with Bryan went the same way. He ended the call, apparently not wanting to hear the details. His grief, like everyone else's, was deep and unrelenting. I felt especially bad for my dad who'd put up with my bad mood earlier in the day. He staggered to his bedroom and crawled into bed but couldn't sleep. He thrashed and moaned, oblivious to Georgie's whining at the front door. My canine seemed to be looking for me.

And I saw it all.

Tears stream down my cheeks. "Parents shouldn't have to bury their children," I tell Ginny. "Children should bury their *parents*. That's the way it *should* be."

CHAPTER FORTY-SIX

Today, May 30

Ginny's reaction to my story is agonizing to watch. She falls back onto the bed, curls herself into a fetal position, and clamps her palms over her ears. The gut-wrenching cries I heard earlier return. The baby hears her mother and starts to whimper, now bothered by Ginny's distress. I walk across the room to pick up Laurel and cradle her until she quiets.

"Now you know why I can't take you to Tennessee." I look at Laurel. Perhaps, like Ginny, she is the most beautiful girl ever born.

"You told me you grabbed someone's hand. I figured the guy in the truck, the one who dragged you to the shore, saved you or a medic." Ginny sits up and takes several deep breaths.

That man did pull me to safety. He did try to resuscitate me. Worked hard to clear my lungs, to get my heart pumping. So did the ambulance crew and the doctors. But they didn't save me.

"I grabbed another hand, Ginny. I grabbed the Big Man's hand. God saved me, but not in the way you, my family, or my friends would have preferred." Even now—after traveling through space and time, different dimensions—I can't quite believe it. Me, the skeptic. The one who ignored the Big Man and believed the world's definition of goodness and value, never understanding or appreciating my own.

The Big Man wouldn't let me return to my old life. He wanted me with Him. I learned this before I visited the hospital, my parents' place. Before I came to see Ginny. I'll admit feeling ripped off. I started arguing. Surely, He had something more for me. *Give me another chance*, I begged, still enraptured by the world and its offerings. He chuckled and said I had one more lesson to learn.

"That's why I'm here. He wanted to show me just how important a friend could be, to appreciate my own gifts, and to remind you of yours. You were light-years ahead of me a year ago when you told me your plans and insisted that I consider my own purpose. You got a little sidetracked and need someone to steer you back onto your path. He told Uriah to escort me."

"Uriah?" She opens her mouth and then closes it. She must not be able to process my words, this supernatural story that would have made me scoff a year ago.

"Yeah, him. Over there." I look toward where Uriah stands on the other side of the door jamb.

"There's no one over there."

Of course, she can't see my guardian angel, the one who was assigned to me since my birth. He couldn't take the final steps with me in my journey to self-discovery, but he never left my side through life's ups and downs, detours, and dead ends. Uriah's almost imperceptible nudging prevented near-miss, head-on collisions and encounters with strangers who meant to hurt me. "I'm not God," he told me at the river. "And I'm not your 'better angel' either . . . You know, the voice you ignored. That voice belonged to the Big Man."

I had disregarded God himself.

"When I walked through your doorway, you were happy to see me," I say. "You called it a dream. You were right. I did come in a dream. And when you get up, I'll be gone. You'll remember the intensity, the details, and you'll probably wonder if any of what I said was true. I want you to check the internet," I say before revealing my full name and address. "My accident will be plastered all over the news and social media."

My story will be used as a warning against swimming in waters that appear outwardly calm. But I see my story differently. My time had ended. My purpose fulfilled.

"The Big Man gave me a rare gift," I tell Ginny. The chance to see her one more time, knowing I'd be the friend she needed. He had no other choice because she stopped listening to Him long ago. He used me, and He used a dream, to get to her.

Whether she fulfills her life's purpose is her choice. While I initially fretted about failing, I now understand I've done my part. Regardless of what she decides, I am, and will always be, her very good friend. Our relationship evolved exactly as planned. Another epiphany that brings me peace.

She looks at the wine stain, the bag of pills on her pillow. She doesn't bother wiping the tears.

I now feel the pull toward my new life. Music had always played an integral part in my existence on earth and Uriah has assured me I can dance and sing to my heart's content . . . but now I'll jam with a better singing voice. I smile at that thought. I glance at the sleeping baby, relaxed in my arms. I lay her in her crib and walk toward Ginny. She rests her head on her hand and closes her eyes.

"You're not going to see me again. Not like this." I sit next to her on the bed. My big, booming voice is on hiatus. Perhaps for eternity. "We will see each other again, but not for a long time. That's the way it's supposed to be. The plan for our souls. I've done my best. Now it's up to you."

From the corner of my eye, I see Uriah. He gestures for me to follow him. The bed creaks as I stand.

"Please don't go." New tears stream down Ginny's cheeks.

"I have to, Ginny." I lean over to wipe her tears with my thumb. "Remember what I said. Your past is your past. Don't let it define your future. Be the woman you were intended to be."

The walk toward the door seems to take forever. As I step over the threshold, I glance over my shoulder just as the same physical sensation that I'd experienced earlier begins anew.

Ginny's curled in her bed, fast asleep, wearing her dirty black clothes. The pills lie in her hand. A cracked wine glass, an empty baby bottle, and the wine bottle I had retrieved from the floor earlier sit on the nightstand, amid the books and papers. The floor is littered with clothes, shoes, and the other empty wine bottle whose vestiges have left a red stain on the rug. And her sleeping baby is tucked away in her crib. The scene looks exactly as it did when I stepped across the portal and into her dream.

CHAPTER FORTY-SEVEN

Ginny, May 31

I sit in a wooden pew that is polished smooth by decades of use. I don't know the name of this church or how I found it. I've been on autopilot, headed west via the backroads across the South, getting as far away as possible from Atlanta, Jacob, and my life there.

I had needed a fill-up, so I pulled into a gas station on the outskirts of a small town. Only then did I notice the white clapboard church across the street. I was drawn by its simple, unadorned beauty. The need to sit quietly and reflect overcame me. I wanted to think about TC and give thanks to yet another miracle in my life.

An elderly pastor must have noticed me standing on the steps, holding my sleeping child. He opened the door and invited me to spend as much time as needed inside the sanctuary.

"Are you sure?"

"Of course, I'm sure," he said. "Everyone deserves a second chance." He smiled and caressed the top of Laurel's head. "Don't let your past define your future, young lady. If you need anything, I'll be in my office." He pointed to a door and wandered away.

As I sit here, at peace, I marvel at the words the pastor spoke, so like those TC had spoken. Another sign. Confirmation. I know I'm on the right track in my journey to recovery. It may not be easy, but I am determined to see it through.

It began the moment Melinda burst into the bedroom this morning, shouting, her eyes wide in fear. "Wake up. Oh my gosh, wake up. What have you done? Where's the baby? Where's the baby?" Her eyes darted around the room.

I don't know if it was the dream or the wine I had drunk, but it took a few minutes to orient myself.

"Calm down. She's in her crib." I sat up and rubbed my eyes. The pills rested on my pillow, and only then did reality shake me from my stupor. Had I really intended to swallow those things? It had certainly crossed my mind before falling asleep. No point in dwelling on something that didn't happen. It was nice to feel whole and clear-headed again. I slipped the baggie underneath the pillow and noticed a wine bottle resting on the nightstand. Hadn't I swept it off the table in a fit of drunken rage last night? So, who put it back on the table?

That was when I remembered.

"Melinda, I need your help." I walked over to the crib and greeted Laurel, the only bright spot in my relationship with Jacob. I looked over my shoulder and saw Melinda standing in the middle of the room, taking in the chaotic jumble of broken glass, bottles, and stains.

"I'll explain everything once I've had a cup of coffee." I felt light and unburdened, sidestepping a pile of clothing on the floor. Melinda hadn't moved. "Come on. Time to get this show on the road."

Except for the magazine left on the island, the kitchen looked spotless. I brewed a pot of coffee, fed Laurel her bottle, and asked Melinda about work, postponing the inevitable. "My phone's upstairs," I said, taking a sip of coffee. "Look up Tyrus Cal 'TC' Chaver. Would you? He lives in East Tennessee."

"How do you know this guy?" Melinda scrolled through the browser's results. "According to local news, he died last night in a swimming accident." She pushed her phone across the counter for me to see.

I bit my lip and my eyes filled with tears. I wanted to break down. Here in black and white was confirmation to what I already knew. If TC hadn't visited last night in my dream, then how would I have known his full name or to search him online? But something still nagged. How had that wine bottle ended up on my nightstand? Didn't TC put it there when he visited in my dream?

I massaged my head. *What's wrong with me?* A miracle had happened. Granny would have assured me of that. He did visit me last night, and he left a little reminder of our time together as evidence so I would believe.

"Who is he?" Melinda asked.

"A very dear friend," I said, wiping my eyes with a tissue Melinda had pulled from her pocket. "He is the only person who could make me laugh, show me truth, and remind me of what's important in life. He finally understands his specialness, and why he was placed on earth."

"You never mentioned him before." Melinda took a sip of coffee.

"We met at a music festival last year before I moved here. Haven't seen him in the flesh since. But I know one thing. He, or someone like him, would be the perfect guy for me."

Melinda's eyes opened wide. But the shake of my head told her I would not go there.

"Well, if you're not going to reveal the details, how then did you know to search his name?" She crossed her legs and arms and leaned back.

"Intuition." I offered no details of my time with TC. No one, including her, would believe my strange dream story. Furthermore, I didn't want to sully the memory with endless chatter and speculation. Better to keep the experience locked safely in my heart, available for whenever I felt low and needed a friend.

"It's funny how that works. You just know what you know." Melinda scratched her temple. "You asked me to stop by this morning. What's going on? What did you mean by getting this show on the road?" She raised her eyebrow.

In my drunkenness, I had asked her to stop in. I wanted her to find me lying dead in my bed. I wanted her to take Laurel home with her. I ran my hand through my hair, horrified by my own idiocy. Jacob would have never consented to Melinda caring for my child. Who knows where she would have ended up.

But instead of that outcome, I was alive. Grateful. Unashamed of my story. As I talked, Melinda listened in stunned silence. Now she knew everything. The burden was lifted, and it felt freeing, much like the sensation I had after I told TC about my childhood. He had been right about so many things.

Melinda shook her head slowly as she traced the rim of her coffee cup.

"Spit it out, Melinda. Nothing you can say will surprise me or change my mind."

"Did Jacob tell you I'd drop by now and then to check on you? I could have called or texted, but my instincts told me to pop in unannounced. Jacob always turned me away, wouldn't let me step inside. He said you were either napping or out shopping with the baby."

I harrumphed. "Of course, he didn't tell me." I rubbed my chin, trying to remember the last time I left the house. "I haven't gone anywhere in days. That changes today. I am leaving." I glanced at the digital stove clock. "I want to be on the road in a couple of hours. Promise me that you won't tell Jacob anything, and I mean *nothing*. I'll get in touch with him when I'm good and ready."

Melinda nodded. "I'm so sorry . . . not that you're leaving him. I knew he was awful, but I'd no idea how bad he was. Last night, I got scared for you and nearly came over, but you'd seemed so insistent that I stay home." She frowned, touching her lip with finger. "I wish I'd listened to my gut."

But had she followed her intuition, I may have never spent time with TC. And that *was* the plan. "No Melinda, please don't beat yourself up. You did the right thing."

She let out a huge breath and her fingers started tapping.

"What else, Melinda?

She sucked in her top lip. "I think he has a girlfriend. At a restaurant several weeks ago, my husband and I saw him with a woman . . . tall, red hair. She may have been a business associate, maybe an employee, but it didn't look that way to me. They were holding hands." The next part of her revelation came out in a rush. "I've wanted to tell you, but I was unsure. I lost a friend once when I opened my mouth . . . and I didn't want that happening to us. I'm so sorry. I shouldn't have assumed you'd react like she did."

I felt myself seething. Not at Melinda . . . at Jacob. His deceit had emptied me of all dignity and self-worth. TC's words came back to me, as did the memories of our time together and what I'd learned. Starting today, I would take an inventory of myself, including the deep-seated hurts that led to my relationship with Jacob.

Sitting in this sterile kitchen, my mind recalled his business trips. The odd hours. Who kept asking about my pain meds? Who offered drinks and seemed pleased when I over-indulged? His hateful accusations and name-calling worked, making me feel inadequate, incapable of taking care of myself, and unworthy of anything better. While I fretted over how to fix our relationship, Jacob schemed. He implied he knew something about Jimmy and my mother. What did he know and how would he use that information to wound me further?

TC was right. He could become more ruthless, and he might never stop—not until I went completely insane . . . or took my life. And then he'd start in on Laurel.

I shuttered at the thought.

"Do you know where you're going?" Melinda interrupted my thoughts. "Never mind, don't tell me. He'll call me first when he discovers that you and Laurel are gone. At least I can be honest in saying that I've no idea."

"Nevada. I must see my mother. We have unfinished business."

"Okay, then." Melinda didn't pry. "Time to move."

While Melinda bathed and dressed the baby, I started packing my Honda Civic that was parked inside the garage. Erasing all traces of my occupancy drove me like a madwoman. I went upstairs, ran past Laurel's nursery, and rushed into the bedroom. I saw it for what it was. A torture chamber where I'd lost all hope and the desire to live. Sweat gathered at my hairline and rolled down my face as I scrubbed the rug until the stains faded and then disappeared. That's exactly how Jacob made me feel—like a mistake, like a spilled drink that needed to be wiped up and forgotten.

When I came downstairs after showering, I saw Melinda in Jacob's study, a room I'd rarely entered because he normally kept it locked. She was sitting at Jacob's desk, jostling the baby.

Papers and folders were strewn across the desk, and the trash can overflowed. A half-drunk cup of coffee sat atop a stack of folders. I pinched my nose as I stepped closer to his desk. "Do you smell that?"

"I do. Smells like something died. A mouse?" She shrugged. "I'm ignoring it."

For as long as I had known Jacob, he'd insist on keeping the house perfect, a reflection of how he presented himself to the world. But in his private study, where no one was allowed, he could let down all pretenses. Here, he laid bare the real Jacob and the true condition of his heart.

"Were you two planning a trip together?" Melinda picked up a marketing brochure and showed it to me. I shook my head. "Business trip, my butt." She laughed mirthlessly.

"I'm more interested in his laptop." I leaned over Melinda's shoulder and started reading a website displayed on the screen. Either he wanted me an addict or would claim I was. His schemes almost succeeded. "Looks like he had big plans for me and my sweet baby."

I picked up my bags, including my cloth satchel, loaded with the Bible that Granny had given me and cash that I'd squirreled away and hid for an emergency. I had enough money to keep us fed and sheltered until I could call Aunt Adele, sort out my finances, and set my plans. It was time to come clean with her too.

I forgot the baggie in my other hand. Getting rid of the pills was my last act, the denouement, in this nightmare story. The wine bottle, which was already tucked safely in one of my bags, would go with me.

"What are those?" Melinda pointed.

"Painkillers. I drank quite a bit last night and considered taking some, but I fell asleep before I could. I knew the mix of alcohol and opioids might kill me. I could see no way out."

Melinda eyed me suspiciously. "Not sure I'm okay with you taking off with Laurel." She put her arm around my shoulder and guided me out of Jacob's study. "I can make an appointment. You need to see a professional. How can I be sure you won't do something drastic? Ginny, I'd never forgive myself."

"Look at me." My voice became forceful, and I spoke slowly. "I have no plans to take my life. Not now or ever. Many people need me. Especially her." I would protect Laurel at all costs. I knew my path forward. I'd shed enough tears. TC's words echoed in my mind. "Can you imagine her life with him? Don't waste your time worrying about me." I took Laurel from Melinda's arms and handed the sandwich bag to her.

"Flush them," I said. "The toilet's next door. If you don't like that idea, then throw them in a dumpster, take them to the police. Say you found them. I don't want them. I don't need a reminder of how hopeless I'd become. I can do better. Much better."

Melinda gave me a sidelong glance and pressed her lips together. She seemed to be weighing her options. Certainly, my confession would be grounds for a medical intervention.

"Just remember who we're dealing with," I added.

"Okay, I get it." She nodded. "But promise me that you'll call when you reach your destination. I won't sleep until I hear your voice and know you're safe." She lifted the bag to her face. "Ginny, these look a little suspicious. Where you'd get them?"

"I have a hunch." Funny how benign the blue pills looked locked inside a sandwich bag.

———————————

Hours have passed since Melinda helped me write a note to tell Jacob that I'd left and wouldn't return. I should get back on the road but need more time to marvel at my precious child sleeping in my arms and consider everything that's transpired in the past twenty-four hours. I'd come within a hair of making an irreparable mistake, and a miracle had arrived—a faithful friend who had thrown my own words back into my face to show me the truth. How smug and all-knowing I must have seemed talking to him about value and purpose.

How the roles had swapped.

Without TC, I may have allowed the thief in the night to steal my life and ultimately Laurel's life too. The dysfunction would end now.

I touch the rubber bracelet on my wrist and remember Granny's words. Special people do enrich our lives, even if it is only for a short time. Without them, we might not live up to our potential or the plan for our lives. I needed to get on my knees and thank God for TC and the gift He gave me. A chance at a redo. A chance at *life*.

I contemplate the hymnals and last Sunday's church announcements. The cross. I look at the ceiling and wonder whether TC is talking up the angels, jamming to the music. I can rest easy, knowing he finally realized his specialness, the gifts he shared so readily with everyone he had ever met.

"We're going to be okay," I whisper to Laurel. "We have everything we need."

I stand as the church bells ring and remember the difference he made. I would always think of him, and I would thank my God every time I did.

The End

Acknowledgments

When I started this journey, doubt and discouragement were constant companions. Writing fiction is hard. But my sister, Debbie Keesey Beall, wouldn't let me give up. When I'd gripe, she'd say, "Just birth this baby."

I did, but not without a lot of help from editors. Thank you Molly Jo Realy, Larry Leech, Tessa Hall, and Rebecca Andersen for guiding me, showing me gently where I'd gone off the rails. Without them and Mascot Books, *Always Think of Me* wouldn't be resting in your hands now.

And it wouldn't be a reality without beta readers and friends— Taryn Queen, Marcia Messer, Debbie Terry, Carol Shipley Pennington, Theresa Shreffler Kidwell, and Karen Luck Delph. Nor could I have traveled this road without web designer extraordinaire, Stephanie Walker, a loyal friend and encourager, and Dave

Stonehouse, who designed the cover.

I'd be remiss, too, if I didn't mention my husband, Kevin Berry, who has stayed by my side throughout this journey, as well as the best man in our wedding, Bob Leahy. Before Bob passed away, he'd always ask, "Kees, when are you gonna write that book?" Well, Bob, here it is.

To all of you:

> "I thank my God every time I think of you."
> —Philippians 1:3

Author Q&A

1. As a child, what did you want to do when you grew up?

I'd always wanted to write a novel, especially one populated with vivid, colorful, and completely relatable characters. Many authors cite Harper Lee and *To Kill a Mockingbird* as the source of their inspiration. That certainly was the case for me. I could see Scout, Atticus, Jem, Calpurnia, and Dill. I could hear them speak. I could imagine living in Maycomb, Alabama.

2. Have you always written?

I am lucky. I earned a living as a writer, first as a newspaper reporter and then as a freelance writer and communication consultant. Great career. Great experiences. I met Native Americans, bootlegging coal miners, super-smart scientists, and engineers. My consultant job also prepared me for my career blogging about real people who overcome adversity. I've always enjoyed writing personality profiles, and the blog has allowed me tell others' stories. I wouldn't change a thing about my career choices.

3. What inspired you to write this book?

Tragedy inspired me to write this book. When our son died, my heart broke. I'd never experienced such mind-numbing pain. I couldn't understand why God took him from my family and me. Those questions forced me to consider our purposes in life and how our failure to carry them out could stop someone else from achieving his or hers. Those are central themes in this book. Writing this novel was cathartic and made me realize that my writing might be better used trying to offer hope to those who hurt.

4. Can you describe your writing process for the book?

I'm laughing. I don't know if I could describe my process. I had an idea of what I wanted to say and how I'd say it, but I didn't follow a specific method. More slapdash than anything else. Maybe I'll be more disciplined next time. Maybe it won't take four-plus years to finish a manuscript!

5. What were your sources of inspiration for the book?

As I mentioned, tragedy inspired this book, but so did my volunteer work with young mothers who'd lost custody of their kids because of addiction and other issues. These young moms didn't grow up wanting to be addicts. In many cases, past trauma contributed to their addictions. Their stories, plus research and interviews with mental-health professionals, informed some of the scenes in the book. When I started writing, I was also struck by the uptick in suicides. I wondered what was at play. If these people understood their value, would they have ended their precious lives?

6. Do you have a favorite character from the book?

Of course, I love TC who is loosely based on my son. Other favorites include Aimee and Granny Smith. Both are no-nonsense. Both have distinctive voices. They love hugely. It took me time getting to know Ginny, but as the months went by, after many, many revisions, she became very real to me. Her innocence and resilience stand out, and I can understand why TC fell for her.

7. Are any of the characters based on real people or people you know?

In addition to TC, other people did come to mind while I wrote the novel. TC's best friend, Bryan, as well as Dusty, Adrian, and TC's neighbors are loosely based on real people. So are TC's family members. The others are completely fictional. Georgie's not a person, but that crazy canine is real. As they say, truth can be stranger than fiction.

8. Can you tell us more about the title? How did you come up with it? What is its significance?

Always Think of Me is the fifth title! I struggled mightily with the title. Those that worked had already been used by other authors or ran the risk of offending people. Ultimately, I chose the title because it speaks directly to TC's internal struggles and his inability to figure out his specialness.

9. Were there any challenges in writing this book? What were they?

I'm laughing again. Many years ago, I took a fiction-writing class. My instructor loved my characters, but she said my stories had no plot. She asked, "Why am I reading this?" As I said, I'd written professionally since graduating from college. But journalistic writing is far different from writing fiction. Learning the fundamentals was an on-the-job experience for me. I am so grateful to my editors. Without them, I wouldn't be answering these questions now.

10. What do you think happened to the characters after the book ended?

Great question. But I'd prefer that readers answer the question. What do they think will happen? I hope they'll let me know. Who knows, their opinions could end up in a sequel!

Reading Guide Questions

1. TC is a party guy who meets his opposite, the shy and unassuming Ginny, at an outdoor music festival. Why do you think they were attracted to one another? Do they belong together? Why or why not?

2. Why are the secondary characters (Granny Smith, Jacob, Mom-Mom, Bear, and Aimee, for example) important to this story? Do they remind you of yourself or someone you know? How?

3. Ginny has secrets and TC is riddled with insecurities. How do these secrets and insecurities hinder them? What did they learn along the way? How do they change because of the events of the story?

4. What do you think the biggest themes are and how did they speak to you?

5. Do you believe the book touched upon broader social issues? Why did they stand out to you?

6. What feelings did this book evoke in you? Did this book leave a lasting impact on how you think?

7. Share a favorite quote from this book. Why did this quote stand out?

8. If you were making a movie of this book, whom would you cast?

9. What do you think happens to the characters after the book ends?

10. Did the ending satisfy you? How would you have concluded the story?

About the Author

Harper Lee inspired Lori Keesey to become a writer. So captivated by Scout in *To Kill a Mockingbird*, Lori wanted to create characters just as engaging as this spunky little girl. Many years passed—and hundreds of novels were read—before Lori realized her goal. A former journalist, Lori has written for daily newspapers, trade publications, and magazines and worked for NASA in public outreach for nearly twenty years as a communication consultant. She graduated from the University of Maryland, College Park, where she met her husband, Kevin Berry, the father of her three boys. Lori was born in Washington, DC, and now calls Walland, Tennessee, home.

lorikeesey.com

 ljkeesey   X LoriKeesey
 lori.keesey   in Lori Keesey